Never Again, No More 2:

Getting Back to Me

Never Again, No More 2:

Getting Back to Me

Untamed

www.urbanbooks.net

Urban Books, LLC
300 Farmingdale Road, NY-Route 109
Farmingdale, NY 11735

Never Again, No More 2: Getting Back to Me

ISBN 13: 978-1-64556-090-6
ISBN 10: 1-64556-090-2

First Trade Paperback Printing August 2020
Printed in the United States of America

10 9 8 7 6 5 4 3 2 1

Distributed by Kensington Publishing Corp.
Submit Orders to:
Customer Service
400 Hahn Road
Westminster, MD 21157-4627
Phone: 1-800-733-3000
Fax: 1-800-659-2436

To Da'Ja, Mary, Keshia, Thelma, Velvie, Annie, and Christina: women who've meant the world to me and now watch over me.

Acknowledgments

I begin my thank-yous as I always have and always will, thanking my Lord and Savior Jesus Christ. None of this would be possible without you. Thank you for this talent you've given me and the vision to see it through.

To my husband, Chris, and my children, thank you for loving me enough to share your time and space with this craft. Without your blessings and support, I could not write one single word. You come first in my world and everything I do is for you. I love you from the bottom of my heart and the depths of my soul.

To my pillars, my dad and Aunt Irene, thank you for your guidance, support, and your love.

To my family near, far, and extended, I love you all and thank you for always being in my corner, fam!

To my A1's,*in my DMX voice* there is Sabrina, LaKesha, Chinek, Chia, about three Tam's, Vulyncia, Gina. Diane, I met her through my girl Patrice, by way of Stacey, LaDonna, Denise, Kiana, Kisha, Jessica, and Kathy. And if I left someone out, blame my head, not my heart, and please don't @ me, LOL! Thank you, ladies, for humbly supporting me not just as an author but as my friend.

To my brothers, Kenny, Dom, Smiz, and JC, thank y'all for holding your sis down!

To N'Tyse and the Literary Champagne Suite crew and Urban Books, as always, thank you for believing and helping me deliver on this dream. The opportunities are limitless, and I'm looking forward to every one of them.

Acknowledgments

To all the supportive interviewers, authors, and readers who have helped me along this literary journey, I appreciate every share, tweet, retweet, like, love, comment, review, and purchase. You all give me literary life! Thank you all so much.

Y'all ready for round two? Hold on because you're about to enter Untamed Territory.

Prologue

Trinity

Previously from Never Again, No More

As I drifted off, my mind began to reminisce about the awesome night I'd had with my ex, Terrence, or rather my personal love-name for him, Dreads, and I felt myself smiling. I loved Dreads, and I wanted him so bad. I knew I had to figure out a way to get back to him, but real talk, a part of me still felt obligated to my man, Pooch. He'd been there for me when I couldn't depend on anybody else, and I'd just betrayed him in the worst way. Did it mean I still wanted to be in the relationship? Absolutely not. I wanted Dreads. If I was truthful with myself, it'd always been Dreads for me, and it always would be. I'd choose him a hundred times over. But like Dreads said, if I was nothing else, I was loyal, and that was the part that made me feel bad for the exit I would soon make from this relationship with Pooch. If only I knew exactly how to do that . . . safely.

Ugh! It bothered me that I didn't know what or how I was going to do anything. The only thing I knew for sure was that even though I had love for Pooch, in my heart, I was in love with Dreads, and I longed to be with him.

With thoughts of Dreads on my mind, I didn't even hear my cell phone ringing with another call from Pooch.

Charice

"Baby, I don't think there is anything else I can say or do to show you how much I love you and want to be with you other than to show you that my commitment is permanent. Love is strange. It strikes at the oddest times in the most unexpected places. But once you have it, you hold on to it, and you cherish it for life. That's what I want to do for you, baby. I want to love you for a lifetime. I want to love the triplets for a lifetime. I want to love our future babies for a lifetime. I want to be married to you for a lifetime. Will you accept this ring as my commitment to you? Charice, will you marry me?"

Nodding my head rapidly, I cried, "Yes! Yes! Yes!"

Lincoln teased me earlier that he would have me up all night, and now, I had to agree. Oh yes, tonight was most definitely going to be an all-nighter! After all the turmoil I'd endured since tenth grade with my triplets' father, Ryan, from giving my whole heart to him for him to shatter it over and over, to breakups, to makeups, to him not supporting me or the kids for his NFL career, I finally had a real man who loved me just as much as I loved him. I was so very happy that I, Ms. Charice Taylor, was about to become Mrs. Charice Harper!

Now we just had to break the news to Ryan. How could we tell him that Lincoln, his teammate and best friend, and his babies' mother were not only dating but officially engaged?

Lucinda

"Wait, Pooch," I called out before he hung up. I couldn't believe I was going to ask this. But my daughter Nadia's picture on my keychain stared back at me, and for her, I'd do the unthinkable. "Um, do you, um, do you need any, you know, dancers at Moet?" I asked timidly, hiding my eyes as I even asked the question.

"I mean, we always auditioning. If you got talent, we'll put you on. Of course, you know they make good."

"Can I audition?"

Pooch paused for a moment and then slowly said, "You do realize by 'dance' I mean strip? Moet is a strip club, Lu."

"I know that. I'm desperate."

"Damn," he grumbled before continuing. "Well, if you're serious, meet me and my manager, Greg, down there at eight tonight. We'll audition you on the stage. You gon' have to strip. Thongs and sexy heels only. No tops, not even a bra. You got to show us some true skill, something we can claim as your specialty."

Wait. I knew I would do anything for Nadia, but that pushed the limits. He couldn't possibly mean I would have to strip in front of him. Nope. "Pooch, I ain't auditioning in front of you! You're my best friend's man!"

"Your choice, Lu. You called me. Greg and I make that decision together. Trust me, it's only business. If you feel like you can't do it, then don't be there. But I'm trying to lace your pockets, mama."

He was serious. *Wow.* I'd hit a true crossroads. I sat there for a moment in contemplation. "I don't have to get down with y'all to get on, do I? 'Cause I'm not betraying Trinity like that. Hell, I'm not even sure I want to betray her by the audition."

"Hell naw. I'm a businessman, Lu. Too many of these skank-ass bitches get down with these grimy-ass niggas. I ain't bringing my babe back shit, and I'm scared shitless of that fuckin' package."

"A loyal thug."

"You know how I am about Trin any-fuckin'-way. So, look, all I'm saying is you got an audition, so show up and you could have a job. Don't show up, and that's your choice too, but then don't call me again, because money I have to blow, but time I don't," Pooch said seriously.

"I hear you," I said, still undecided.

"So I'm going to say see you at eight o'clock. Whether you do or don't is up to you, but you've been put on notice. Remember that shit."

"Yeah, I know. Thanks," I said plainly.

"It's all love," he said and hung up.

Holding my head in my hands, I sat there for a few minutes. Then I called information to get the unemployment office's number and made an appointment to go down there about my unemployment. At least that was taken care of. It was a start.

After I hung up, I noticed a message on my cell phone. I retrieved it and was reminded about my overdue light bill. Disconnection was set for next week if I didn't have their money. When it rained, it fucking poured. I shook my head at the message and my predicament. Anger consumed me. *Fuck it. Fuck my deadbeat baby's daddy, Raul. Fuck my old job at National Cross. Fuck school. Fuck my entire life.* Wrong or not, I had to do what I had to do. I couldn't allow Nadia to go without because of my fucked-up life. Rolling my eyes at my phone, I deleted the message and cranked up my car.

I headed downtown to go shoe shopping for some sexy heels. I had an appointment to keep tonight at eight.

LaMeka

"What are we doing here?" Misha asked.

"You are going back to Mom's. I can't deal with you," I said angrily.

"No, Meka, please," she pleaded.

"Get out of my car," I said sternly, looking at her.

"LaMeka—"

I looked straight ahead as she slowly opened the door and slid out.

"I'm sorry, Meka. I don't know how to make it right—"

"Go home, finish school, and grow the fuck up," I interrupted and then drove away. I didn't even have the heart to make sure she made it in the house first.

I drove until I pulled up to a twenty-four-hour shelter for abused women and children. The pastor had told me about it. Now that the adrenaline rush from the incident at my house—when I found out that my now-estranged boyfriend, Tony, had slept with my sister, Misha, and he tried to kill us both in his coke-induced high—had worn off, I felt weak from the loss of blood. I got out of the car somehow and staggered to the door of the shelter, which was half open. My pastor was standing in the foyer, engrossed in a conversation with some lady.

"Pastor Gaines," I said weakly, stumbling inside.

"Oh God, LaMeka," he yelled. My legs finally gave out, and Pastor Gaines caught me just before I hit the floor.

"My babies are in the car. I'm too weak. I need a place . . ."

And suddenly everything went black.

Chapter One

Lucinda

As I sat on the other end of the phone call, I was happy but sad. Here my girl Charice was finally confiding in us about her new man and that they just got engaged five days ago while I was waiting to go inside to perform at Club Moet. My stage name: Spanish Fly.

At the audition, I was drunk as fuck, but I managed to perform for them. Obviously, I got the gig, as I referred to it, because it sure as hell couldn't be considered a job. Pooch gave me the nickname Spanish Fly afterward because I have a tattoo of a butterfly that covered my entire ass. Each butt cheek had a wing, and when I dropped and did my backward split, it spread like it was flying away. I felt so disgusted when I performed for my best friend's man and even lower as I saw Greg and him smiling and critiquing my moves, then realigning their dicks, trying not to get a hard-on. Men could say whatever the fuck they wanted, but their dicks don't discriminate against pussy.

Pooch told me that was my signature move and to end every show with it. Then he asked Greg to show me the ropes. Luckily, Greg and Pooch thought with the head on their shoulders and not the one between their legs, regardless of how turned on they were. They kept it strictly business with me after the performance. However, I could bet you a dime to a dozen, Pooch dicked down Trinity real good that night. Surprisingly, Pooch kept his word and didn't put my business out, so none of my friends and family knew. I was sure eventually they'd find out from dudes on the block, but that's the only way. I wasn't volunteering shit, and apparently, neither was Pooch.

Back to the situation at hand. Charice had called Trinity and me on three-way and told us all of the details of her vacation/proposal. We were shocked out of our minds to find out her new man was Lincoln Harper! How this bitch ended up with kids by one NFL star and engaged to another—her baby daddy's best friend, no less—was beyond my stretch of imagination. This heifer was going to live the good life no matter what. All I wanted was a little bit of the financial comfort that she had. Just a little bit. I didn't have to be balling out of control. I would settle for an education and a decent job that paid well enough to pay my bills and leave me with a fair amount of money for extras. That's all. Instead, I was an unemployed, uneducated, single mother who stripped for a living.

I knew Charice was excited, but I had to go. She was my girl, and I was happy for her, but admittedly her newfound love bothered me because of my current circumstances. It was like shit was working out for everyone around me and not me. I wanted to be included. I wanted to be the one to bear good news instead of always griping about my troubles. And honestly, it was so hard to fully be excited for someone else when the weight of the world was on your shoulders. It may have been wrong, but it was my truth.

I congratulated her again so I could end the call. But before I could disconnect, she made me promise not to say a word to anybody until after they had officially broken the news to Ryan, who didn't know about their relationship either. I just shook my head and promised. I wanted to tell her she should've told him sooner, because I had no doubt in my mind that those two dudes would kill each other. Ryan may have been an ass in high school and college, but now he loved Charice, like *loved* her. Part of me felt bad for him because he was forever trying to get back with her and was totally oblivious to the fact that Lincoln was sneaking in from the back door.

Honestly, even though I felt bad for Ryan, that part had made me want to high-five the hell out of Charice. It takes a bold and bad bitch to pull some shit like that, and she did it without even trying to be malicious. That's what made that shit so cold. She wasn't trying to be mean, and neither was Lincoln. They honestly loved each other. But the reality was it also made that situation that much more dangerous.

Shit, but enough about her. I had my own problems. I had to figure out how the fuck I could stop stripping and find something that I wasn't afraid to tell my friends and family about. I ain't gon' lie now, stripping paid the bills. After my show, I normally did private table dances for a few of my regulars, and that's how I made good for the week. On average, I pulled $1,000 to $2,500 a week. Sundays and Mondays were my days off, and I worked Tuesday through Saturday night. I was going to start getting my unemployment check soon, and I was slated to start classes this summer. So even though Charice's news made me feel a little bad, I could admit that not everything was so bad, but stripping was definitely not good.

After hanging up, I walked in the dressing room and put on my leather panty covers, bustier, and black heels. As I brushed my hair, a set of girls came in the back.

"Girl, Spanish Fly, the club is packed, and the niggas is ballin' tonight," Alize shouted as she counted her money.

"Oh yeah?" I asked just to make small talk and threw back my third shot of Jose Cuervo.

"Hell yeah," Chocolate Flava yelled as they high-fived each other. "One of them niggas asked us to do a private party at his house! That nigga is paying six Gs. You need to be down with us. We could split it three ways. You know niggas be crazy for y'all Spanish chicks, and then there's that damn sexy-ass split you do," Chocolate said as she walked over and threw her arms around my neck. "That shit gets me hot myself, boo," she said, gliding her hand across my titties. "Real hot."

"Ah shit," Alize said. "Do I need to leave up out of here?" She laughed with some of the other chicks.

I slapped Chocolate's hand away. "Nah, I'm good, and I like dick only."

"That's 'cause she ain't never had Flava lick that cat before," another chick named Black Pearl said.

Flava looked up at Pearl with a sexy glint in her eyes, then sexily waltzed up to her, and they kissed. "Don't knock it 'til you try it, Spanish Fly," Pearl added as the other chicks hooted and hollered.

I downed another shot. See why I had to get away from this environment?

"Leave her alone. Y'all know she the goody-goody," Alize said to the others. They dispersed. Once they went about their business, Alize walked up to me and sat down beside me. "Why you do this shit?"

"Huh?" I asked her, looking at her with a confused stare.

"Bitch, you heard me," she said, smacking her lips before she continued. "You ain't like the rest of us. We do this shit 'cause we like it. Say what you want, but I'm using what my mama gave me. Ain't no shame in flaunting what you got to make it. To me, it's only shameful if you think it is. I don't give a fuck. I'll get down every which way to stay on top. Dancing, fucking, it don't matter, shit, male or female. If he or she got that green, I will dance, shake, fuck, and suck whatever they ask me to. But this shit ain't you. So why do it?"

Alize caught me off guard with her question. I'd never gotten close to any of the girls because I knew I was different. She was right. They did this because they wanted to do it. I did this out of necessity. I didn't think I was better than them. I just wanted better for myself and my daughter. However, listening to Alize, it was the first time I felt comfortable enough to share my personal feelings with any one of them. To be honest, I needed it. I couldn't talk to my family or, hell, not even my girls because of Trinity's relationship with Pooch. Being able to talk to someone was a welcomed and needed release.

"I got fired from my job, and I got a baby to support. That's why," I said plainly. "Y'all do what you want. I ain't knocking it. I'm just here to dance and get my money. After that, I go home to my baby. She don't know what I do, and she don't need to know. All she needs to know is that her *mami* loves her and will always make a way for her. That's all that matters to me."

Alize nodded. "I feel you. I ain't got no kids, but I feel you. I wish my mama felt like that about me. Maybe I would feel different today," she said with sadness evident in her voice.

For the first time, I realized all of us had a story to tell. Maybe my reason seemed more genuine than the next female's, but ultimately we were all women lost in this man's world, trying to get in wherever the fuck we could fit in. And for the briefest of moments, Alize was not just some chickenhead stripper I worked with. She was a misguided woman simply trying to make it, like me.

"Bitch, you getting me all emotional, and I gotta go dance soon," I joked to lighten the mood.

She laughed, picking up on my lighthearted banter. "Hell, you was the one telling that sad-ass story."

Nonchalantly, I shrugged. "You asked."

Standing, she nodded and patted me on the shoulder. "You look good," she assured me. "I'm sure the deejay is about to call you to the stage." She picked up the hairbrush and brushed my hair down in the back.

"Yeah." I glanced down and then looked up as our eyes met in the mirror. "Thanks for the talk. I needed it."

"Ain't no thang. We all do sometimes," she said and set the brush down.

Just then, the deejay announced that I was next. "That's my cue," I said, standing up.

Stepping back, Alize eyed me up and down, then placed her hands on her hips. "Damn, bitch, you let me know if you change your mind about switching teams. I want first taste." Alize licked her lips. "Damn, you look good."

"If I ever bump my head and do that, you'll be the first to know," I joked, walking toward the backstage entrance.

"Bitch, don't make me trip you up on the stairs and make you suffer a concussion," she joked, turning to go to the front.

Alize was right. The joint was packed tonight, and these dudes looked as if they were ballin' for sure. I walked out and did my thing to "Blame It" by Jamie Foxx. When I ended it with my signature move, the bouncers had to keep this one dude who was drunk out of his mind from storming the stage. I had so much money on the floor and on my thongs and garter, it was insane. As I walked to the back, I counted it up and found I had made $2,000 in my stage show alone. *Damn!*

Greg walked in the back. "You got some regulars wanting private dances, Spanish Fly," he told me.

"I'm coming," I said, tossing a shot of Cuervo before walking out.

"Damn, baby, you look good." Greg licked his lips. "Too bad it can only be business between us."

"Yeah, whatever." I ignored him and walked out on the floor to one of my regulars. He gave me 500 bones off the rip, and I began twisting and dancing my ass off. I moved on to the next dude who had graced me with another hundred bones when one of the waitresses, Tiffany, tapped me on the shoulder.

"Spanish, those dudes want you. It's the guy in the blindfold's birthday, and they want you to give him a dance," she laughed.

"Them dudes got money, Tiff?" I asked her.

"Shit, the one who asked gave me a fifty spot as a tip for one ice-cold beer, so I would say so. Don't nobody tip us waitresses like that unless they're a celebrity."

"A'ight then," I said, making my way over to the group of men. "They tell me y'all are checking for Spanish Fly," I said as I approached them.

"Hell yeah. We missed your performance, but I've seen it before. You gotta do something special for my mans right here. It's his twenty-eighth birthday. He's a professional now, and he doesn't really hang out like this no more. Show him what the fuck he's been missing," the one who requested me said, while the other men hooted.

"His birthday, huh?" I asked erotically. "Why y'all got him in a blindfold?"

"Shit, I had to keep you a secret until I could secure the dance," he replied as his boys gave him daps.

One of the dudes smacked my ass. "Damn, look at that shit jiggle!" he shouted, sticking a fifty in my thong.

"I told you, dude," the first guy said.

I walked over to the birthday boy and whispered seductively in his ear, "Are you ready to get caught in the Spanish Fly trap?"

He nodded eagerly. "Yes," he said, trying to keep his composure.

"Hell yeah! Damn! I wish it was my birthday!" the guy who gave me the fifty hollered.

I began dancing on the birthday boy to get him hot, and he was shifting in his chair something awful as his boys started throwing money at me. I scooped it up. I bent down with my ass tooted in his face when his boy lifted the blindfold. I spread my cheeks and made them clap for him.

"Ooh shit!" he said excitedly as his boys hollered in pleasure.

More money fell, and I collected it all. I turned around to straddle him, and when our eyes met, I nearly choked. It was Mr. Sharper, my old boss! My heart rate was going a mile a minute, and suddenly I felt like a cheap slut.

He sat forward. "Lucinda?" he asked, confused.

"Oh shit," I said nervously. "Mr. Sharper."

"Dawg, you know Spanish Fly?" the guy who requested me asked as the others looked on in shock.

"Lucinda?" he asked again in amazement as I covered over my titties, turned, and ran away. "Lucinda!" I heard him yelling, but I kept running.

When I reached the dressing room, I paced back and forth nervously and drank a long swig from my bottle of Jose Cuervo. I couldn't believe this shit! Of all the strip clubs in Atlanta, this dude had to show up at Moet! I never knew Mr. Sharper was so young. Hell, I never looked at him that way because I went to work to work, unlike the rest of the females who were constantly trying to get at him. That's why they harped so much on me being his pet. The majority of them wanted him for themselves. He was a successful, good-looking, chocolate black man who I never in a million years would've thought I would cross paths with again, especially not at Club Moet!

Soon Greg came busting through the door. "What the fuck is you doing?" he yelled. "You ran off from some patrons?"

"I'm sorry, Greg. I am, but I can't go back out there tonight," I said to him as I gathered my things.

"What the fuck you mean you can't go back out there? Yes, you are," he hollered.

"No, I'm not," I said sternly.

"Look! I don't know what your beef is with them dudes. Did some ill shit go down?" he asked. "Me and Big Crunch will handle it."

"Nah, they didn't get out of hand."

"Well then, Spanish," he said, grabbing me by my arm and spinning me around, "you better get to explaining why you running off."

"Look! I know one of them dudes. I never thought I'd see him here, and I just prefer to go home tonight," I told him.

"I don't give a fuck if you saw your daddy, Spanish. This is a business. Sex sells, so go and sell it!"

"I'll sell it on Tuesday," I told him.

"You won't have a job on Tuesday if you don't get out there!"

"I'll holla at Pooch," I said dismissively.

"I already did," he interjected. "Pooch said if nothing ill happened, you needed to go finish up. He's not going to have his customers not being satisfied because you getting a conscience. So if you don't go back out there, by direct orders from Pooch, you are fired, Spanish Fly."

Fuck me! That fucking Pooch could be a heartless-ass bastard. No wonder Trinity fucked Terrence that night. Pooch and I used to be down like four flats on a Cadillac. I knew him back when his moms still called him Vernon. He forgot it was me who stopped Big Mike from whooping his ass on the playground by letting him feel on my butt.

And it was me who fed him the info about Trinity needing her rent paid so he could use that information to push up on her. I'd hand delivered his woman to him after years of his ass not being able to hook up with her, and he did me like this? Me? I should've known that *puto* only cared about his money, though. At the end of the day, he was and always would be a true-blooded hustla.

Panic kicking in, I made a desperate-ass move. "Yo, Greg," I said coyly to him. "How can we make this square between us? I'm sure there's something I can do so that you won't, you know, tell Pooch," I said, leaning on him sexily, slowly licking my lips. "I'll do anything."

Greg smiled and rubbed his hands together. With his ugly ass! But I was in a fucked-up situation, and I needed my so-called job. "Meet me in my office in fifteen minutes. I'm sure we can work some thangs out," he said, gripping my ass.

"All right, boo." I planted a wet kiss on his lips.

Greg licked his lips and shook his head. Then he turned to walk away. "Oh, and if you have a change of heart, don't bother coming back," he said and walked out.

I grabbed a paper towel and wiped his nasty kiss off my lips. I didn't know what to do. If I followed through with this, I'd become another ho in the streets, and then these dudes would expect me to do anything to get down. If I didn't, I'd be fired again, and I'd be broke in a couple of months with only my unemployment check to sustain me. I'd even quit Susie Q's for this damn gig. I exhaled as I sat down in a chair in the dressing room and took another swig of Jose Cuervo before putting my hair up in a ponytail. Looking at myself in the mirror, I concluded, "Sometimes a woman has to do what she has to do," and I prepared to go and fuck the shit out of Greg.

Just as I stood, some rosary beads that Nadia had given me fell out of my bag, and I picked them up. It was as if I heard God Himself ask me, "Where is your faith?"

I jumped because the voice was so real. I looked around, but there was no one there. It was just me and the beads. Tears instantly streamed down my cheeks, and I pulled out a picture of Nadia. That's when I knew I couldn't do it. Whether I was fired or not, I was getting the hell out of Club Moet. Alize and the rest of these broads could have it. I was better than this. Pooch just didn't realize he did me the biggest favor in the world. Never again, no more did I have to walk through these doors and degrade myself. No matter what happened, neither stripping or fucking was the answer for me. Spanish Fly was officially retiring, and Lucinda was about to get on the job hunt.

I dressed and made my way to Greg's office. When I opened the door, he was sitting at his desk with a box of Trojans.

"Ready, Ms. Fly?" he asked with a huge-ass smile on his face.

"No, I'm not. As a matter of fact, tell Pooch thanks, but no thanks anymore. I quit," I said, turning to walk away.

"Spanish Fly!" he yelled. "I gave them niggas a hundred bones back to get a dance from Chocolate Flava! Get your ass back here!"

I turned around, took out a hundred spot, and threw it at him. "Now we're even."

"Don't come here looking for work no more! Fuck you, Spanish Fly!" he called out as I shut his door.

Alize clapped as I walked by. "I knew you couldn't hang, goody-goody."

"You got it. I'm good." I threw my hands up.

"Let me go rock this nigga world right quick so he won't be lying on you to Pooch. I'm your witness that you gave up the money he dished out."

I frowned. "You're going to fuck him?"

"Oh, hell yeah. Black and ugly or whatever, that nigga got a king-size dong, and he knows how to make me holla for a dollar! But this one is a favor for you. Trust me, that nigga is grimy."

I hugged her. "Thanks, Alize."

"Ain't no thang. We have to look out for each other in this game. Now get the fuck out of here and go home." She smiled. "Oh, and if you do bump that head of yours, I'm waiting."

I laughed as she walked into the office, and soon I heard kissing and moaning. *Yuck. Man, help comes from all places. Now I have to get the hell out of this place.* As I walked out the door and down the sidewalk, I heard someone yelling my name. I turned around and saw Mr. Sharper. I exhaled and kept walking, but he caught up to me.

"Lucinda, wait," he yelled, touching my arm.

"Look, Mr. Sharper, I've embarrassed myself enough for one night. You don't have to chase me out here," I said with an attitude, not bothering to look at him.

"Can you just wait a second, please?" he asked with slight irritation in his voice.

I turned to face him. "Okay," I said nonchalantly.

"I just didn't want there to be any awkwardness between us. I wanted you to know that I don't judge what you do."

"Well, outside of this club and the insurance company, you wouldn't see me. But you won't see me at either one now," I replied.

"Why?"

"After I refused to come back out, I had an option: sleep with the manager so he wouldn't rat on me to the owner, or get fired. I chose neither. I quit."

He smiled. "Good for you. Truth be told, you didn't seem like the kind of woman who'd be in this place anyway. Not from the person I saw at work."

"Yeah, it wasn't for me. After I got fired, I made a desperate move and started working here. It was truly one of the worst decisions I've ever made, but it'll get better. It always does. If there's one thing that Lucinda Rojas is good at, it's survival," I explained.

He shook his head. "Lucinda, I'm sorry about that. I wish I could've done something so you didn't have to turn to this. I feel so bad, and believe me, you are missed around there."

"Mr. Sharper, it's not your fault. You did what you could do for me, and that's more than enough."

"Will you stop calling me Mr. Sharper? That was at work," he laughed. "Truth be told, I hate that. It makes me sound old as hell."

I giggled. "Yeah, I had no idea you were only twenty-seven . . . well, twenty-eight now. I mean, not that you look old or anything, it's just like you said, calling you Mr. Sharper makes you seem so much older, and it's extremely formal."

"Why don't you say how you really feel?" he said sarcastically.

"I'm sorry. I just keep it real. Besides, you don't want me to call you Mr. Sharper, but I don't even know your first name," I chuckled.

He extended his hand for a handshake. "My name is Aldris. Aldris Sharper."

I shook his hand. "Aldris. Kinda like Idris or Al—" I was saying.

"Al Sharpton!" he laughed, cutting me off. "Don't even go there. That's exactly why I do not go by Al."

I burst into laughter. "I'll bet you don't, especially if you used to rock some long, permed hair!"

"Hell to the no," he laughed.

"Hey, but Idris Elba is a compliment. That dude is too fine for words," I said, shaking my head.

"I'll take your word for it. I'm not even trying to feel that way about ol' dude," he joked.

I looked at the time. "I better get out of here. My daughter's grandma is watching her. I should go ahead and pick her up."

He nodded. "Okay. I didn't mean to hold you up."

"No, no, you're cool. It's all good," I assured him.

"It was good seeing you again," he said.

"You too," I agreed as I turned to walk away. "Oh yeah, have fun with Chocolate Flava." I giggled.

"Whatever," he chuckled. "Hey, wait. I almost forgot."

"What's up?" I asked, turning back around.

"Listen, I know some contacts in the medical field. Maybe I could look around for you or just keep my ear to the ground and let you know when opportunities come up. I know it's not my fault, but I feel like I owe you. I hate what happened, and I just feel like a hard worker such as you deserves a chance," he explained.

"Well, that's cool. I'd really appreciate that."

"Can I have a contact number so that if I do find something, I could let you know?" he asked with a little sarcasm.

"Shut up," I said with a laugh as he handed me his phone. I plugged my phone number in his contact list.

"Cool. I'll keep you posted," he said and put his phone back in his back pocket.

"Thank you, Aldris," I stressed for effect.

"Good night, Lucinda." He chuckled.

"Good night."

Once in my car, I couldn't help but pray that he really did help me, but for now, I was going home to enjoy time with my daughter. Even though I had no job and limited income, I felt so free and liberated. For some reason, I felt as if my life were finally just beginning. Whatever the feeling was, I hoped it lasted a long, long time.

Chapter Two

Trinity

Guilty pleasures. That's what I was experiencing nowadays. I wished in all sincerity that I could say Pooch was the source of the pep in my step and the glide in my stride, but that honor went to my baby, Terrence. Ever since our night of lovemaking in Suwanee, I'd been high as a kite, and he was making damn sure I wasn't coming down. Don't get me wrong, I didn't jump in full-fledged at first. In fact, that next weekend when I dropped the kids off at Terrence's house, I told him that it would be safer for us to be cool and remain friends, but he wasn't even trying to hear that shit. That nigga talked a good game about waiting for me and shit, but ever since the moment I gave his ass the green light, he had been no holds barred. I didn't even want to admit it, but that conversation ended with the best fucking oral sex of my damn life! And I ain't just talking about receiving it either, you know.

Since that moment, it'd been on like fucking popcorn! I'd been sneaking like a thief in the fucking night. Between hiding classes and fucking Terrence, I was surprised I hadn't had a heart attack. I was scared shitless of getting caught, but I was addicted to fulfilling my dreams, and I damn sure was addicted to Terrence's love and dick.

Terrence's loving had gotten so good to me that fucking Pooch felt like a chore. The key was not to act like it was

a chore. Whenever that nigga told me to bend over, I was
on all fours in an instant and screaming like it was the
best thing I'd ever felt in my life. No need to change
the routine. At one point, those screams were for real,
and even though now they were just a facade, I wasn't
about to let that nigga think I wasn't enjoying it. While I
was fully aware that I was playing with fire, I was being
damn sure careful not to get burned.

The question remained, why was I even still with
Pooch? I wish I had a straight answer for that, but really
I didn't. It was a combination of a lot of things. For one,
probably the most important one: fear. I was scared for
Terrence's life and mine if I told Pooch I was leaving
him for Terrence. Hell, even if I just left him and he later
found out I was with Terrence made me nervous like a
muthasucka. Then, of course, it was guilt. Okay, I knew
Pooch was a hustla and his attitude fucking sucked, but
deep down, I honestly felt like that nigga was true to me.
That was rare for a nigga in general, but especially for a
street nigga with money as long as Pooch's.

Bitches were hatin' on me big time. They wanted what
I had—security—which was another reason I was still
here. But if you think I had to deal with hoes running
up on me, catching Pooch dippin' and slippin', or the
ever-famous baby-mama drama, you can think again.
Outside of the expected hatin', I'd never had a bitch who
had said, "Yeah, I fucked your man." To me, that was a
clear sign that he wasn't fucking around on me. Either
that or he was paying them hoes off for real, but knowing
Pooch, I truly doubted that. Like I said, I felt guilty that I
was doing him dirty, but not guilty enough to stop.

Shit, if you want to be real with it, I felt in some ways he
brought it on himself. I would never have given Terrence
a second thought if Pooch truly valued me as a person.
True, he respected me as his woman, but to him, that's
all I was: his woman, the operative word being "his." I

was just as much his property as his businesses, his drugs, and his money. He ran me like he ran them, the way he fucking wanted, and that was it. So guess what? I found somebody who gave me what I needed while Pooch continued to give me what I wanted. It was a fair trade. Problem was, the more I got what I needed from Terrence, the less I wanted anything Pooch had to offer me. In the end, what I needed and what I really wanted were all wrapped up in the same package: Terrence.

"Trinity!" Pooch yelled, startling me.

I jumped and rolled over on the bed. "What? You scared the shit out of me."

He came and sat on the bed. "What the fuck you so jumpy about? I've been calling your ass for at least five minutes."

"I was just reading the magazine. I didn't hear you," I lied. I closed up the magazine that I was pretending to read and sat up next to Pooch. "What's up?"

"I swear I don't know where your mind be at," he said, shaking his head. "But check it. I have to get ready to go out of town tomorrow."

I frowned. "For what?"

He rubbed his hands together. "I'm tryin'a expand my empire, and I gotta get up with Tot about venturing into it with me. I need more product to service my customers."

"Why would you want to expand? Everything is kosher. Why rock the boat tryin'a be greedy?" I asked.

"It's cool, but every business needs to expand to survive."

"This kind of business should stay small to survive."

He sucked his teeth. "I ain't come to you for you to be my consultant and shit. I'm just letting you know I ain't gon' be here this weekend. Don't you worry about the streets. I got this shit on lock. This is what I do. Shit," he said with irritation.

"I'm just concerned about you, baby," I said, but honestly, I just didn't want no heat around us.

He kissed me. "I know, baby, but you know this is who I am. This is what I do. I got this. Let me handle these streets. You just keep yourself looking pretty and being my lady. A'ight?"

I nodded and stood up. "A'ight. When are you leaving and coming back?"

He stood up and pulled me to him. "I leave tomorrow around noon, and I'll be back at about six Sunday night."

"Cool. Listen, speaking of looking pretty, I want to go get my nails done. Can you watch the kids for me while I go do that?"

"Yeah, I got 'em."

I looked confused. "Huh?"

"I said I got 'em. You sure you don't need your fuckin' hearing checked?" he asked me with the most serious expression on his face.

I laughed. "No, I heard you. I just can't believe your answer. You actually said yes."

"What the fuck was I supposed to say?"

I shrugged. "A lot of times I ask, and you be like no because of this, that, and the third. I'm just shocked."

"Shit, that's because a lot of times I have this, that, and the third to do," he replied, irritated. "Why the hell you even ask me if you feel like I'm gon' say no?"

"Asking never hurts. I'm just saying usually your answer is no."

"A nigga try to help, and I'm gettin' slack. Ain't this a bitch?" He shook his head in disbelief.

"I'm not giving you slack. I'm just shocked. That's all I'm saying," I said with a slight attitude.

"Whatever. While you wasting time being shocked and shit, you better get to going before something do come up and you be draggin' they asses to the nail salon with you."

I shook my head as I stuck my feet in my flip-flops. I could always count on Pooch to spoil a sincere moment between us. Like I said, his attitude fucking sucked.

"I'm 'bout to go. If you need me, you know where to hit me," I said, grabbing my cell phone and waving it as I got my purse.

"A'ight," he said and pulled me to him for a kiss. "Damn. When you get back, I'm gon' have to hit that shit right quick. It's been a couple of days. You being stingy on a nigga and shit."

"No, I ain't. You ain't asked," I said to him.

"Since when I gotta ask?" He looked at me crazy.

I rolled my eyes. "I'm just saying you ain't made no moves."

"Well, I'ma make a move when you get home," he said, kissing me on my neck. "Fuck! I can already feel that pussy slidin' on my dick," he said, grabbing his crotch. "Hurry back."

I giggled. "A'ight baby." I walked to the door.

"Oh, and get red polish on the toes this time."

"Red?" I asked, turning around in my tracks.

"Yeah, red. It's a color like blue, white, and green," he quipped.

I rolled my eyes. "I know that. Why you want me to get red?"

"You used to get red all the time, and I thought it was hella sexy. Now you keep getting this damn orange or peach-looking color. It's cute, but I like red," he said.

"It's called Jasmine, and I happen to like it," I said with an attitude. *And so does Terrence.*

"Yeah, well, get red this time. You can go back to your Jasmine next time," he said nonchalantly. "Besides, it ain't like you paying for it," he commented arrogantly.

"Oh, so now you throwing up your money in my face?" I asked.

"Nah, babe, I'm not throwing it up. I'm just lettin' you know since you seem to have such a fuckin' attitude about it. I don't know what the fuck is up with that lately, either. You need to check that shit."

"Red it is," I said, throwing up my deuces. "I'm out," I added before I cussed his ass out for real. My patience was short as hell with him lately, but like I said twice before, his attitude sucked.

"Trinity," he called out as he walked out behind me.

"Yeah," I said, not even bothering to turn around.

"I love you. Remember—"

"I know. Remember that shit. I do," I interrupted and walked to my car.

Once I was down the road, my cell phone buzzed. I swore if it was Pooch texting me to start some shit, I was going to fucking flip for real. I picked up my cell when I got to the stop sign, and I read the message. It was from Terrence asking me to call him, so I hit number one on my speed dial. Yep, he was numero uno.

"Hello?" his deep baritone voice floated through my phone. It was like music to my ears. All of my tension instantly eased away.

"Hey, baby," I cooed.

"Hey, you. That was quick. Pooch must not be around."

"No, he's actually watching the kids while I go get my nails done if you can believe that," I giggled. "I was so shocked."

He chuckled. "I'm not. It's his territorial senses going off on him. He can't pinpoint it yet, but a nigga knows when someone is moving in on his territory."

"Please don't say that. I'm nervous enough," I said with exasperation.

"Let me quit messing with you before I give you a heart attack," he said. "Are you getting my favorite color?"

"Hell no. This fucking asshole wants me to get red. Talking about that's what he wants. He is so fucking aggravating."

"Then leave," he said matter-of-factly.

"Terrence," I warned.

"I won't go there," he said, giving up. "Am I going to get to see you this weekend?"

I smiled. "Actually, you will. Pooch is heading out of town tomorrow. He's trying to expand his business."

"Oh, really? He just bold with it, huh?"

"Yeah, I told his ass, but you know what? Fuck it."

"He's a grown man. He can handle it. So fuck him and let me handle you," he said seductively.

"Oh, baby, and you definitely handle it very well."

He laughed loudly. "Hell, I know, but it's nice to hear it. I'm more than happy to oblige."

I shook my head. "You so fucking cocky."

"And I don't have a reason to be?"

"Yeah, you do with your arrogant ass."

"Damn. I miss you and my babies. I wish you all were over here," he said sweetly to me. "I want to do a family day with you and the kids this Sunday. Let's have a picnic in the park."

"Well, Pooch will still be out of town, so I will have Princess too," I said, thinking out loud. "I don't know, Terrence. You know how Pooch hates us to be around each other."

"You just said that nigga is gon' be out of town. Plus, you know I love Princess, so what's the problem?"

"I guess nothing really. I'm just being paranoid."

"I would say that you wouldn't have to be paranoid if you would leave him, but you don't want to hear that," Terrence said sarcastically.

"I know. Listen, I just pulled up at the nail salon, so let me go."

"A'ight. Get all jazzy for me. I suck red toes too."

I burst into laughter. "You's a fool!" I shouted into the phone.

"A fool in love," he said sweetly.

I sat back, blown away by his sentiment. "Aww, I love you too."

"Go. Go get jazzy. I'll holla at you," he said, obviously choked up.

"A'ight. Bye, baby." I blew a kiss into the phone.

I didn't know what the hell I was gonna do about my situation with Pooch. One thing was becoming very apparent to me. Both Terrence and my feelings were getting way too deep to keep putting off what we really wanted. Case in point, the last damn thing I wanted to do was leave this damn nail salon and go back to Pooch. I wanted to go be with my Terrence. I loved him.

Chapter Three

Trinity

"'I'm easy like Sunday morning.'" I sang a very bad rendition of Lionel Richie's song as I floated around, finishing my house cleaning. I couldn't help but smile.

Pooch had been gone since Friday, and I had been thoroughly enjoying myself with Terrence. It was our first time spending the night together since before we broke up. I wasn't crazy now. I knew Pooch would be on the lookout, especially after what happened the last time he left town. To this day, I still trembled over the fact that Terrence and I could've gotten caught by Pooch or his people when we were sneaking around with each other when I was supposed to be out partying with my girls. Had it not been for Terrence's quick thinking and my girl Lucinda's willingness to lie for me, we would've been. Needless to say, after that incident, I was cautious.

On Friday night, I'd had Terrence pick up the kids and had my mom pick me up and drop me off at a hotel where Terrence had rented adjoining rooms for us and the kids. That way, my car stayed put all damn night. Pooch called me a couple of times and was content that I was chilling at the house, so once he was all squared away, Terrence and I got down to business! And oh yes, he did suck red toes too.

Besides the lovemaking, we talked about life, school, his job, and marriage. Yes, marriage. We both wanted to get married one day, and of course he kept insisting that he wanted to marry me, but I didn't get my hopes up. I was just enjoying the simple pleasures he gave me that I never got from Pooch, such as being held and caressed and feeling so appreciated, so loved, so respected. Before daybreak the next morning, a cab picked up Princess and me, and I was in my bed before anyone could blink their eyes. Thug niggas usually slept until midmorning anyway. While Terrence had our two that Saturday, I used my time to do my coursework and the majority of my cleaning. However, we were on the phone all night having phone sex. Without even fucking touching me, that man made me cum harder than Pooch did. Now that was some shit.

The one thought that kept coming to mind was that I wished Terrence had never broken up with me. When he had to do his bid, if he'd only told me that he'd broken up with me because he felt he'd be holding me back, I would've fought for him, for us. I could've explained that I was with him. I'd would've done the time with him instead of feeling like he didn't want me and the kids anymore. It's not that I didn't appreciate Pooch for stepping up to the plate as my man, and there was no way I regretted our daughter. My kids were my world, and I loved Princess, I truly did, but it would've been so much better if Terrence was her daddy and I'd never hooked up with Pooch. With Terrence, it was as if time stood still and we picked up right where we left off. I wanted to be free to love him and be the woman for him he so desperately wanted, but I was bound to Pooch. Like I said before, once you were in that circle, you were in it, and by having Pooch's child, I was in it beyond waist deep.

I was so excited to meet Terrence at the park for our picnic. On point as usual, I had on my ankle-length olive green and cream cotton sundress that dipped low, exposing some cleavage, with matching flip-flops. With my classy ponytail pulled back neatly with a regal effect, my MAC makeup poppin', and my Opulence perfume dabbed in my key areas, I knew that I looked and smelled scrumptious. Terrence smiled when he saw us approaching. He ran over and grabbed Princess. He looked good with his jean shorts and short-sleeved striped Polo shirt, and Brittany and Terry were cute in their Polo outfits as well. We were so fucking fly that we should've taken a family picture. Yeah, the same one Pooch forbade me to take.

"How are two of my favorite women doing?" Terrence asked as he kissed Princess on the cheek. We walked to join the kids.

"We're great. I'm a lot better now that I'm with you."

He smiled. "It could be like this all the time."

"You never miss an opportunity to express that to me, do you?"

"Nah, not at all," he said and laughed.

We sat down on the blanket and enjoyed our sandwiches, chips, and drinks while having a great time with each other and our kids. After we ate, the kids played on the playground equipment. We put Princess in the baby center so she could play as we sat on the bench and watched her.

"Thank you for this. I miss this," Terrence said, looking over to check on Brittany and Terry.

"I miss it too, Dreads," I agreed, playfully pulling one of his dreadlocks.

"You love running them fingers through this hair," he joked. "But you'd chop mine off if I touched yours."

"I can't mess up yours, but God knows you could mess up mine."

He turned to face me. "I wish you would really consider leaving him and marrying me. Let's be a family, Trinity.

We don't have to stay in Atlanta. We could leave, us and
the kids. Start over. Start fresh."

"What about your job and my coursework?" I asked
him.

"Fuck that. I got that. You know I got y'all no matter
what. Just trust me enough to let me be that man for you.
You're scared of Pooch and maybe even a little scared to
put your trust back in me. I fucked up when I got locked
up and shit. I regret every fucking moment of leaving you
and my seeds out here to fend for yourselves. If I could
do it all over again . . ." he said, his voice trailing off. "Just
let me do it over again, please."

I pulled my Dolce & Gabbana shades on top of my
head and leaned forward. Although what he proposed
was enticing, could I really do it? Could I leave Pooch,
run away with Terrence, and let go of the fears that he
called me out on? I wanted to, and more than anything, I
needed to. Terrence leaned forward, staring at me as if he
were waiting for me to grant him permission to breathe.

"Terrence, I—" I began. Suddenly, to our surprise, I was
snatched up by my arm.

"What the fuck?" Terrence yelled, jumping up to see
the culprit.

"What the fuck are you doing here with him?" Pooch
yelled.

Stunned, I couldn't answer him. It was only one o'clock
in the afternoon. This nigga said he'd be home around six.
What the hell? How did he find me?

"Get your hands off her!" Terrence yelled as he pulled
me out of Pooch's grasp and protectively stood in front of
me. "Who the fuck do you think you are, grabbing on her
like that?" Terrence asked, boldly getting up in Pooch's
face.

Oh God! I was terrified! They stood toe to fucking toe
as if this were one of those highly anticipated fights, like

the Mayweather and Pacquiao bout. Barely an inch separated them, and both had hatred in their eyes. A mixture of adrenaline and anger coursed through their veins so that their muscles bulged out of control. With their jaws locked tight, the only thing the other one was waiting for was for someone to make a move. I looked at the parking lot, and Pooch's still-running SUV was parked directly behind my Mercedes with the driver's side door wide open. From the passenger side, Big Cal watched.

"Didn't I tell you to stay the fuck away from my girl?" Pooch asked, staring intensely at Terrence.

"Since when do I ever listen to you? We have children. We're enjoying time with our kids. Regardless of how you feel or what you think, she's bound to me for life. Not by one but two of my seeds!"

Pooch let out a sinister laugh. He stepped back an inch and clapped his hands together. His nose flared. "And them kids is the only reason you still breathing, bitch. I suggest if you want to continue making them happy, you stay away from her."

Terrence sucked his teeth slowly and deliberately and cut his eyes at Pooch. "Nigga, please. If you wanna do something, let's get to it. I don't give a fuck about that shit you talkin' right now."

"Oh yeah?" Pooch said real cocky-like.

"Oh yeah." Terrence nodded.

Deathly afraid of the situation, I forced myself between them. "Pooch, listen, please. He just mad right now. He don't mean it."

"Fall back, li'l mama," Terrence said, trying to pull me back but never taking his gaze off Pooch.

Pulling my arm away, I forced Pooch to look into my eyes by grabbing his chin and pulling his face down so that we locked eyes. "Please, Pooch. For me." I turned to face Terrence. "Let it go. You've got the kids to think about, please," I pleaded as sweat and tears rolled down my face.

Reluctantly, they both eased up and fell back.

"Get my daughter, and get your ass in my truck, right now," Pooch peered at me and demanded, pointing his finger in my face.

"Trinity—" Terrence began.

I put my hand up. "Don't. Just take Brit and Terry, please."

He nodded as I scooped up Princess and hightailed it to Pooch's truck. "Final warning, muthafucka," I heard Pooch issue to Terrence, and by the time I locked Princess in the car seat, Pooch was at the truck.

"Big Cal, get out and drive her Mercedes. Give him the fuckin' keys, Trinity," he demanded, and I obeyed.

I was about to get in the passenger side when Pooch yanked me by the arm, dragged me to the back, and pushed me in the seat next to Princess! "Get your fuckin' triflin' ass back there with the baby," he said, seething.

"Pooch—"

"Shut up," he screamed, causing me to jump and Princess to cry.

He slammed the door and jumped into the driver's seat, and we pulled off with a screech. Except for a phone call Pooch made, which was to ask his sister if she was home, we rode in silence all the way to the house. He didn't say shit to me, not a word. I refused to make eye contact through the rearview mirror, so I sat there with my head down.

"Get out of the car," Pooch sneered once we got home. He turned to Big Cal and threw him his keys.

"Princess is still in the car," I said to him.

He ignored me. "Take Princess to my sister's house and chill out until I call you," Pooch commanded Big Cal, who looked at me with sorrowful eyes, got in the SUV, and dipped with my baby.

Now I was officially scared shitless. Pooch unlocked the door, grabbed my arm, pulled me all the way to his office in the king suite, and threw me down on the sofa. Perched on the edge of his desk, he calmly pulled out a Cuban cigar, clipped the end, lit it, and pulled a drag from it. He folded his arms and eyed me suspiciously before he pulled another drag. I didn't know what to do, so I sat there just staring at him in fear.

He put the cigar between his index and middle finger and pointed it at me. "Do you know how many bitches would love to be in your shoes? Hmm? Do you?"

I only nodded.

"Do you know how good I am to you, Trinity?" he asked, puffing on his cigar.

"Yes," I said weakly.

He laughed evilly. "I don't think you do, so let me break it down for you. I may not be sentimental and shit, but I'm loyal. I give you everything your heart wants and desires. I've treated you well. Right?" he asked tensely, but I didn't answer. "Right?" he exclaimed, looking at me with an intense expression on his face.

I nodded.

"So when I say something, I expect it to be followed. I told you to stay away from him. Now I come back in town early to surprise my lady, but I get a phone call from one of my dudes that you two are up at the park, looking mighty fuckin' cozy, having a nice li'l family picnic together. This cat knows you and Terrence, but I still don't fuckin' believe this shit, because you would never do some shit like that behind my back. Never.

"But as sure as the sun is shining this afternoon, I roll up to see your car and his, and I look over and see this nigga rapping in yo' ear like y'all a fuckin' couple and shit," he said with another sinister laugh. "This shit is so funny to me because a couple of weeks ago, some chickenhead broad told me she saw you in the Compound grindin' like a muthafucka on Terrence, and I thought the silly ho was lying on you just to get next to me. I didn't even confront yo' ass wit' it, because that's how much confidence I had in you," he said, pointing his finger at me.

My nerves went from being frazzled to straight shot! I started trembling, and I swore I was going to pass out. Here I was guilty as fuck of everything I'd been accused of, and I had no idea where this little interrogation session was going. It would be different if he'd yell at me and get it over with, but this shit? This shit was cryptic.

He pulled once more on his cigar before putting it in the ashtray and walking over to me. He looked at me sideways, then slowly paced back and forth in front of me. He stopped directly in front of me and gripped my chin so that I was looking directly into his eyes.

"With all this information, I'm going to ask you this, Trinity, and I'm going to ask you this . . . one . . . time," he growled. His eyes burned with anger, and his jaw was so tight it bulged out on both sides. "Are you fuckin' wit' that nigga Terrence on me? Hmm?"

I shook my head. "No, Pooch, I . . . I would never—" I stuttered nervously.

Before I could finish, my face was met with a backhand slap. Instantly, I grabbed my face because it felt as if it split in half. Tears of fear and pain poured from my eyes.

He grabbed me by my face, squeezed it, and bent down so we were nose to nose. "Don't. You. Lie. To. Me! Don't you ever fuckin' lie to me," he screamed, holding my face.

"Pooch, please," I begged in a whisper, my voice stolen by fear.

"We gonna try this shit again," he said. I tried to pry his hand free, but it was firmly affixed to my face. Every vein in his neck and arms bulged. If I didn't know better, I would swear he was geeked up. But no drugs were needed. His rage was pure, and the inferno burned from a betrayal felt deep within. "Was you up in the Compound dancing wit' that nigga? Are you fuckin' wit that nigga, huh, Trinity? Huh?"

Figuring it was better to tell a partial truth, I nodded. "I dance . . . I danced with him, but that's it," I stuttered. I also figured it was best to admit to the less-offensive crime.

He let me go, started rubbing his head with both hands, and paced back and forth with hard footsteps again. I didn't know what to say or do. My face felt like it was virtually on fire, and I felt the swelling increasing under my eye. This nigga literally was flipping the fuck out! I was ready to bolt for the door when he started hitting himself on the forehead and talking to himself.

"I'm a good nigga. I try to be. Them niggas be saying don't put all yo' trust in no broad. That's what they be tellin' me, and I be like nah, not my babe. Not my Trinity. Shit. Not my Trinity. She's loyal. This is my ride or die bitch here. I shoulda known something was going on. She getting all jazzy more and more. Coppin' an attitude wit' me when she normally wouldn't. Even the sex, it's been good, but something just was never quite right about it to me. She don't have the same emotion as before," he said to himself while continuing his antics.

"Pooch," I said barely above a whisper. "I'm sorry, baby. I am."

It was as if my words brought him to the realization that I was still in the room with him. Suddenly, he turned and looked at me. Disbelief and malice danced in his eyes, and in that split second, I knew that malice had won. "Sorry," he huffed. He turned his back to me and popped his neck to one side. "Oh, you're gonna be sorry," he said angrily.

Before I could react, he was on me so fast and had slapped my other cheek with his open palm and sent me falling across the sofa. "Please, Pooch, stop!" I screamed.

He snatched me up by the throat and pressed his forehead deep into mine. He was so enraged, spit flew out of his mouth. "The next muthafuckin' time I catch you wit' that nigga, I will kill you! Do you fuckin' hear me, li'l mama? That is what he calls you, right? Li'l mama?"

Gagging and coughing, I replied, "Yes."

He let go of my throat and punched me in the mouth. "You gon' learn to respect me!"

The snot, tears, and sweat that were already rolling down my face mixed with the blood that now trickled down the side of my mouth. I held my bleeding mouth as panic settled in. I tried to move away from him, but he grabbed me by the hem of my dress and snatched me back, his hand finding its way around my throat again. My neck felt hot, and the pressure from his hands felt as if it was crushing me.

"Is this my pussy?" he asked. I nodded since I couldn't speak from his hands being wrapped around my throat. Then he let my throat go. "That's right, and you gon' prove it to me," he said, unbuckling his pants.

I shook my head fearfully and put my hands up. "No, Pooch, please!" I screamed, trying to scoot back out of reach, but it was no use.

He balled up his fist and raised his hand as if he was going to strike me. "Make one more muthafuckin' move and I will kill you!"

I stopped moving.

His pants dropped to the floor, and he yanked down his boxers and stroked his dick twice, ready to take back what was stolen from him. Still feeling as though I could plead my way out of this, I begged him to stop, but he pulled me by my knees and threw my legs apart. Then he ripped my thong off. Hocking a glob of spit, he launched it on his dick, smeared it, and rammed it into my dry pussy. Although I yelped in pain, he held his hand over my mouth and kept pumping out of control like the madman he was.

"I told you that you gon' learn to respect me!" he panted huskily as he raped me on the sofa. "Fuckin' bitch! This is my pussy! Mine!" With a hard jolt, he released inside of me.

Without another word, he stood up and pulled up his shorts. Then he walked in the bathroom to wash off and came back to where I was curled up in the fetal position on the sofa. He walked over to me and knelt down. Though I was fearful, I dared not move, but he only kissed my forehead. "I love you, Trinity," he said, stroking my face and hair. "I love you . . . to death."

His declaration shot a cold tingle down my spine as the severity of the last statement took root in my soul. I could do nothing but stare at him as silent tears rolled down my face. My face and body hurt from all of the violation, but worst yet, my soul felt empty on the inside.

As he stroked my face, his voice fell into a soft, soothing tone. "See what you made me do? I never wanted to do you like this. You're my babe," he said and kissed my swollen lips. "Now this is what I want you to do. Call Terrence and tell him to keep his kids for a couple of days. Then go to the bathroom, clean yourself up, draw a nice, warm bath, and soak. I'll come in, dry you off, and put you to bed so you can rest. It's been a long day for you, but I had to teach you a lesson. I think you get it now. I hope so. I love you, and from now on, you're going to do what?" he asked as if he were speaking to a child.

"Remember that shit," I answered hoarsely.

He smiled. "Good. I have to go call Big Cal and have him bring Princess home. I'll watch the baby for you while you get yourself together." And with that, he walked out.

After a few minutes, I sat up and limped across the room to get my cell phone. My hands were trembling as I pressed number one on my phone.

"Trinity!" Terrence yelled. "Is everything okay? Are you all right?"

"Terrence," I said, trying to speak clearly.

"What's wrong? What did he do to you?" he asked frantically.

"Nothing," I whispered. "Keep the kids a couple of days. I'll call you when you can bring them over. I have to go now."

"No! Hell no! Did he put his fucking hands on you? I'll kill his ass! I put that on my muthafucking life," he screamed into the phone.

"Please," I whispered weakly. "Let it go. Just take care of Brit and Terry. Tell them I love them and I'll see them in a couple of days. Please," I begged.

"Baby—" he said, now sad and frustrated.

"I have to go," I cut him off. I hung up and turned off my cell phone. I walked to the door and swung it open to find Pooch standing there.

"Good job," he said as he walked past me back into his office.

I turned to look at him as he sat behind his desk and finished his cigar. Realizing that I was dismissed from his presence, I slowly turned to leave his king's suite.

"'I'm easy like Sunday morning.'" I whimpered Lionel Ritchie's song as I limped down the hall.

No matter how much I loved Terrence, I couldn't be with him. Pooch had proven how lethal he could be, and he warned he'd be worse if I violated his trust again. I wasn't going to because I had to live for my kids. But one thing was for certain, I hated Pooch. I hated him with all my heart.

Chapter Four

LaMeka

I still can't believe I nearly died. My mind replayed the events after Tony tried to choke the life out of me that night. I was rushed from the shelter to the hospital, where I was treated and held for two days. Pastor Gaines stayed by my side the entire time. He even got in contact with my mom, and surprisingly she came. That was the most I could ever remember her being concerned about me. She said that Misha had confessed the entire story to her about what happened, and she wanted to make sure I was okay. I almost busted Misha out about Joe, but it wasn't the time for that shit. Besides, regardless of what Misha did to me, Joe was still a bastard of a man to fuck with a baby. Furthermore, he was even lower to sleep with his girlfriend's daughter. So instead, I listened to my mom and remained happy that she was even around, because God knows I needed someone to be.

I couldn't bear the thought of my friends knowing where I was, so I didn't bother to tell any of them, and I asked my mom not to tell either. However, to ensure I kept my job, Pastor Gaines did stop by the day care, and they completely understood my situation.

For the first time in my life, I broke down and told my mom and Pastor Gaines all the hell I'd been going through with Tony. Much to my surprise, my mom was extremely supportive and offered to be there for me. I was shocked to hear that my mom had put Joe out for good. She actually admitted with Misha being away, she had a lot of time to reflect on the hell she'd put us through growing up. She confessed it was the same way her mom treated her, and even though she vowed not to do the same, somewhere along the way, that's just what she had done. She vowed to be a better mother starting with kicking Joe out and helping me in any way possible. She'd offered to let me move in, but I needed to take it one step at a time. I didn't trust her, Misha, or Tony. Hell, the shit they took me through was enough to make me not trust my own damn self.

However, Pastor Gaines was truly a blessing to me. Once I was released from the hospital, I stayed at the shelter for a couple of days before he was able to get me into a transitional house. Due to Tony Jr.'s autism, I was informed that I'd be able to stay there for one year rent free. Ain't God good? I even met with the counselors from the shelter to get therapy for my ordeal. At first I was nervous, but Pastor Gaines was there to help me.

"Pastor Gaines!" I said, opening the door and motioning for him to come inside. "Come in. What brings you by?"

"Hello, LaMeka. I was just checking on you to see how you've settled in and to see if you were going to the counseling group meeting," he quizzed me.

"Well, everything is coming along here at the house. I'm so appreciative of everyone at the shelter and at the church who has donated clothing and furniture for us. It has truly been a blessing for my sons and me. I saw Mr. Smith the other day, and I thanked him for fixing my driver's side window," I told him.

"Good. I'm glad everything is coming along for you, but you still haven't told me whether you're going to the group session."

Lowering my head, I folded my arms. "Honestly, Pastor—"

"Here we go. Let's hear your excuse," he chimed in.

I shook my head. "No, I wasn't . . . It's just that I get my counseling from you, and I don't see why I need to go around a bunch of people I don't even know."

"Well, I thank God that my counseling and advice has helped you, but you've been involved in a very serious domestic dispute. I'm sure you have some residual effects, or you will in the near future. Tony meant a lot to you, and what you went through with him was not only physical, it was mental and emotional. I'm not saying that ministry isn't needed. All I'm saying is that God put qualified individuals in place to give you the kind of specialized assistance you need. My advice would be to take advantage of it."

"I hear you. I do. But I just don't want people in my business like that. I haven't even told my closest friends about this."

"Maybe that's because they haven't gone through what you've gone through, so you know they won't fully understand."

He had a point. "True, but still, I'd rather tell them before telling a group of strangers."

"LaMeka, believe it or not, sometimes it's easier to tell people you don't know than people you do know. People you don't know don't tend to judge you or the situation. Plus, you'd be around other women who have been in the same situation. You're a strong young lady, and your strength could be just what another woman needs to make it through. There is a blessing for everyone in every situation. Let them bless you, and in turn, you will bless someone else," Pastor Gaines said convincingly.

Again, great points. Honestly, I hadn't considered things the way he pointed out, and while I hated to admit it, it made sense. How could I not go after that convincing argument? "Okay, I will go," I decided.

Although I was apprehensive about attending the group counseling session, I kept my word that I'd given to the pastor. At first, I sat back and remained quiet. However, the more I listened to the other women's stories, the more it helped me see that I wasn't by myself. In fact, there was a woman there who had a child with special needs. During the break, I introduced myself to her, and it felt good to relate to someone not only about the abuse, but about our children, also. I even opened up to the group and admitted my trust issues.

I realized Pastor Gaines was right. I did feel better having a stranger to talk to who could relate to me than trying to explain all of this to a friend. They understood in a way that no one else could. In the end, I was happy that I went, and I was going to make every effort to go back.

Even though it'd only been a couple of weeks since the incident, I was making some good decisions in my life. I'd decided to utilize the help to assist me with Tony Jr.'s medical condition, and I was more determined than ever to get my GED. Now with great counseling and medical help, I was determined not to let anyone or anything deter me. That was, until I saw the one person I vowed to catch a case for— Kwanzie.

Trouble was so easy to get into.

I was coming from a doctor's appointment with Tony Jr. when I saw that heifer in the parking lot. "I vowed on my kids' lives that if I ever saw your ass again, I'd beat the shit out of you," I said, walking up behind her.

I was all set to pop her ass dead in the grill, Tony Jr. present or not, but the sight before me scared me more than anything in my life. Looking like pure hell, she had to be at least ten pounds lighter. Her face was sunken in with dark and gloomy eyes, her clothes were raggedy, her hair was thinned out. It was official. She was a certified crackhead. I stepped back because as much as I wanted to whip her ass, she looked like death. I was scared to be near her.

"I don't want no trouble," she pleaded with me.

"After the shit you did to me? Bitch, please," I yelled at her, moving Tony Jr. behind me. "I should whip your ass right here and now!"

Tears flowed from her eyes. "I'm different. I'm getting off that shit, and I'm sorry."

"You must want some damn money or something for being all kind to me. You weren't talking that shit when you were up in my house, fucking my man."

"Look, I haven't seen Tony in weeks, and it's for the better. He's on that shit heavy. What I did was wrong, and I'm sorry," she apologized.

I pushed her. "Fuck you and your apology."

She put her hand up. "Please don't," she screamed frantically.

"Why not?" I said, about to charge at her.

"I have HIV! I don't want you to get my blood on you!"

Her words stopped me in my tracks. My entire body felt as if it went into immediate shock, and instantly, bile formed in my throat, and I threw up. My throat felt dry, my stomach did somersaults, and I couldn't breathe. *Did this bitch—who I was forced to have oral sex with—just admit that she had the package? Oh God, no! She's been fucking Tony! Oh God, my sister fucked Tony!* I immediately thought back and realized that I did get a test and it was negative, but what if it was too soon to detect it? Was I infected because of Tony's actions? *Oh my God. Oh my God!*

"You liar!" I screamed as the tears that welled up threatened to spill over.

"It's true," she cried. "That's why I'm here."

"How? Was it from Tony? When did you find out?"

She showed me her arm. "I got hooked on heroin. When I got clean, one of the other junkies told me they heard that my dealer had the package. I had been sharing needles with this cat, and he all but told me he'd given me this death sentence," she said as fresh tears ran down her face. "I came to the hospital and got tested. I have it too. They got me hooked up with a program to kick my habit, counseling and treatment for my status. I ain't gon' lie. I've stayed away from Tony because I think word got out to him that I have it. I'm scared of him, of what he'll do to me. I just hope that you don't have it," she confessed.

I'd been using female condoms with Tony ever since that day. Not that I even wanted to screw him. I just knew he'd make me. We'd actually only had sex three times since the whole Kwanzie incident, but still, I was nervous about whether I had it. Just as importantly, I was worried about my sister. I didn't know how long she and Tony had been fucking around, but none of that mattered because he was raw with her. I saw it with my own two eyes.

Hearing the news, I couldn't do shit but turn and run away. I picked up Tony Jr. and held him as I tried to pull breath down into my chest. My entire life flashed before my eyes. Who would look after my children if Tony and I both had it and something happened to us? I couldn't even think of dying and leaving my children here, motherless and fatherless. I couldn't have the package. I couldn't. As soon as I was in my truck, I shut the door and held Tony Jr. tight as I furiously rocked back and forth and cried.

As if understanding my situation, Tony Jr. reached up and rubbed my face. "It's okay, Mommy. I love you, Mommy."

I held him closer and cried into his shirt. "I love you too, li'l man. I love you so much. Mommy is always going to be here for you. Always," I said, trying to convince myself that everything was going to be all right. But my heart was paralyzed with fear. There was a possibility, a strong possibility, that I had HIV.

Chapter Five

Trinity

Three days later and I still hadn't moved. I wasn't fit for shit, much less caring for a baby, so I had Pooch drop Princess off at my mom's house for a few days while Terrence kept our children. Just as they did when Pooch bathed me on the day of my beating, silent tears slid down my face every time he touched me. This was the man I put my trust in? This was the man I ran to thinking he'd be a good man to me? I thought that Pooch loved me, but now, more than ever, I realized he only loved what I stood for in his life—being his bottom bitch. As long as I was his slave, servant, ho, and trophy girl, we were all to the good. To him, my position was underneath him, not even behind him, and damn sure not beside him.

Only moving to use the bathroom, I'd been in the bed in the fetal position since that fateful day. In my mind, I kept replaying the horrifying events in Pooch's office.

"Do you know how many women would love to be in your shoes?"

"When I tell you something, I expect it to be followed."

"You gon' learn to respect me!"

All of Pooch's comments just weighed on my soul. His actions weighed on my mental. I'd never been put in a situation where I was afraid to be me.

Pooch fussed a lot, and of course he meant busi-ness with other people, but I never figured he'd actually do this to me. I'd always prided myself as being his one soft spot. Even if he had caught me cheating with Terrence, I thought his anger would be directed toward Terrence, never me. Not even after he'd warned me that he'd hurt me did I truly believe that he would. My worst fear had always been about him doing something to Terrence or taking his money away from me and my kids, but never physically hurting me. Never. My self-confidence, my pride, my strength, and even my womanhood was taken from me that day, and my face and neck still bore the battle scars. My body still hurt from the violence he unleashed on me, and I was stuck in limbo between depression and submission. I just lay there, scared to move from the one spot that had brought me peace of mind even when Pooch curled his bastard ass up next to me.

"Trinity?" Pooch asked quietly as I stared blankly at the wall. "You have to eat," he said, bending down with a bowl of soup in his hands. He stroked my hair, but I just looked past him, never blinking. "Trinity, can you hear me? Are you okay? Talk to me, babe."

"I just want to lie here," I said hoarsely.

"You have to eat, and you need something to drink," Pooch said.

For the first time since the incident, I looked into his eyes. Hell, he actually looked scared for once. Not of me, just for me.

"I don't want it," I said softly.

"You don't have a choice," he said sternly. "Now, open up."

Out of fear, I did what I was told. Opening my mouth, I sucked the ice-cold water through a straw. It did feel good going down my throat. Pooch sat me up, and I grudgingly ate the soup he fed me.

He wiped my mouth and asked, "See? Don't you feel better?"

I only nodded.

Just then, the doorbell rang. Pooch went to answer it, so I lay back down. Terry ran into my room and pulled on my arm, so I sat up slowly and lazily.

"What is it, Terry?" I asked, not focusing on the fact that my son was home.

"Mama! Mama! Please hurry quickly! Pooch and Daddy are going to fight," he yelled.

Just then, Brittany burst into the room, crying. "Mommy! Pooch pulled a gun on Daddy!" Brittany cried.

"What?" I screamed, snapping out of my trance.

Instantly, riddled with fear, I jumped up with lightning speed. My pulse thumped in my ears as sweat beads formed on my forehead. My hands felt cold and clammy. With wobbly legs and unsure steps, I scrambled in a hurry. My body felt as if it were floating. This was the last fucking straw! If Pooch had hurt Terrence, I would kill him myself! I was so scared of what I was about to see, yet I took the stairs damn near three at a time as I made a mad dash down the hallway to the front foyer.

"Pooch!"

Pooch stood there with his 9 mm Glock gripped in one hand with it pointed it directly at Terrence's chest. Terrence's chest heaved up and down as anger rose inside of him. He refused to back down from Pooch. The sense of fear nearly consumed me as I watched the scene in horror.

"Pooch, put it down," I screamed in tears. My voice finally caught their attention as they looked at me.

"Trinity," Terrence yelled when he saw me.

"Please put the gun down," I pleaded, pulling on Pooch's arm. Pooch's nose flared as he continued to point the gun at Terrence.

"This muthafucka is real disrespectful. Telling me he ain't leaving until he knows you're all right. How he gon' come over here and try to rule my house? Not my house," Pooch yelled.

"You're scaring my kids! Put it down!" I begged.

Terrence backed up a little. "I just wanted to make sure you were all right." He turned and looked me over. "What the fuck? What happened to your mouth? And your neck has bruises!" Terrence gasped. Instantly, he became enraged and looked at Pooch. "You muthafucka!" Terrence screamed at Pooch. Suddenly, he charged toward him.

"Terrence, no," I screamed as Pooch pulled the trigger. I closed my eyes, waiting to hear a bang, but there was nothing.

Terrence laughed, standing right up in Pooch's grill. "Safety's on, bitch." He punched Pooch square in the jaw and knocked the gun out of his hand.

I picked the gun up as Terrence and Pooch began a slug fest on the floor. I ordered Terry and Brittany to go upstairs and not to come down until I told them. They did as I said as I struggled not to get hit. I turned around to find Terrence whopping Pooch's ass! With Pooch pinned against the floor, he popped his ass from cheek to cheek with thunderous blows.

"You want to hit women, bitch?" Terrence yelled. "Wrong woman, nigga, and definitely the wrong man! I'ma fuck you up!"

"Terrence, stop, please," I screamed.

He stood Pooch up, and as he yelled, he punctuated everything he said with punches. "The next time"— he punched Pooch—"you put your hands on Trinity"— he punched again—"I'll kill you." Pooch's lips were bleeding, his jaws were swollen, and he had a huge cut underneath one of his eyes.

"Terrence, please," I pleaded, walking toward them. "Please stop," I said faintly, suddenly becoming light-headed. The room was spinning, and I was falling.

"Trinity!" I heard them yell hysterically.

"Oh God, babe!" I heard Pooch scream.

"Call 911, nigga! Trinity! Baby!" Terrence yelled as I felt him scoop me up. I couldn't respond. Everything was so groggy, and then there was nothing.

My body felt sore and tired, and my throat felt a bit parched. As the thought came to me to get comfortable, I heard a constant beep in the air and felt a burst of cool air around my nose. When I reached up to touch my face, I felt a long wire or tubing or something, which caused my eyes to pop open and look around. I jumped up, confused and out of my mind. "Where the hell am I?" I asked warily, scrambling to get up.

Feeling a hand against my shoulder, I heard a strange man's voice say, "Easy, easy, Ms. Atkins."

I looked over in his direction and realized he was a doctor. "What? What happened? Where am I?"

"You're in Grady Memorial Hospital, Ms. Atkins. I'm Dr. Wallace," he said, pulling up a chair beside the bed.

Suddenly, I remembered the fight with Pooch and Terrence. "My kids. Terrence. I have to get up."

"Ms. Atkins, it's okay. There are several young men outside waiting for you. One is named . . . Pooch, I believe he told us, and his friends. There's also a young man named Terrence and your children. They are all right. Their concern is for you."

Looking around, I was hooked up to every gadget imaginable. My body felt tired. "Why am I here, and how long have I been here?"

"You've been here about five hours. You're here because you passed out. Do you remember anything that happened prior to this?" Dr. Wallace asked.

"No," I said, not willing to confess shit about the incident.

"All right. Your boyfriend, Pooch, said that someone tried to attack you a few days ago. He stated that's why you have all of the bruising around your neck and face. Is that true?"

I nodded.

"Did you report it to the authorities?"

I shook my head. "I'm good. I didn't need to."

"You know, Ms. Atkins, a woman in your condition doesn't need to be in an unhealthy situation."

"Wait, what do you mean, my condition?"

"You don't know, do you?" The doctor looked at me in shock.

"No," I said plainly to him.

"You're about six weeks pregnant."

The moment the word "pregnant" escaped his lips, my mind inadvertently tuned him out. *Unfuckingbelievable! Did this doctor just say I was pregnant?* My heart nearly dropped to the floor. No the hell I wasn't pregnant again by that damn Pooch. *Wait a minute.*

"Excuse me. How far along did you say I was?" I interrupted whatever he was rambling about.

"Six weeks. Give or take a week or so. I was going to have a gynecologist come down and examine you to be certain," he said to me. "But I'm pretty sure it's around six weeks."

Instantly, my mind thought back over the past month. Damn, it had been a minute since Mother Nature had visited me, but had it been six weeks? *Six weeks ago, six weeks ago. I was on the pill per Pooch's orders, so how the hell did I get pregnant?* I always took my pill at the same time every night at eleven. *When did I skip?* Suddenly, it came back to me. My ladies' night out! Suwanee, Terrence, the hotel . . . It came back to me like a tidal wave, the moment at the hotel when my child was conceived. I thought about the moments before Terrence's seed invaded my womb.

"Oh shit, li'l mama. Fuck, I'm 'bout to explode," he'd said. I remembered the feeling as he pulsated inside of me.

The doctor must've noticed the dazed expression on my face. "Are you all right, Ms. Atkins?"

"Have you told Pooch or Terrence?"

"No, I haven't. I had to speak to you. I did, however, tell them the reason you collapsed. Your body has suffered from exhaustion, dehydration, and malnourishment. Physically, your wounds will heal, but you cannot take any more trauma. Your iron is low, and your blood pressure is high. You have to take it easy for the baby's and your sakes."

For the first time since he spoke, the reality of life growing inside of me dawned on me. His cautionary warnings about my condition immediately tapped into the motherly instincts inside of my heart, and worry began to settle in the pit of my stomach. "So, what's wrong with me?" I asked, rubbing my belly.

"For starters, you're anemic. We also found that your blood pressure was extremely elevated and believe that you have chronic hypertension, which could lead to pre-eclampsia. I want you to get on a non-salt diet and take iron pills. We're going to provide you with some prenatal vitamins, but you really need to set up an appointment with your gynecologist," Dr. Wallace advised.

"Okay, well, can you not mention the pregnancy? I want to tell the guys myself," I asked the doctor.

He placed a comforting hand on my shoulder. "You do not have to worry about that. I nor any of the staff is authorized to release any information outside of the bare minimum that was released. I am bound by doctor-patient confidentiality. Telling anyone else is up to you, and that's your choice. However, I will advise you that if it is going to be a detrimental situation for you, you should consider telling them in a public place or notifying the authorities first."

"I hear you." No additional explanation was needed. I understood exactly what he meant.

"I'll send the gynecologist down in an hour or so. Would you like to see anyone?" he asked.

"Please send in Pooch, Terrence, and my children."

"All right. If you need anything, just push the call button."

A few minutes later, I heard Terrence and Pooch arguing as they came through the door, and I rolled my eyes. Now was not the time for their bullshit.

"You shouldn't even be here," Pooch grumbled.

"But I am, and I ain't going nowhere," Terrence shot back as they pushed the door open.

My kids ran to me. "Mommy!" they yelled, hugging me. I held them tightly. "I love you guys so much."

"Are you okay?" Terry asked meekly.

"Yes, I am fine."

"Why are you in the hospital?" Brittany asked.

I smiled at her. "Because I was sick, but I'm a whole lot better."

"What was wrong?" Terry asked.

"Yeah, what the hell is wrong? That damn dumb-ass doctor wouldn't tell us shit," Pooch said. When I looked at him, I laughed to myself, because he had been treated for the ass whooping Terrence put on him. No wonder he had all of his crew here at the hospital.

Terrence walked up and hugged me. "What did the doctor say?"

"You know, I've had about enough of you that I am willing to stand in this bitch. Now get away from my woman!" Pooch yelled.

"Please stop!" I yelled. My heart monitor began beeping rapidly, so I slowly calmed my ass down. "Please." Terrence and Pooch were both shocked into silence at my outburst and the machine.

Pooch sat beside me, lifting up the monitor. "Babe, what's going on wit' you?" he asked, genuinely concerned for the first time.

"Um, Terry, Brit, wait outside the door for just a minute," I said.

Terrence directed them where to sit and closed the door. "I think you can leave too, bruh," Pooch said snidely.

"Pooch, don't, please," I said, grabbing his arm. "Let it go."

He shrugged it off. "A'ight. What's up?"

I looked at Pooch through sad eyes. "I'm pregnant."

He snatched his hand away from me and jumped up. "What? Hell no. Come on, man, I told you I didn't want no more kids—"

"I know that, but can you please calm down!" I exclaimed, and the monitor went off again. "Damn!" I took a deep breath while I rubbed my belly to calm my nerves.

Pooch paced, looking from the monitor to me. "Fine."

I pointed to the machines. "It keeps going off because it's monitoring my heart rate. I have anemia and chronic hypertension, which could lead to preeclampsia. I have to watch my iron levels and what I eat, and I have to watch my blood pressure."

"What the hell is anemia and pre-chlamydia?" Pooch asked, mispronouncing the illness. *Only he would associate it with a damn STD. Dumb ass.*

"It's called 'pre-e-clamp-see-ah,'" I said, stretching the syllables. "Not chlamydia. That's a damn STD."

"However the fuck you pronounce it! What the hell is it?" Pooch asked, looking all ignorant and shit.

Disgusted, Terrence explained. "When you suffer from anemia, it just means that your iron is low. Preeclampsia is an illness due to the pregnancy. She probably got it from all those salty five-star meals and stress," he said snidely to Pooch. "Just do what the doctor says, because it can be harmful to you and the baby."

Thankfully, Terrence explained it, because I didn't have the energy to entertain Pooch's antics. It was refreshing to have a man by my side who simply understood and took the time to learn something other than the streets. Simply put, Terrence was just knowledgeable like that. If he had gone to college, he'd have been hell to deal with.

"Well, thank you, Doogie damn muthafuckin' Howser, M.D.," Pooch snarled at Terrence.

Terrence sniffed and pointed at Pooch. "This fucking cat, I swear."

Pooch shot a heated glance in Terrence's direction, then sat down beside me. "Look, Trinity, we already talked about this. I really don't want any more kids," Pooch fussed. "You know that Princess was a mis—"

I put my hand up to shut his mouth. "You know what? I'm tired as fuck, Pooch, and I really don't feel like dealing with this right now. Can we please discuss this at home when I feel better?"

Pooch rubbed his head. "A'ight. We can discuss this later."

"How far along are you?" Terrence asked.

Looking at him with pleading eyes, I softly replied, "Six weeks."

Instantly, Terrence's whole demeanor changed. Instead of being laidback and pissed off, he looked worried and anxious. "Umm, really?" he asked.

He was really asking me if the baby was his. I confirmed it for him. "Yeah, really."

Completely oblivious to the unspoken conversation between me and Terrence, Pooch bit his lip and looked back at Terrence with an attitude. "Look, bruh, I know you concerned, but Trinity needs her rest. Can you take the kids and keep them for a few days? I'm gonna stay with her," Pooch said as a temporary truce between them.

Agreeing with Pooch, I mouthed, "Please," to him.

"Okay." Terrence nodded. "Trinity, I'm gonna holla at you later, fo' sho.'"

"Yeah, tell the kids I love them," I said as he walked to the door.

"Will do," he said and walked out.

Pooch looked at me. "Only because you in here is the reason that nigga still breathing," Pooch said, seething with a look of pure hatred.

I palmed his face, although I really didn't want to touch this woman-beating bastard. But I'd do anything to protect Terrence. Anything. "Pooch, if you love me, I mean truly love me, let it go," I told him.

Pooch huffed, and then shook his head as if he was in deep contemplation. Finally, he exhaled, and I knew I'd just squashed this shit between Terrence and him at least one more time.

"Get that nigga to play his fuckin' position then, and I ain't fuckin' playin'. 'Cause I ain't gon' take too much more of him acting like he yo' man. For real. He the kids' daddy and shit, but I will toe tag that nigga. And even though I owe that bitch an ass whooping about my face, I'll let that shit ride this once because of you and what you going through. But I'm telling you he better fall the fuck back."

"I will talk to him. I promise," I said, rubbing my stomach, happy for Terrence's reprieve.

Pooch smiled at me. "You look happy."

I decided to be honest, at least halfway. I was more than excited to be carrying this baby. I was overjoyed. I loved children, and this was my seed. I told Pooch how I felt for real. "I am. I'm happy about my pregnancy. I know what you said about not wanting any more kids but—"

In a move that shocked me, Pooch rubbed my stomach too. His action stopped me from talking in midsentence. He rubbed his hand across my belly and looked at me with the kindest expression I'd ever seen on his face. It reminded me of the Pooch who asked me to check the yes or no box on his piece of scrap paper when we played on the playground. It was that kinda innocent and sweet expression.

He took a deep breath and exhaled. "Let me ask you something, Trinity," he said as he continued to rub my belly. "Do you think this baby could, I dunno, you know, maybe make us closer? Make us like how we use to be?"

"Huh?" I asked, stunned.

Pooch turned my face so that I was looking directly into his eyes. For the first time, he looked so sorrowful. His eyes reflected a genuineness that I hadn't seen since we were kids, and in that moment, he wasn't Pooch the street king. He was Vernon, the timid guy I'd met and loved as a great friend all those years ago when we used to be nothing more than close friends in the hood tiptoeing around the schoolyard. He kissed my lips and caressed my cheek in his hand.

"I know you been unhappy wit' me, Trinity. I do. I'm a rough-ass nigga wit' some high-ass standards. But I love you so much, and I just get so fuckin' crazy because I don't want to lose you. I'm sorry I put my hands on you, but I can't stand the thought of you being wit' or catching feelings for another nigga. Not even if he came before me," he said and paused to let me marinate on the fact that he was referring to Terrence. Then he continued. "If you want the baby, we can keep it. I'll try to do better. I swear I will as long as you just love me like you used to," Pooch confessed.

Daaamn. I never thought I'd see the fucking day. Maybe Terrence's ass whooping knocked some sense into this fool for real. Honestly, I thought he sensed that deep down, I truly loved Terrence, and more importantly, he knew that Terrence truly loved me. And more than anything, he knew that Terrence was the kind of man I wanted in my life. He may have acted crazy and wasn't all that book smart, but Pooch wasn't dumb by any stretch of the imagination, especially not when it came to reading people.

Unfortunately, he was fighting for something that was long lost. The moment he put his hands on me was the moment Pooch destroyed anything we'd ever had, still had, and would ever have. He'd crossed a line with me, and never again, no more would I love Pooch. On top of that, I knew what he didn't—this wasn't his baby. But now was not the time to be stupid. So I lied.

"Yeah, that would be great." I smiled at him.

Smiling, he kissed me passionately. "Good. I guess we having a baby, babe," he said excitedly. "Shit, maybe I'll have me a boy—Pooch Jr."

He laughed, and I forced a smile.

"I'm hungry as hell. I guess I better send them niggas on their way and get some food. You want something?" he asked, handing me my purse.

"Nah." I shook my head, reaching inside and grabbing my cell phone as he stood up, stretched, and walked to the door.

"A'ight. Get some rest then," he said as he walked out the door. "Keep your cell phone close."

Pooch couldn't have been gone five minutes when my cell phone rang. You already know who it was. Terrence. To paraphrase Ricky Ricardo, Lucy had some 'splaining to do. I already knew how this conversation was about to start.

"Hello?" I answered.

"You ain't getting rid of my seed," Terrence said point blank while I simultaneously mouthed the words. As I said, I knew what he was about to say. I just knew Terrence like that.

With a deep sigh, I confirmed, "No, I'm not, so please take the bass out of your voice."

His deep breath let me know how relieved he was to hear those words come from my mouth. "I'm sorry, baby, but this shit is so fucking frustrating. We gotta make some hard decisions and moves, you know that, right?"

"I know."

He paused, realizing that I wasn't in the mood to deal with this. "I'm sorry. You're tired and shit. I'ma let you rest. Me and the kids will check on you."

"A'ight, and thank you."

"You don't have to thank me about the kids. These are my children—" he was saying.

"Not for that, but for understanding and keeping the peace. You always do what's right, even when it kills you, and for that, I thank you."

"I'm a real man. Real men do that."

"So I've noticed," I said and yawned.

"You and my baby need y'all's rest. Be easy, li'l mama."

"I love you," I said to him.

He chuckled lightly. "That's good to know. I was kinda wondering, but I love you too, li'l mama. Now get some rest."

I blushed. "Dreads, you ain't never got to wonder about that again," I said sweetly to him. "A'ight, I'm going to rest now. Good night."

As I was ending my conversation, my line beeped. "Hello?" I answered.

"I'm at Sonic. You sure you don't want no ice cream or pickles and shit? I know y'all pregnant women be craving shit like that."

"No, Pooch. I'm good. I'm resting," I said with a slight attitude.

"Okay, a'ight, damn," he huffed, blowing away his irritation. "I'll be there in about twenty minutes, babe. Get your rest," he told me and hung up.

I deleted Terrence's phone call, pushed my cell phone under my pillow, and lay down. Life was weird. Just three days ago, Pooch had virtually beaten my ass into submission and sent me into depression, and now with the news of my pregnancy, I suddenly held all the cards. Terrence was ready to marry me and be a family, and Pooch was even taking shit off of me and accepting my pregnancy in the hopes that we could get our relationship back on track. I rubbed my belly and closed my eyes.

"Mama's gonna get it right for all of us this time, little one," I said softly.

Now the only problem was how.

Chapter Six

Charice

Our vacation/engagement getaway had been nothing short of perfect. However, once we got back to the States, reality set in. We had to come out with our relationship. We called Lincoln's parents first. They were overly excited, as I figured they would be, but they vowed to keep the information low-key until everyone was aware. I wanted to tell LaMeka too, but I couldn't get in contact with her, and I had every intention of finding out why. At any rate, I told my other two girls, Lucinda and Trinity. While Lucinda only congratulated me and got off the phone, Trinity let me have it.

"What do you mean, Ryan doesn't know yet?" she asked as soon as Lucinda hung up. "You mean he doesn't know about you getting married, right? Please tell me you don't mean that he doesn't know about your relationship."

"I'll take the second answer for two hundred, Alex," I said in my *Jeopardy!* voice. "Listen—"

"Oh hell no, cuz," Trinity hollered into the phone. "Are you crazy? Do you realize what is going to go down when Ryan finds out?"

"I realize that, but lest I remind you that you have no room on your moral barometer to talk about me, Miss Suwanee," I said sarcastically. "Just please keep it to yourself."

"A'ight. You've got a point. I'm just concerned."

"I know. I'll be all right," I told her, but I wasn't even sure if I was telling the truth, not just because of Ryan, but because of my parents as well.

As it turned out, I had every reason to be concerned. You should have seen how my parents took the news when we showed up on their doorstep. Lincoln flew down, and I called a dinner with my parents while Ryan's mom had the triplets so that we could discuss our relationship and break our big news. My parents' reaction was not the one I expected. Let's just say that my vacation had to be the calm before the storm.

"Hey, baby! You're back from your . . . trip." My mom answered the door excitedly until she saw Lincoln standing beside me.

"Hey, Mama!" I said excitedly while hugging her. "Can we come in? Good grief, you're in the way."

She stared back and forth at us. "Umm, yeah, sure come in."

My dad walked into the foyer. "Hey, baby. Lincoln Harper? Damn," he yelled in shock. "What the hell are you doing here? I mean, it's a pleasure to meet you, but I'm just confused," he said, looking at my mom.

"Don't look at me. I have no idea," she said. Her hands were lifted in the air as if she wanted no part of the current situation.

"Maybe I should've said something, huh?" I whispered to Lincoln.

He nodded and mumbled, "It would've helped."

"Are you going to tell us what the hell is going on here?" my mom asked with her hands on her hips.

"Mom, Dad, can we all sit in the family room?"

My dad nodded. "Sure."

We entered the house and followed my parents into the family room. It felt as if we were walking the green mile it was so quiet as we moved from room to room. Lincoln and I settled on the large sofa as my mom and dad settled on the love seat. There was no small talk as my parents sat. They simply stared at both of us in wonderment and a bit of confusion.

Lincoln spoke first once we settled in the family room. "First off, let me just say that it's an honor to meet you both. I wish the circumstances were better."

"Circumstances? What circumstances?" my mom asked, looking at me tensely.

"Mom, remember when I told you that I had someone in my life, but I asked you not to pry and not to talk about it?"

"Yes, I remember," my mom said, still slightly clueless. Suddenly, a look of realization, then anger, passed between my parents.

"Well," I said, taking Lincoln's hand before they could implode, "Lincoln and I have been dating since December. We thought it was best to keep our relationship a secret until we were ready to tell everyone. You know, given the circumstances," I explained.

"How in the hell did this happen?" my dad asked. "Please fill me in, because I'm lost."

"You ain't the only one," my mom agreed.

"Mom, Dad—" I began with exasperation.

Lincoln patted my knee, causing me to take pause. "Please let me explain." He sat forward and looked directly at my parents. "Mr. and Mrs. Taylor, you must be shocked. Believe me, my parents were too. It's no question that Ryan is my teammate and one of my best friends. I know that will be a hard row to ho when that time comes. However, Charice and I met when she first brought the triplets down to stay with Ryan. There was an instant attraction and chemistry even then, but of course, due to the situation, we didn't pursue it.

"The next time she was in Dallas, we had a chance meeting at a hotel lounge, and we refused to fight the feelings we were experiencing. We took things slow, getting to know each other and enjoying our time together. I won't lie. The fact that I am in a bad position with Ryan eats at me, but I can't hide how I feel about your daughter. I love Charice, and there's nothing I wouldn't do for her or the triplets. Nothing in this world," Lincoln said, smiling at me as he gripped my hand tighter. I felt my cheeks flush.

After a long pause, my mom spoke, waving her hand in the air. "Well, we can't tell you how to live your lives. But you two are sure about this?"

I nodded. "Yes, Mama. I love him."

"And I love your daughter. I'm crazy about her," Lincoln said, kissing me on my cheek.

"And Ryan is okay with this?" she countered. "All things aside, he's changed, and he truly loves and cares for you, Charice."

"Umm, we haven't exactly told him yet." I bit my lip and waited for the blowup.

"Say what?" they yelled in unison.

"There just never seemed like a right time."

"You mean to tell me that you two have dated to the point of falling in love and you haven't said anything to Ryan? Nothing at all?" my dad asked.

We shook our heads.

"Well, thank the good Lord you two aren't talking about getting married. At least he'll have time to adjust," my mom blurted.

Lincoln and I looked at each other. "Mom, about that—"

"Wait a minute!" She jumped up. "I know good and well you're not telling me that you're engaged."

"Umm, well, actually, Mr. and Mrs. Taylor, I asked Charice to marry me on our trip to Paradise Island . . ." Lincoln said and paused out of uncertainty.

"And I accepted," I finished.

"Wait a minute! You mean to tell me that you went to Paradise Island with Lincoln, who you told me was a friend, got engaged, and no one knows about this relationship?" my mom asked, hands on her hips.

"When you make it sound like that, it seems so horrible," I said.

"Answer the question!" she hollered.

"Yes, that's what happened," I admitted.

"Unbelievable!" My mom threw her hands up.

I turned to Lincoln. "This is not working out how I thought," I said before turning back to my parents. "Look, it seems bad and rushed, but please, we are grown adults. We didn't just do this on a whim."

"Of course it doesn't seem that way to you. You've known about it for six months!" my mom exclaimed. "Have you told his parents? I'm sure they must be livid!"

"Actually, his parents knew about us already, so they were happy to hear the news," I admitted willingly, even though I was adding more fuel to the fire.

My mom shot us a hard glare. Then she focused her heated stare at me. "You trusted his parents with the news. His parents—who have a relationship with Ryan—but not us?"

"Mrs. Taylor, I told my parents on my own volition. I didn't even tell Charice that I was going to tell them," Lincoln defended us.

"Then that makes you the one out of the two of you who has some common sense. I'm sure your parents had fun getting to know my daughter the way a parent is supposed to," she shouted as my dad consoled her.

Lincoln stood up and walked over to them. "In hindsight, I should've encouraged Charice to tell you all. For that, I am sorry. I guess we were so consumed by how Ryan and the kids would react that we didn't consider your reaction. I know that all of this has taken you by surprise, but please believe me when I say I truly love your daughter, and I would love it if I could have permission to marry her."

"Now you want permission?" my dad asked sarcastically.

I joined Lincoln's side. "Dad, he's being polite. Don't take this out on him, because it was my bad and not his. His obligation is to his parents. Now I am sorry for not telling you guys. I really didn't expect our relationship to develop this quickly. However, it has, and I love him. Whether you guys approve or disapprove, I'm marrying him. I'm begging you to please look past my mistakes to see my happiness and be a part of it," I said as I rubbed Lincoln's back.

My mom, who'd had her back turned toward us, turned to face me. "You're serious about this, aren't you?"

I smiled and nodded. "Yes, ma'am."

The scoff that escaped her couldn't be missed, but there was a glint of understanding in her eyes. Grudgingly, she shook her head, then nodded in acceptance. "I could kill you, but I love you. You have to give me some time to get used to this, but if this is truly what you both want, I will support you."

"Thank you, Mama," I cooed as we embraced tightly. "You always have my back."

"Yes, I do, so please stop blindsiding me with information," she told me. Then she hugged Lincoln. "You better take care of my baby."

He laughed and hugged her in return. "I will. That is a promise."

"Let me just tell both of you that if you pop up at my house with a grandbaby I know nothing about, I'm whipping y'all's asses!" she cautioned.

"We promise we will not do that!" Lincoln and I both laughed. I turned to my dad. "Dad, we cool?"

He shook his head. "No, we ain't cool. Your mother may be cool with this, but not me. Not at all," he said and stormed out, heading toward his office.

"Daddy!" I yelled after him to no avail. I'd never seen him react this way. Usually, the roles were reversed. My mom was the stubborn one, and he was the forgiving one.

"Why is he acting this way?" I turned and asked my mom.

"You're his little girl, Charice. You may be grown, but you're always our little girl. You remember how hard your dad took your pregnancy and the Ryan situation? Even now, it's still hard. He just puts the best on the outside for his grandkids. He's always been your protector and provider. He doesn't want to see you go through any more changes. Then you waltz in here and declare that Lincoln—who we know nothing about—is filling that space, and you all but demand that we accept that. It's a lot for him. You're his baby, his only baby."

Remorse instantly filled me. My mother was right. Regardless of Lincoln or any other man, my dad always had been the rock and quiet warrior I'd gone to for understanding and solace. He always would be that. He never let me see him sweat, the only exception being his fight with Ryan. True enough, Lincoln was the love of my life, but my daddy was my daddy. I needed him to know that, no matter what, he would always be my daddy.

"Hey, you," I said quietly as I walked into his office.

"Hey," he said plainly and sat back in his chair.

"Daddy, can I talk to you?"

He threw down the newspaper he'd been reading. "Sure, Charice," he said.

I sat beside him. "I was wrong with how I handled everything."

He nodded. "Mm-hmm."

I cut straight to what I knew the issue was. "He's a good guy. He's nothing like how Ryan used to be."

"So you say."

"I know this time, Daddy. I learned a lot from you and, honestly, from Ryan. Now I know what I need in my life and what I want. I also know what I won't tolerate. Lincoln is a gentleman. He makes sure I know I'm his one and only, and he takes good care of my heart. I love the man in him, and he loves the woman in me. He reminds me a lot of you."

"That won't make me like how you handled it."

"But does it make you feel better about my decision?"

He exhaled. "I don't know."

"You'll always be my daddy. Nothing will ever change that. I just need for you to allow Lincoln to take his rightful place as my husband. I trust him, and if he messes up, my daddy will be right there," I said, leaning my head on his shoulder.

Suddenly, there was a knock on the door. "Come in," my dad said.

Lincoln gingerly walked in and cleared this throat. "Mr. Taylor, I'm sorry to interrupt, but I just felt I needed to say something—"

"My daughter is talking to me, and you just waltz in here to make a statement?" my dad interrupted.

With his head bowed, Lincoln placed his hands in his pockets and stood by the door. He took a moment as if contemplating his next words before he gazed up and looked my father in the eyes. "I'm sorry for the intrusion, sir. I value your time, and I value your time with your daughter. I simply want you to know that I will take care of your daughter because I love her. I swear that on my life. I am not like Ryan, nor am I here to replace you," Lincoln pleaded to him.

"And you're quite sure about this?" my dad asked.

"Yes, sir," Lincoln answered. "Very sure."

My dad turned to me and hugged me. "I love you, sweet pea. If he makes you happy, then I am happy for you."

He hadn't called me sweet pea since I was in middle school, and it caused a girlish grin to grace my face. "Thanks, Daddy."

He winked at me. "You're welcome, my love," he said and kissed me on my forehead. He got up and walked over to Lincoln, silently accepting him by extending him a handshake.

"Despite my reaction, I have a good feeling about you. I'm going to put all things aside and trust in what you have told me."

Lincoln smiled widely and shook his hand. "Thank you, sir. I appreciate that, and again I am sorry for how everything was handled."

My dad nodded. "I can accept that. I give you my permission to marry my daughter."

"Thank you so much, Mr. Taylor. I promise you won't be disappointed," Lincoln said excitedly as I stood next to him, grinning from ear to ear.

My dad opened his arms for a hug, and Lincoln obliged. "Good. And I better not be disappointed, or I'm going to cut your balls off," my dad whispered in his ear. I pretended not to hear.

Lincoln pulled back quickly and swallowed hard. "Yes, sir."

"We're clear on that?" my dad asked him.

"Very," Lincoln nodded.

"Good. Now let's go see what my beautiful wife is cooking," my dad said, walking out of his office.

"Did you hear what your dad told me?" he whispered.

"Uh-uh, sure didn't," I faked and walked down the hall quickly with Lincoln on my heels.

I loved Lincoln, but I agreed with my daddy on that one. Besides, I wasn't getting on my dad's bad side for anyone.

All may have been well that ended well on that note, but if the meeting with my parents was an indication of a fraction of the tension we'd have to go through with Ryan, then I knew we were up for a damn battle. Trust me. Every time Ryan called or saw the kids, he always tried to push up on me. He was utterly relentless. So many times, I wanted to just burst out and say, "I'm with Lincoln!"

I felt bad for Ryan, but this new and improved Charice, the one who finally found life outside of Ryan Westmore, really didn't give a damn about his hurt feelings. I'd gone through the internal emotional struggle about my relationship with Lincoln, and then I realized I really didn't owe Ryan anything after all the times he had hurt me in the past. I wanted to claim my heart's independence from Ryan, and hiding my relationship with Lincoln was like still being trapped in Ryan's web. I'd been tangled in his web of deception for eight years, and it was time to, as Mary Mary would say, "Take the shackles off my feet so I can dance!"

But I understood Lincoln's position. Ryan was his boy. He still confided in Lincoln about his love for me, and I knew how foul Lincoln felt. Because of that, I had continued to give Lincoln the time he needed to best prepare himself for the revelation to Ryan. After Lincoln shared that, their friendship would never be the same, perhaps even nonexistent. Still, it was time.

I hadn't seen Lincoln since we'd told my parents two weeks ago, so I decided to fly out to Dallas for two reasons: to surprise him with a visit and to make plans to break the news to Ryan. Yes, I needed to see my man. The two weeks we'd spent apart felt like utter torture, but I'd be lying if I said that his absence was the primary reason for the impromptu visit. Now that we'd moved beyond dating to engagement, we could no longer continue to withhold information from Ryan. The sting of our newfound love would hurt, but now that we were mixing families, the revelation was a necessity.

He was so ecstatic when he opened the door Friday morning to find me standing there that he decided to skip his workout with the team so that we could spend time together. We discussed some things we wanted for the wedding and got down to our personal form of working out: lovemaking. Umm! It was so good we lingered in the bed from exhaustion until late morning.

Waking up first, I rolled over and rubbed his chest. "Good morning, baby."

Smiling sweetly, he yawned. "It's more like good late morning," he chuckled. "Ma, you put your thang down last night."

"You know how ma does it," I giggled and kissed him.

He pulled me close to him. "I can't wait until we're married."

I squeezed him tight. "Me either. Then I won't have to surprise you. I'll already be here."

He caressed my hair. "I love you, ma."

"I love you too, pa," I said and sat up. "But if I lie here anymore, I'm going to grow attached to this bed. I'm going to grab a shower, and then I'll make us some lunch. How about that?"

"Can I shower with you?" he asked seductively.

"Two things are going to happen if you do that."

He tried his best to look innocent. "What are the two things?"

"Either there won't be any showering in the shower, or there will be, but we'll get funky again by moving it back to the bed," I laughed. "So, you stay here."

"What's so wrong with the bed?" he asked, faking innocence.

"I know you love this honey love between my legs, but we have to take a break, Lincoln. I need to look over the books for the nonprofits," I told him. "And I wanted to discuss some more things with you. We can play later," I added vaguely. I didn't want to spoil the mood with the "Ryan conversation."

"But I don't wanna be a grownup right now. I wanna plaayy," he whined in the cutest little boy voice that he could muster up.

I burst into laughter. "Well, I'll tell you what. If you're good, ma will throw in an extra treat for you later."

His eyes danced with excitement. "Cool with me. Go shower."

"Spoiled ass," I laughed, heading to the shower.

Though I'd have rather lain in bed with him, my reason for getting up was twofold. Lincoln had been pining over a new Sharp ninety-inch flat-panel television for his—our—entertainment room, and since the investments I'd made with some of the money Ryan had given me had produced a decent return, I ordered the $9,000 television for Linc out of my own pocket. It was being delivered today, so I needed to be decent when the installers came.

I smiled to myself as the multiple showerheads cascaded a fury of hot water down my body. I loved his shower—our shower. I had to get use to the fact that all of this was now mine too. At times, I still couldn't believe it. Lincoln and I were getting married.

While I finished my shower, I heard the doorbell ring. Upset that I was missing my own surprise, and so Lincoln wouldn't refuse the damn thing, I hurriedly got out and threw on the first thing I saw—one of Lincoln's wife beaters, a pair of my short shorts, and my flip-flops—and bounded down the stairs. Grinning from ear to ear, I headed down the hall to the foyer. Once I entered the foyer, I overheard someone tell Lincoln that he forgot a team-building golf game, and Lincoln anxiously said that he'd catch up with them later. It didn't dawn on me until I was in plain sight of everyone standing in the foyer that it wasn't the installers at all, but Lincoln's teammates, Marcus, Lamar . . . and Ryan!

"Dawg, how could you forget the golf game? You planned it—" Marcus stopped in midsentence as I appeared. Their attention turned to me.

"Charice?" Ryan's confused expression said everything.

Standing there like a deer caught in headlights, I threw my hands over my mouth. "Oh shit," I mumbled.

Lincoln, with head bent, let out an exasperated sigh. "Shit," he muttered.

The air in the room turned stale. My skin was flushed, and even the little bit of clothing I wore made me hotter. I wanted Ryan to know, sure I did, but not like this. Never like this. This was cruel. This was embarrassing. This was cause to kill a muthafucka. Nobody deserved anything like this. Lincoln looked as if he were utterly defeated, and Ryan looked stuck between confusion and pure rage. Marcus's mouth hung agape in shock, and Lamar kept looking back and forth between Ryan, Lincoln, and me, trying to figure out the connection.

Finally, Lamar spoke first. "Charice? Isn't she your kids' mother?" the rookie asked Ryan.

"Yes, she is," Ryan said tensely. "Now, I want to know what the fuck you're doing here."

Just then, a Best Buy delivery guy came up to the open doorway. "Excuse me. I have a delivery for a Lincoln Harper."

"I didn't order anything," Lincoln stated abruptly with a bit of irritation in his voice.

The deliveryman looked at his clipboard. "No, you didn't. It's from a Charice Taylor. She had it delivered for—"

I bolted past Lincoln. "It's my delivery," I confirmed. "Can you all reschedule it?"

"Ma'am, this is a three-hour job. The television is the largest—"

"I understand," I said, cutting him off. "But now is really, really not a good time. Please take it back to the store, and I will reschedule."

Frustrated, he huffed. "Okay, can you please just sign this? I need to verify that this is the correct address and that a delivery was attempted," he stated, and I signed the necessary paperwork with Ryan standing next to me in the open doorway, his anger burgeoning.

At the most inopportune time, the deliveryman began to recognize everyone. "Hey, you're *the* Lincoln Harper, and you're Ryan Westmore! OMG and Marcus Cottrell! Man, can I have your autographs?" he asked, and they obliged.

"Man, Mr. Harper, you are one lucky man. I wish my girl were able to order me this television. Sharp's ninety-inch flat screen is the truth," he bragged to my dismay as Lincoln signed his autograph.

"Thanks. We'll reschedule," Lincoln said quickly and closed the door on the deliveryman.

Before Lincoln could turn around good, Ryan started in on him. "Dude, you're my best friend—my brother from another mother. Tell me that my babies' mother being here like this is some kind of misunderstanding or surprise for me," Ryan hollered. "And why are you here in that outfit at his house, Charice?" he all but yelled at me, though neither one of us were really decent. Lincoln only had on a pair of gym shorts with no shirt on and some tennis shoes.

Marcus shook his head in dismay. "Come on, dawg. Man, please tell me you ain't playing foul like that."

Lincoln stood there and just stared at Ryan with the most apologetic look on his face and shook his head, unable to speak. What could he say in this situation? Lincoln turned to look at me. I couldn't stop the tears from falling, and I mouthed the words, "I'm sorry."

"Say something," Ryan screamed at Lincoln.

"Ryan, I . . ." Lincoln hesitated, swiping his hand over the top of his head.

I walked up, stood beside Lincoln, and turned his face to mine. "It's okay. I'm with you." Lincoln looked as if his heart were ripping in half, yet we wrapped our arms around each other, and together we faced Ryan, who paced back and forth.

"Ryan, I'm sorry. Charice and I . . . we're together as a couple, and we wanted to tell you this in private. I never meant for you to find out—"

Without notice, Ryan charged for him. I jumped out of the way just in time to see them topple back on the floor.

"Oh my God! Stop! Ryan, please," I screamed as they tried to pummel each other.

"You muthafucka," Ryan bellowed.

"I don't want to hurt you," Lincoln yelled, suppressing him.

"Come on, dawgs," Marcus screamed. "Stop this shit!"

"We're a team, man," Lamar added.

"Can you two please stop them? Somebody is going to get hurt," I yelled as Ryan and Lincoln continued to tussle.

Ryan struck Lincoln with some hellacious punches, and Lincoln had to pop him a couple of times just to back him down. I could tell he really didn't want to fight Ryan, but if someone didn't stop it, Lincoln would have no choice but to actually fight back, and then there would really be a damn situation in here. Finally, Marcus was able to pull Ryan off and pin his arms down.

"Come on, dawg, for real. Let it ride. Don't catch no case. You've got a career to think about," he coaxed.

Ryan spat blood on the floor, and I ran to Lincoln, checking out his swollen jaw and his eye, which was already turning blue. "Baby." I petted him.

"'Baby'? For real, Charice? Tell me not for real," Ryan heaved.

My emotions were everywhere as I faced Ryan. "I'm sorry, Ryan, but it's the truth. Neither one of us did anything to try to hurt you, but your heart can't help who it loves."

"So all this giving me advice on how to get Charice back was just a front, huh, bruh? You wasn't man enough to tell me that you been sticking it to my babies' mother? How long have you been fucking my babies' mother, Linc?"

"Ryan, we wanted to wait until we were sure this is what we wanted," Lincoln said. "I was going to tell you."

"It shouldn't have happened at all, muthafucka! You were supposed to be my best friend! Linc, she is my kids' mother. I'm supposed to be happy that you get my girl and I don't? Fuck is wrong with you? You couldn't find your own woman, so you go after mine?" Ryan yelled as he paced back and forth under Marcus's watchful eye.

"For real, dawg, how would you feel if he went for your baby's mother?" Lamar asked snidely.

"You keep your rookie ass out of this! Besides, I wouldn't give a fuck," Lincoln yelled back.

"No, you wouldn't, because you been too busy sticking it to my babies' mother to care," Ryan hollered. "When was you gon' tell me, dawg? Huh? Let me see, maybe when you were walking down the fucking aisle, is that it?"

Lincoln paused. I was sure to the others it seemed as if he was simply at a loss for words, but I knew that Ryan's words stung him, coming from an all-too-real place. The fact was we were about to walk down the aisle, and that was exactly the situation in which Lincoln had chosen to tell him.

As if he'd tapped into our thoughts, Marcus tried to coax Ryan by saying, "We need to go. Nothing is going to get resolved today." He put his hand on Ryan's shoulder.

Ryan snatched away from him and approached me. "Ricey, I did some fucked-up things to you. I know it. But this is me. This is us," he said desperately, caressing my face in his hands. "We deserve a chance to be together as a family. We have three children together. They adore me and you. Give us a chance. I don't know what this muthafucka filled your head with, but I know you. I know your heart. Please don't do this. I'll prove how serious I am." He grabbed my hands and kneeled down on one knee. "Please be my wife . . ." He felt my ring finger and looked down at my hand. "What the fuck is this?"

My tears continued their relentless path down my face. I just wanted to lie down somewhere and die. "Um . . ." I couldn't find the words to say.

Lincoln exhaled. "We were going to tell you."

"I know this is not what I think it is," Ryan said, his voice quavering. "Tell me it's not, Ricey."

I took a deep breath, wiped the tears from my eyes, and released the information that was sure to send Ryan completely over the edge.

"Ryan, I'm sorry. We've been dating for a little over six months. Lincoln proposed to me, and I, umm, I accepted. We're getting married," I managed to say in a shaky voice.

"Six . . . six months," Ryan said as if someone knocked the wind out of his chest. He stood on shaky legs and staggered backward. "Married?"

"I'm so sorry."

"That was before the Super Bowl," Ryan whispered. "You've been pushing up on her since you met her?" Ryan asked in disgust. "You muthafucka!" he yelled, charging at Lincoln again.

Ryan wrapped his hands around Lincoln's throat, trying to choke the life out of him. Marcus and Lamar were trying their best to pry Ryan off as Lincoln fought against Ryan's tight grip.

"I'm gonna kill you! You muthafucka!" Ryan yelled with pure malice. I'd never seen him so enraged and jealous in my life. He was literally trying to kill Lincoln.

"Please, stop, Ryan," I cried. "Please don't hurt him!"

Finally, Lincoln kneed Ryan in the stomach, and he doubled over, holding his stomach in pain. Lincoln rubbed his throat as he coughed and gagged. Marcus and Lamar tried to restrain Ryan from getting to Lincoln again.

"Let's go, man," Marcus yelled at Ryan.

"Hell no! This muthafucka gonna pay." Ryan tried to break free. He was like a caged lion with his eyes on the prey.

"I don't want to hurt you physically, man," Lincoln said between coughs. "I've hurt you enough. Please listen to them and leave. I'm not going to let you keep popping off on me, for real, dawg. We'll deal with this when cooler heads prevail."

"If you think I'm ever gonna calm down about this, then you done lost your fucking mind. I swear I'm murking for you, nigga. Every fucking chance I get. You better strap the fuck up, nigga, 'cause I swear it's fucking on every time. Every time," Ryan yelled.

"I'm sorry, but I can't change it," Lincoln apologized.

"Then leave her! Prove you are really my dawg. Prove you are truly sorry, and just leave her alone," Ryan yelled.

Lincoln shook his head angrily. "Foul or not, hate me or not, if I have to fight you every day for the rest of my life, then so be it, because what I will not do is leave Charice. I love her, and she will be my wife!"

"Fine, it's your funeral," Ryan snarled and broke free from Marcus and Lamar.

I jumped in front of Lincoln before Ryan could get to him, stopping Ryan dead in his tracks. "If you're going to hurt him, if you're going to kill him, then you're going to have to do the same to me! I'm not going to let you touch him anymore, Ryan. I love him, and I will not let anything happen to him. Nothing!"

Ryan cocked his head sideways and looked at me. "It's like that, Charice?" he asked, brokenhearted, as tears found their way to his eyes for the first time. He pointed to himself. "You picking him over me?"

"Yes," I said confidently. "Please, just go." I began to cry and fell back into Lincoln's embrace.

"It's okay, baby," Lincoln said, kissing my head. "I love you."

Ryan shook his head, not caring that he was crying too. "Charice," he whimpered. He held his chest as if someone had just snatched his heart right out of the cavity. Without any notice or further words, Ryan turned and ran out of the house with Marcus and Lamar following.

Slowly, I moved toward the door, closing and bolting it behind them. A wave of hysteria came over me, and I slid to the floor in a mess of tears. Lincoln rushed to me, picked me up, and carried me to our bedroom, where he laid me on the bed and held me as I cried.

"We'll be okay now. Nothing is going to happen to us. We'll be okay," he kept repeating over and over again.

But I wasn't so sure. I wasn't sure at all.

Chapter Seven

Lucinda

It'd been a month, and there was still no change on the job hunt. I felt a little discouraged, but I wasn't going to let it get me down. Besides, I was fulfilling my dream of being enrolled in college. Financially speaking, my severance pay had run out. However, I was getting my unemployment checks, and I had a couple grand left from the money I made at Club Moet.

Speaking of good ol' Club Moet, the funniest part about the whole situation was that Pooch actually called me to come back. Seemed his patrons missed me more than he thought they would. I found great pleasure in telling him no. In more Club Moet news, I'd bumped into that crazy Alize at the mall, and she gave me the scoop on Greg's grimy ass. He tried to steal from Pooch by claiming that he'd lost money on my stunt move, but Alize told Pooch that I'd given Greg the money in full that he'd paid out. Once Pooch confronted him, he gave up the money, and Pooch gave Greg the ax. He was lucky that's all he got. It was one thing to lie on me, but it could've been his funeral for stealing from Pooch. Now some new cat named Big Cal, who was his right-hand man, was running the show. Apparently, he was real cool, and the girls liked him twenty times better than Greg. That's what happens when you try to be grimy.

I even got a request from Magic City to come and join their stripper clique. I guessed the word spread quickly about ol' Spanish Fly, but I denied them, too. The money was appealing, but I wasn't going to sell my soul for cheap tricks anymore. I was slowly learning to trust in God. Whenever I removed myself from the picture and let Him guide me, things always tended to work out. I had no clue how I was going to make it, but I wasn't going down the path I had been headed down to get there. Of that, I was certain.

I was also certain that Raul came to my job that day so that he could get fired from his. It was the only logical explanation. He knew that National Cross would press charges, which they did, and that he would get locked up, which he was, for disorderly conduct and trespassing. He also knew that if he got locked up, then he'd get fired from his job, which he did, and getting fired meant not being able to pay child support. See what I mean? How completely selfish is that? He would rather lose his job and get a record than take care of his child? Nadia didn't ask to come here. Our irresponsible actions brought her here, and it was both of our responsibilities to see that she was well taken care of. He was so busy trying to get back at me that his dumb ass didn't figure that I would get fired too. That's what happens when you plan dumb shit.

Well, if he thought he was off the hook, he could think again. I contacted my attorney, who was more than happy to march into the judge's chambers and get an order to keep Raul locked up. That's right. Before Raul could be released from his ninety-day jail sentence, he had to pay back support for those three months. I only wished I could've seen his face when that news was delivered to him. Oh well.

Chillin' out in my favorite lounging outfit—a tank top and a pair of booty shorts—I enjoyed this Sunday break. My mama had the day off, and she decided to spend some time with Nadia, which gave me the perfect opportunity to study and do homework. Just as I'd finished one of my assignments, my cell phone vibrated. I didn't recognize the number, so I let it go to voicemail. As soon as I drank a sip of my iced mocha, the same number called me again.

"Either they know me or desperately need to contact the person they are looking for," I deduced before answering. "Hello?"

"Hello, may I speak with Lucinda?" a man's voice asked.

"This is she. Who is this?"

"Hi, Lucinda. It's Aldris."

I smiled. "Oh, hi, Aldris! How are you? This is quite a surprise."

"I'm good. I can't complain. How are you?" he replied.

"Not bad, actually. I'm in school now. In fact, I was just sitting here doing some assignments."

"That's great, Lucinda! I'm glad to hear it."

"I told you I'd be all right."

"You did," he concurred. "Does this mean that you have also found a job?"

Leave it to him to bring up my point of pain. Rather than get upset about it, I let it go, because he was only checking on me. "Unfortunately, no. I'm still searching, but I know something will come up."

"That's exactly why I was calling you. I didn't mean to disturb you or call back-to-back like that, but I may have an opportunity for you," he said excitedly.

"Really?" I asked with high anticipation.

"Yes, really," he confirmed. "Is there any way you could meet me somewhere so we could discuss it?"

"Um, I'm sure I could. Is there somewhere in particular you'd like to meet?" I asked, grabbing my pen and paper just in case I needed to get directions.

"Great! I just got home from church, and I'm starving. I have a taste for a good, juicy burger," he told me. "Are you hungry?"

"A little."

"Will you meet me at the Varsity in Kennesaw in, say, forty-five minutes?" he asked.

"I can do that." I looked down at my inappropriate attire.

"Good. Bring your appetite, and I'll bring the wallet," he joked.

"You don't have to—"

"I know what I don't have to do, Lucinda. I'm offering, and you're going to accept it," he interjected sternly yet with respect.

"My bad, dude. You got it. I forget how much of a gentleman you are," I accepted.

"Yes, I try. So please allow me to be a gentleman to you. Can you do that?"

"No doubt," I answered.

"Good. I'll see you in about forty-five," he said, and we hung up.

I was pleasantly surprised that Aldris called, and I appreciated that he didn't use this opportunity to make me feel low or embarrassed about the whole strip club incident. Hell, he didn't even mention it. That's not to say that he wouldn't. I just liked that he was able to act as if he had not seen my ass clapping in his face.

Since the last time he saw me I looked like a straight-up hooker, I wanted to make a better impression. I was determined to make him remember Lucinda and not Spanish Fly, so I chose khaki Capri pants, a round-neck fitted yellow T-shirt, a green high-back, short-sleeved mini jacket, and tan wedges. The ensemble tastefully graced my size-eight figure. To finish, I added light makeup and green eye shadow to accentuate my hazel eye color. My curly locks, caramel skin, and attire were sheer perfection. Exactly fifty minutes later, I arrived to find Aldris inside, waiting for me.

He stood as I approached the table. "I'm sorry. I hope I'm not too late," I apologized for my slight tardiness.

"Oh no, I only just got here about five minutes ago," he said as we sat down. "You look great."

"Thanks." I blushed. "And you look good yourself. You dress down very well." I admired his royal blue Polo shirt, knee-length dark denim jeans, Nikes, and his dark blue Yankee baseball cap. But I shouldn't have expected any less. This cat was always sharp. "You look twenty-eight today," I added.

He burst into laughter. "Oh, you got jokes!"

"I'm just saying." I shrugged and laughed along with him.

We continued to joke around about my comment while we walked to the counter. I ordered two chili dogs with a medium Coke, and he ordered a chili cheeseburger, chili dog, fries, and a large Coke. He pulled out a twenty spot to take care of the tab and grabbed our food.

"Good Lawd, my dude. Can you eat all of that?" I asked, amazed at the amount of food he had as we made our way to the table again.

He chuckled at my question. "I'm a big eater. What can I say? Besides, I couldn't decide between the burger and the dog."

"I'll bet your chick stays in the kitchen."

"Actually, I don't have a chick. I do a little something-something, but mostly my home-cooked meals come from my mom's house on Sundays."

"Oh, you go to her house every Sunday?"

"Sometimes. Of three sons, I'm the only one who moved back to Atlanta after college, so I try to go over and check up on her as much as possible. In return, she cooks me some killer meals."

"Three boys? I know the refrigerator stayed empty."

"Who you telling? It was like a war zone in there over the stove and the refrigerator. My pops didn't have a chance," he said with a chuckle.

"When you're there, I bet he still doesn't have a chance," I joked.

He shrugged. His expression turned solemn. "Actually, I wish he were there. I'd sacrifice all the food for him. He died of a stroke two years ago."

A gasp escaped me. "I'm so sorry. I didn't mean to offend you. That's what I get for opening my big mouth," I apologized sorrowfully.

He touched my hand, which caused my words to halt in my throat. "It's okay. You didn't know, and I brought him up anyway. I'm at peace with it. He's in a better place."

My eyes fluttered up from our hands to meet his gaze, and I smiled at him. "I admire your strength."

"Shit, I admire yours," he countered, lightening the mood while soliciting a light blush of shock from me.

"Me?" I asked, pointing to myself.

"Yes, yours," he replied and took a sip of his soda. "I have to admit I've had a good life, so I know the efforts of hard work, but not struggle. I've never had to. That's what makes me admire you. No matter what, you keep on trucking, and you're a hard worker, too."

"Hell, I've never known a person who didn't have to struggle. It's nice to find someone who can actually say their life was good."

"It's due to my parents. They were married for thirty-five years before my dad passed. My mom is a retired RN, and my dad was a sergeant in the military for fifteen years before he retired and worked as an IT technician for the remainder of his life. They were the classic couple. They met in high school, got married right after they graduated, and my dad went off into the military. My mom finished nursing school, worked, and tended to us boys, which I'm sure was a feat, especially since we're all two years apart. My oldest brother, Daniel Jr., is thirty-two, Levi is thirty, and I'm the baby at twenty-eight."

"Wow. That's so wonderful. I swear I wish I had a family like that," I said sadly.

"It is great. My parents raised some great boys, if I do say so myself. Dad taught us to love and respect God first, then family, and to always be a provider, protector, and a loving husband. All of us graduated and are doing well. Daniel went into the military and has a wife and two little boys. They are in living in Germany right now. Levi is a computer systems analyst and lives in Savannah. He's getting married next year. His fiancée and he have a one-year-old daughter, who is my mom's pride and joy, especially since she's a girl. And I pride myself on being the closest to both my mom and dad. You know the baby of the family gets the shine," he teased. "But enough about me. Tell me about you," he requested, then bit into his burger.

"When you come from a good background, it's a little easier to discuss than when you don't. So how about you just tell me about this opportunity instead?" I said, attempting to skirt the conversation by shoving a French fry in my mouth.

He sat back and stared at me in disbelief. "I just sat here and told you damn near my entire upbringing, and you won't give me a little bit of info? That's not even fair. I'm not telling you jack until you give me something," he joked with a smirk on his face.

"Come on. That's not fair." I threw my hands up with laughter. "You told me to meet you here for the info. You're the one who walked down memory lane."

"Oh, and your little comment about my 'chick' staying in the kitchen didn't start this whole conversation? You think you're slick, Lucinda," he chuckled.

Shaking my head, I shrugged. "My story is nowhere near as nice as yours," I warned.

"Then tell me what you want. It can't be all ugly. You turned out to be a good woman."

"Flattery will get you everywhere." I blushed coyly.

"Okay, okay," I caved. "At twenty-one, I'm the oldest of eight children."

"Wow!" he screeched in sheer amazement. "Eight kids?"

"Yeah. I'm more amazed that my parents aren't together since it's obvious that they did enjoy each other," I said half-jokingly. "Jose is eighteen, Lucy is seventeen, Ana is twelve, Jorge and Emmanuel are twins, and they are ten, Luz is eight, and the baby, Peter, he is seven."

"I don't see how your mom does it. To have a twenty-one-year-old daughter and a seven-year-old son, that's like starting over," he said, shaking his head.

"Hell, everyone who doesn't know us swears Nadia is her child because she just kept having children," I kidded. "But, jokes aside, she manages well. She's the person I admire because I'm about to go crazy trying to provide for one child. How she manages seven is beyond me."

"I feel you on that," he agreed, eating his chili dog.

"My dad—and I use that term loosely—left my mom when Peter was four years old. He ran off with this chick named Maria, who is now his wife. That woman—and I use that term loosely as well—is only two years older than me. Now where they do that at? Anyway, they have a one-year-old daughter named Eva together, and Maria has a four-year-old daughter named Rosemary. So in all, I have eight siblings and one stepsister. My mom works as a housekeeper by day and a CNA by night. My dad is a local truck driver. He makes decent money, and we were doing okay up until he left. He's more focused on his new family and doesn't think about my siblings at home, or me, for that matter," I shared.

He shook his head. "I just can't see it. After all those years and children, that in itself is enough for a man to stick beside his woman. My mom used to tell me all the time that having a baby is as close to death as you can get without dying. To me, I figure if a woman, especially your wife, loves you enough to bear your kids, especially eight of them, that should stand for something."

"Your mom is a wise woman, and I agree with her. As for my parents, I don't know all the details, but I know my mom loved my dad. I noticed the arguments and the shift in the household. When your parents don't get along, you can tell it. My dad cheated, and when my mom found out, she lost it. I'm not sure if they tried to make it work, but the next thing I knew, he moved out, they got a divorce, and he married Maria."

"Damn," Aldris said, sounding disheartened. "Tell me about this Raul character, Nadia's dad," Aldris requested with a scowl on his face, yet obviously wanting to change the subject. "Has everything worked out on that end?"

I took a deep breath and shook my head. "I know you were trying to spare me, but I was enjoying myself until that *puto*'s name came up. Hindsight is twenty-twenty, but it would be so much easier if foresight were twenty-twenty instead," I said as he cracked an apologetic smile. "I have no doubt in my mind that he plotted that whole scenario to get fired from his job so that he wouldn't be able to pay child support. I haven't confirmed it, but it's the only logical reason. But he got a nice surprise, because he's not getting out until he's all caught up with his payments. I wish I had the mindset then that I have now. I never would've messed with Raul to begin with. It was a high school love, and we were doing things we shouldn't have at that age, and like so many other young girls, I got caught up. Unfortunately, Raul proved to be like so many other young boys: irresponsible," I explained between bites of food.

Aldris shook his head. "So many young men are so misguided these days. Guys like that are so quick to defend their mothers and then go out there, make a baby, and leave their child and the mother to fend for themselves. It makes no sense to me. That's why I volunteer as a big brother for the Boys Club. A couple times out of the month, I meet up with Raheem, my little brother, and I take him places so we can have fun and have serious talks. Since I don't have a son, I feel like that is my way of making sure one young man grows up to be a real man."

I was taken aback. I had no idea that he was a big brother. "You're just an all-around good guy, huh?"

"I wouldn't say that. Just because I haven't been caught up doesn't mean I wasn't out there doing what it takes to make a child. Trust me. I could've easily been a high school boy with a child."

"But you would've handled your responsibility," I interjected.

"Very true."

"Well, anyway, why don't you tell me how you got into the health insurance business?" I asked, ready to move on from that topic.

"I'd always been curious about the medical field because my mom is a nurse, but the politics of the health care industry are what really interest me. I went to college and received my bachelor's and master's in health care management. I started out as an account representative for United Cignal and then moved over to National Cross HealthCare and worked up to be a manager. What about you?"

"Job hunting to get out of my mom's house with Nadia is how I ended up at National Cross," I clowned, though I was being serious.

"Lucinda, you keep it real all the time. There ain't no cutting corners with you, I see," he declared, rolling with laughter.

I shrugged. "I am how I am, and that is straight up. What you see is what you get over here. I told you our lives were very different. Your life was so clean-cut, planned, and organized. Mine was on the other end of the spectrum. I appreciate your kindness, though. You're a cool dude. That's why I'm surprised that you don't have a chick."

He sighed and gazed off as he finished up his burger. I bit my chili dog, observing him quietly. What I said affected him, and I wanted to know what it was since he wanted us to have this personal conversation. "Oh, so I've finally hit a nerve that Mr. Aldris doesn't want me to touch. Since you playing a hundred and one questions today, you're going to have to spill it," I told him matter-of-factly.

Returning his gaze to my direction, he released a slow, deliberate groan and conceded. "I did ask for it, huh?"

"Yep, it was you who said you weren't telling me jack until I gave you something. I believe that was the same Aldris who sits here. I'm not listening to anything else until you spill your beans."

"Now that's not fair," he chuckled.

"Oh yes, turnabout is always fair play," I playfully protested.

He wiped his hands, then leaned back, preparing to tell me the story. "I had a woman. Her name was Jennifer. We went to the same college, and we met while I was working on my master's degree. I can't even speak a bad word about her. She was beautiful, educated, and she loved me like no other woman I'd ever known besides my mom," he said, getting quiet.

"What happened?" I pressed. "You're a good dude, and she sounds like she was a good chick."

He took a sip of his Coke and continued. "Me," he admitted honestly. "I cheated on her. I cheated a lot.

Hell, I was young, in the prime of my life, and I wasn't ready for a relationship. Anyone with a pretty face, a nice waist, and a fat ass caught my eye. I'm not excusing my actions. I'm just trying to let you know where my mind was at back then. After two years of dating, my mom said I should marry her. Hell, Jennifer was hinting around it herself, even though she'd caught me cheating once before. She forgave me like a lot of women normally do, so I felt pressured to ask her to marry me, and of course, she said yes. We even moved in together. I swear I tried my best to fly the straight and narrow path, but after three months, I was on the prowl again. She caught me twice with the same girl, once at a restaurant and the next time in our bed. That was the last straw for her. She took my ring off and moved out. A month later, she transferred to another college back in her home state of Virginia, and she's never spoken to me since.

"I felt like shit afterward. No other woman satisfied me, nor did they do any of the things she would do for me, and I realized for the first time what I really had in her. Right then and there, I vowed never to treat another woman like that in my life, and I haven't. But like you said, turnabout is fair play, or as I'd like to say, karma is a bitch. The last two females I was in a relationship with only lasted between three and six months, and both of them dogged me out. Funny thing is, last year, I heard from one of our old college buddies that Jennifer is married and pregnant with her first child, and to this very day, she can't stand the sound of my name. So that's my story."

Most females would probably be upset with him about his past, but I wasn't. Truth be told, all of us have to grow into maturity in different areas in our life, and a lot of times, someone else gets hurt in the process. That's why I tried to work with Raul for as long as I did. I tried to give him time to accept his responsibility, but for Nadia's welfare, I could no longer wait. Besides, there's a difference between someone wanting to and making an effort to change, and someone who was just being an ass. Raul wasn't trying to change, but Aldris did. That's the difference.

"I really respect that about you. It's honorable. It takes a strong man to admit his shortcomings and work to fix them. Sometimes you have to go through hell to get to heaven."

He smiled. "I like that. I might have to cop that from you."

"Go ahead. I'm sure I copped it from somebody," I giggled.

"Thanks for not judging me based on that, too," he said sincerely.

I rolled my eyes. "Hey, I owed you one."

He gave a knowing chuckle and put his hand up as if to say, "Let's not get on that subject."

"Don't mention it."

To lighten the mood, I teased him. "Could you mention to me why you had me meet you here in the first place? That would be nice."

"You are a handful! I swear to God, woman," he said as we shared a laugh. "But check it. My homegirl Suzette Hall is the office manager for the Doctors of Orthopedic Medicine."

"Yeah, I've heard of them. They are like ranked in the top ten in the nation of orthopedic doctors," I added.

"Right," he concurred. "Their practice has grown tremendously, and they've decided to start an at-home claims processing center where people work on their claims at night. She called me because she needs three full-time employees and three part-time employees to hire."

"What?" I asked in amazement.

"Yep. Potential candidates have to have at least two years of experience and have to be willing to work between the hours of five p.m. and six a.m. Full-time is forty hours a week, and part-time is a minimum of twenty-five hours, no more than thirty-five hours per week. If you're full-time, you can get benefits, and get this, the starting pay is $17.50 per hour. Plus, you get paid once a week, and she's doing immediate hiring, so you don't have to wait to work," he explained excitedly.

"You've got to be shitting me!" I nearly climbed out of my seat.

"No, I'm not, and here's the best part: I told her about you and asked her to keep a full-time and part-time position available. She promised that she would. In fact, I bragged on you so much that she promised me that if you interviewed with her and she hired you, she'd pay you $18.50 per hour."

Without warning, I jumped up and hugged him, nearly knocking him over. "Thank you! Thank you! Thank you! Oh God! I can't believe this! I'm so nervous and excited," I said, squeezing him tight.

He hugged me back. "You're very welcome."

I noticed the other patrons looking at us as if we were crazy, so I eased back in my seat. I pushed my other chili dog back and waved my hands. "I'm so jacked up on adrenaline right now I can't even eat."

"See why I wanted to relax, eat, and then discuss it?" he asked, and I nodded. "I have her office number, and she's expecting your call tomorrow to set up an interview. You must have a desktop computer, and she gave me a list of all the necessary computer capabilities. Oh yeah, and as far as you getting fired, don't mention that to her. I told her you had to quit because you were going to college during the day to get your degree. I have you covered."

My mind was racing a mile a minute. I couldn't believe how Aldris had come through for me. This dude was freaking awesome. *See what happens when I step aside and let God direct my path?* Here I was fired from one job and quitting the other, and now I was in college and on my way to a decent-paying job during the hours I needed. Yes, I was claiming it. I even had enough money to buy a computer thanks to my gig at Club Moet.

"Wow, this is so awesome! You're awesome, and I can't thank you enough," I said, taking the contact information from Aldris as well as the computer requirements. I looked at the specifications and realized it was Greek to me. "Um, I have to go buy a computer, and since your dad was an IT guy, do you know what any of this means?"

"I know what all of it means. I'm great with computers. It runs in the family," he said, looking at the list. "This is talking about your memory and drives—" he began as he pointed to one of the items on the list.

"Look, dude, I have no idea about drives and stuff. RAM and cleaning out cookies is about the extent of this chick's IT skills. If you don't mind . . . I mean, if you have some time today, would you mind going with me to pick out a good computer?" I interrupted.

"That depends on two things."

I furrowed my brow. "It depends on what?"

"First, it depends on if you can stop calling me a dude and yourself a chick. I'm all for slang, but there's just something about when you say that you're a chick, I don't know, you make it sound like you think you're unworthy of being called a woman. And that is definitely not the case. I'm a man and you, Miss Lady, are definitely one hell of a woman," he clarified with a sweet compliment.

He caught me so off guard that I gave a casual shrug at first. "I never really thought about it. I guess in a way you're right. That's just my expression because I'm just a down-ass, round-the-way kinda chick."

He snapped his fingers. "That's it! See what I mean? You're not just that. Okay, yeah, you are cool and down, but you are more than that. Don't put yourself in a box like that, because you're a woman first who is cool and down."

Blushing intensely, I glanced away momentarily to regain my composure. "Okay, I get your point. I can feel you on that." I wasn't offended, because he made a lot of sense. Accepting what he'd said and moving on, I asked, "What else does it depend on?"

"It depends on if you'd let me take you out again, but this time on a real date," he stated, and I noticed a little nervousness in his voice. He looked at me with his brown puppy-dog eyes, and I knew that's how he'd pulled many a woman. The look on his face was hopeful yet fearful of my answer, but most of all, he looked sincere.

To say I was shocked was putting it mildly. *Did he really just push up on me?* He was fine as hell. No, I mean really he was. About six feet tall, with a muscular build, low-cut Caesar, and neatly trimmed goatee, he reminded me of the football player Reggie Bush with facial hair. There was no question that we enjoyed one another's company and that our conversation flowed like water, but a date? Was I really ready for a date with Aldris? I hadn't dated anyone really in over a year. My focus had been on raising Nadia, getting an education, and making money so much so that I hadn't even considered being with a man. Then to go out with a man like Aldris? Our backgrounds and lifestyles were so dissimilar. He was that dude who went to the strip club as a birthday gift, and I was that chick who stripped there. That's what I meant.

I put my head down as I contemplated it. "I don't know what to say, Aldris. I really don't know about that." I fidgeted nervously.

He reached across the table and lifted my chin. His touch sent a jolt of energy through me that I'd never felt in my life. I didn't know if it was attraction, nervousness, or lust—hell, maybe it was a three-in-one combination—but whatever it was, it felt damn good. Once he noticed that I was nervous too, he stared at me with sheer determination in his eyes, as if nothing was going to deter him from getting what he wanted.

"You wear nervous well. Underneath that tough-girl facade is a woman, an amazingly beautiful woman, inside and out, whom I'd love to get to know, but for now, I'd settle for one chance at an actual date."

Shit, I'd never had a dude—I mean, a man—say no shit like that to me. As rough and tough as I was on the inside, that little bit managed to touch the little girl in me who just wanted to be loved. And that was hard to do for such a round-the-way chick—woman—like me. I smiled shyly, taken aback by his words. I was so caught up I agreed without a second thought. "I'll go out with you on one real date."

"All right then." He stood as I realized that I'd agreed. His smile was so infectious that I could do nothing but bask in his warmth. I didn't have the heart to change my mind. "Let me get you a to-go box so we can go shop a bit for some of the best deals on computers, and you can land this job," he said excitedly before going to the counter.

As I watched him glide to the counter, I felt giddy yet afraid. I had no idea what I was getting myself into with Aldris. Not to mention, part of my reservation was because I wasn't sure if he was attracted to me or Spanish Fly. Again, the last time I saw him before today, my huge

ass was all up in his face at Club Moet. I also wasn't sure
of his motives. Perhaps he simply wanted to help me,
but I wasn't used to having generosity being extended to
me without asking for repayment. However, I was going
to try not to overanalyze everything. Even if it went nowhere, Aldris and I would remain cool people, and that
was good enough for me. But for now, my focus was sole-
ly on landing this job not only for myself but for Nadia.

Chapter Eight

Charice

The bright bulbs went off in my face. Mad as hell, I pushed the camera back. "Move! Excuse me! Please leave us alone," I yelled, trying to escort my children inside their private school.

"Mommy, why are these people following us?" Charity asked.

"Just hush and keep moving," I replied.

"Charice! Can you give us a comment about your relationship with Lincoln Harper?" one reporter asked.

"What is Ryan Westmore saying about your engagement?" another asked, flashing more cameras in my face.

"I'm trying to take my children to school. Please leave," I bellowed in frustration. I pushed open the front doors and allowed them to slam shut in their faces.

Well, the cat was officially out of the bag now, and boy was it out big time. Now my life was riddled with turmoil. Ryan hated Lincoln and wasted no time expressing that to me and anybody else who would listen, with the exception of the press. He didn't want Lincoln around the triplets or me, and not a day went by when Ryan didn't try to convince me to leave Lincoln and be with him. When I refused, it turned into a shouting match over the stipulations he wanted to put on me about the triplets with regard to Lincoln.

To add to our problems, Lincoln had been in more than one argument with other teammates about dating me, and he and Ryan had come to blows in the stadium parking lot. The media was hounding all of us like crazy. My home was no longer private, and even Lincoln's parents and my parents were dragged into the mess by the paparazzi. Now they were cornering me at my children's school. What the hell?

The media ran all kinds of crazy headlines about it: A COWBOY'S LOVE AFFAIR, COWBOY'S LOVE TRIANGLE, and the most beloved title, TWO COWBOYS AND A COWGIRL. I had bitches writing me letters asking how I snagged two NFL players as if I were some sort of groupie. It was all beginning to be far too damn much for me.

"Just one statement, Charice," a reporter said, interrupting me as I rushed out of the school.

"Leave me the fuck alone. How's that for a statement?" I hurriedly got into my SUV and slammed the door. I took a deep breath and pulled off, leaving the sea of reporters behind.

You would've thought that this story would've stayed centralized in Dallas, but I thought it was more popular here in Atlanta. Everyone was trying to make it seem as if my motives were malicious when the truth of the matter was that Lincoln and I truly just found each other and fell in love. Was that just too simplistic to believe? Oh, and my family? They just kept giving me the "I told you so" speech, and I was tired of hearing that, too.

To top things off, Lincoln and I were both on edge and under a lot of stress between our families, Ryan, and the media, and it seemed the only thing we could do when we spoke was take it out on each other. We argued over the stupidest shit, like why it took so long for me to call him back, or him acting as if he didn't have the time to talk to me when I did call. It seemed as if no one understood where I was coming from except my girls.

After I finally got LaMeka's mom to admit to me that she was in a transitional home, I knew it was time to catch up, so I called a mandatory girls' gathering. It seemed that we were all going through some shit, and if I couldn't count on anyone or anything else, I always had them. And right now, I really needed them.

"Is the coast clear?" I asked, pulling up into the backyard of LaMeka's transitional house. She closed and locked her privacy fence behind me. "These fucking reporters have been hounding the shit out of me."

"You good," LaMeka confirmed. I hopped out of my SUV, pulled off my Chanel shades, and headed inside with her.

"Thanks." I smiled wearily to them. "So, ladies, what's good?"

"That shit is all over the news and entertainment reports about you, Lincoln, and Ryan. What the hell happened?" Lucinda asked me.

I sighed and ran my fingers through my hair. "Ryan caught me in Lincoln's house."

"Daaaammnn," all three of them said in unison.

Trinity shook her head. "I'm not gon' even go there, Charice. How the fuck did he manage to do that?" she asked sarcastically.

"I missed Lincoln, so I flew down to visit. Apparently, he'd planned a team-building golf game with the offensive line that he forgot about because I was there. Long story short, I'd ordered him something from Best Buy, and I thought it was the deliveryman—"

"And when you got to the door, it was really Ryan," LaMeka finished, putting two and two together.

"Exactly. But there were also two other dudes from the team."

Trinity again shook her head in disbelief of my predicament. I could almost see the "I told you so" dancing on her tongue. "I know Ryan was embarrassed like a muthasucka."

Dropping my head into my hands, I released a weighted sigh. "Embarrassed ain't even the word for it. More like pissed the fuck off. I've never seen Ryan so angry and jealous. He tried to kill Lincoln! Poor Lincoln was trying not to fight him back, but the other two guys could barely contain Ryan. I finally had to stand my ground and let Ryan know that I chose Lincoln, and when I tell you he looked devastated, I mean that thing."

"Have you talked to Ryan since?" Trinity asked.

"Every day. He's relentless in getting me to leave Lincoln."

"Kinda reminds me of Terrence," she blurted.

Snapping her fingers, Lucinda turned to Trinity with a questioning gaze. "What is the deal with you two anyway? You know, since Suwanee," she asked as we all nodded.

This time it was Trinity's turn to drop her head, obviously upset about what she was about to reveal to us. "So much shit has gone on. Honestly, I'd snuck around with Dreads ever since that night in Suwanee. I thought we were careful. It was the best of both worlds, you know. My man to take care of my home, and my man to take care of me. It was playing with fire, but I felt like I could handle it. I guess being with Dreads made me feel invincible in a way. But that invincible shield got penetrated by Pooch. He caught me a couple of Sundays ago in the park having a family picnic with Dreads and the kids."

A collective gasp swept through all of us. To be honest, I was more shocked to see that Trinity still stood here with us, among the living. Pooch was crazy in love with Trinity, to the point of being obsessed. It was something we all were leery about but never placed stock in because Trinity was loyal to Pooch. Or she had been. But as long as she was loyal to him, there were no problems, because

Pooch simply didn't want Trinity to cheat or leave him. As long as that never happened, we all believed that Pooch would never cause Trinity any harm. But it had happened. Not only was she disloyal, but she'd also cheated, and she'd done both with the number one sworn enemy, Terrence.

We all guessed how that went down, but no one wanted to ask, so I decided to be the one to broach the subject. "What happened?"

"What didn't happen? That's the question," Trinity said sadly. She looked up, and the pools of water developing in her eyes revealed the untold pain that lay behind them. I'd known it was bad, but somehow, I knew—I think we all knew—that it went beyond bad. We all stared at each other and back at Trinity as we braced ourselves for what happened next.

"It all seemed so surreal," she began. Her voice quivered as she swiped tears out of her eyes. "I had to stop him and Terrence from tearing each other apart in the park with all those kids around, and then . . ." She paused briefly as the tears she'd tried to stop finally rolled down her face. "Pooch beat my ass at the house." Her shoulders deflated as emotion overcame her. With her hand over her forehead, she took a deep breath and continued through a tearstained voice.

"He, uh, he raped me to prove that I wasn't gonna give his pussy away," she barely got out before completely breaking down.

We hurriedly gathered around her. Lucinda rubbed her back while LaMeka and I held her hands. "You don't have to go on," LaMeka interjected.

She shook her head. "No, I need to tell y'all this," Trinity said, her voice continued to shake. "Three days later, Dreads showed up at my house, and Pooch tried to kill him. He had that gun pointed straight at Dreads, but the safety was on, and Dreads beat his ass. I tried to stop them, but I passed out."

"Passed out?" we all repeated in shock.

She nodded, wiping her eyes. Her next words nearly caused all of us to pass out. "I'm pregnant."

Lucinda patted her back. "No, Trinity, don't tell us that, *chica*," she said, her voice filled with disappointment. "You know how Pooch feels about kids, and you got pregnant with his child again?" Lucinda asked in disbelief.

Trinity let out a slight groan. "I'm about nine weeks pregnant."

"So? What does that have to do with anything? You know he don't want no kids. You can still have an abortion," Lucinda said. "'Cause you know he's gon' make you do it."

She turned to Lucinda angrily. "First of all, I don't give a fuck what he would want me to do. I'm not aborting my child, and how dare you of all people even suggest that I should?" Trinity fumed. "Besides, that's not even my fucking point. Think about what happened two months ago."

Her words dawned on me. I inhaled sharply, then whispered, "It's Terrence's baby."

Trinity nodded. "Exactly." She threw her hands up.

Not that I doubted what she said, but it's not like Trinity and Pooch had been separated. Maybe she was wrong about this. Maybe she simply wanted this child to be Terrence's. I had to ask because she'd already been through enough with Pooch. A baby, especially a baby by Terrence, could mean her funeral for real. "Okay, listen to me, honey," I said, turning her face toward me. "How can you be sure?"

"That's around the time Pooch got robbed. We hadn't had sex in like three weeks when that shit went down between me and Dreads 'cause he was trying to get his clique straight. Dreads and I didn't use no protection, and that nigga skeeted all up in my shit. And I am pregnant to the exact date that we made love. It's definitely, unquestionably Dreads's baby," she said as tears rolled down her face.

"*Ay, mamacita,* what are you going to do? 'Cause if you're still breathing, then Pooch doesn't know," Lucinda said with her usual bluntness.

Trinity rolled her eyes at her and shrugged. "Gee, thanks with your rude ass." She shook her head before she continued. "Actually, the weirdest shit is Pooch wants me to keep the baby to try to make us close again. But that ain't gon' never happen, especially not after what he did to me. The truth of the matter is I love Dreads, and I'm not killing my baby. But right now, I really don't know what to do."

We all took a moment to process what she'd said. However, we could offer no real solution. No matter what, Trinity's mind was already set, so the only thing that could be done was to support her decision.

Although Lucinda had been the one giving Trinity the most grief over the situation, in true best friend form, she was the first to hug and console her. "I'm with you, girl. Whatever you need, I got you. Just don't let Pooch find out. You know how that *bastardo* is."

Trinity pulled back, and out of nowhere, she gave Lucinda the most disgusted glare before she sucked her teeth. "Yeah, and so do you," she said with a slight attitude.

"What's up with that?" Lucinda looked at her, confused.

With her lips pursed, Trinity gave her a mean side-eye. "Come on, Lu. You know I know." She smacked her lips and pointed her index finger at herself. "How you figure you can keep some shit like that from me? You think I live in the dark or some shit? I am Pooch's girlfriend. Don't too much shit go on with his businesses and operations that I don't find out about."

Lucinda looked so defeated as she put her head down, seemingly embarrassed. "I figured he'd tell you."

"Oh, he didn't, but you damn sure should have," Trinity fussed. She crossed her arms and rolled her neck. "Skeet, Dread's best friend, is cool with Greg. How you figure I wouldn't find out about Spanish Fly? I just thought we were cool enough for you to tell me. You been my bestie since forever. But apparently you and Pooch is a little cooler than me and you," Trinity smarted off.

At this point, I was just as confused as LaMeka, who looked at me for answers that I couldn't offer. I placed my hand up to stop their back-and-forth. "Wait. Hold up. What the hell are you two talking about?" I asked finally.

Trinity looked over at Lucinda, who held a timid expression on her face, and she rolled her eyes again. "Go on and tell her about Spanish Fly. You scandalous, Lu. How you gon' audition for Pooch?"

"You don't know the whole story," she said, her voice trembling.

"Audition?" I asked with a puzzled expression.

"Mm-hmm. Yep, audition," Trinity said nonchalantly.

This powwow just got wilder and wilder. Thank God we were all seated, because between my drama, Trinity's revelation, and Lucinda's scandalous antics, I was sure my legs were too weak to hold me up. My goodness. What the hell was going on with us? It seemed all of us were tied up in some bullshit that we all desperately needed to figure out and figure out quick. LaMeka and I stared at Lucinda in utter disbelief as we waited for her to explain. She had to explain this shit. This could not be life.

Lucinda looked at us as if pleading for us to hear her out. "*Ay, mamacita.* It wasn't like that, you guys. I swear," she cried. "The truth is Raul got me fired from my job, so

I was a stripper at Moet for a little bit," she admitted. "I called Pooch, and he put me down."

"More like you auditioned naked in front of him to get the gig. That's the only way Pooch put you down," Trinity popped off.

"No you didn't," LaMeka and I hollered in disbelief. Oh, hell no! This was too much.

"I had to! I needed the money!" Lucinda shouted with regret. "It's not like I slept with him. It was just for the gig. I swear. I put that on Nadia's life," she cried, looking at Trinity.

As the information Lucinda revealed filtered into our minds, LaMeka gazed at her as if she'd just realized something. "Wait. How did Raul get you fired?" LaMeka asked.

Lucinda sat back and rubbed her neck. She bit her lip, and you could tell just the thought of what transpired ate away at her. Sucking in air, Lucinda explained, "Long story short, that *bastardo* came to my job and picked a fight with me and my coworkers. It was a mess. Security and another manager had to get involved. Raul got arrested, and I had to make a statement. Later on, I was released from my job because my situation was an immediate danger to other employees," Lucinda said, unable to hold back the slow and steady stream of tears that flowed from her eyes as she told the story.

She shrugged and lifted apologetic eyes to Trinity before placing both her hands atop hers. "I did what I thought I needed to do. I didn't say anything to you or to anybody because I was embarrassed. I didn't want anyone to know what I was doing, and most importantly, I never wanted to betray you, Trin. You gotta know that. I didn't want to audition. I just didn't know what else to do. But I never wanted to hurt you or our friendship. You are my bestie for life."

Hearing Lucinda's heartfelt plea softened all of us, especially Trinity. The huff deflated from Trinity, and she released a sigh, then embraced Lucinda tightly. "It's all right," she consoled her, then pulled back and looked at her as she held her by her shoulders. "Honestly, I was more pissed that you felt you couldn't tell me. How could you trust Pooch over any of us? Over me?"

That part. We all nodded in agreement. I got that she was embarrassed and didn't want to tell others, but this was us. The four amigas. Even if she didn't tell LaMeka or me, she should've known she could go to Trinity. They'd been best friends forever. There was nothing that they couldn't share. Trinity would've been there for her hands down.

She hunched her shoulders. "I don't know. I really wasn't thinking. I didn't want you to be mad with me, I guess. But one thing's for sure: it wasn't about trusting him. At the time, I was desperate for a way out of my situation, that's all," Lucinda admitted.

Her explanation made sense. All things aside, Lucinda had always been the type to do what she had to do for Nadia. Besides, who were we to judge? None of us were in good standing with our decisions of late, and I could only imagine being in a financial struggle only to get fired. Lucinda may have been wrong, but desperate doesn't care about wrong or right. It cares about survival. And that's all she had tried to do—survive.

"Are you still stripping?" I asked because whether she wanted to or not, she would accept my financial assistance. I would not allow her to continue to degrade herself at some damn Club Moet.

"Hell no. I got a job," she said with a slight smile.

"Where?" we asked.

"Doing medical claims at home. My old boss, Mr. Sharper, hooked me up." She smiled, starry-eyed.

We all glanced at each other knowingly. Then Trinity grinned. "I know that fucking smile. It got bright as hell when you mentioned that fine-ass Mr. Sharper. Spill that shit."

Mm-hmm, Lucinda's ex-supervisor was fine as hell. And the look on her face told us he'd helped her with much more than a new job. We sat back in anticipation for the scoop on this new development.

A blush flashed in Lucinda's cheeks, and she couldn't help but giggle. "There's not much to say, *chicas*." She shrugged as we all gave her the "spill the tea" look. "I'll admit, Aldris is a good man. He really bent over backward to get me that job, and umm, he wants to take me out."

Finally, something good to celebrate! Her good news caused a smile to grace all of our faces. Excitedly, I asked, "Good! You going, right?"

She shrugged. "I said I was. I mean, he ain't one of these hood dudes we used to fuckin' with. I should want better, but a hood dude is all I'm used to. And full disclosure, he saw me in Club Moet, so I am ashamed of that, too. I don't know. I just don't feel like I'm good enough for someone like Aldris."

To hear she thought she wasn't good enough was disheartening, and Trinity confirmed what we all thought. "You are more than good enough," Trinity said to her. "You may be from the hood, but on the real, you handle yours, and any nigga with two blind eyes can see you a good catch." LaMeka and I chimed in with our agreement.

She put her hands up, shaking her head in disagreement. "Wait, y'all. But he is different. He's educated and successful. What can I offer him?" Lucinda asked, staring blankly at the coffee table.

Placing my hand on her face, I lifted her chin so that we were eye to eye and I could encourage her. "Go out with him and find out."

"I don't know—"

Out of nowhere, LaMeka huffed and blew up on us. "Y'all bitches get on my nerves," she blurted out.

Appalled, we all gasped and looked at LaMeka as if she were crazy. She'd been unusually quiet, but this was totally out of character.

"Fuck is all that about?" Trinity asked.

"Yeah," Lucinda and I agreed.

For a few moments, LaMeka just stood there, staring at us with a blank expression on her face. It was as if she were in a trance. Then suddenly, her eyes blinked rapidly and instantly, she began crying, like really heart-wrenching crying. I tried to lean over and console her, but she pushed me away. She grabbed a Kleenex and dabbed her eyes and then looked at all of us as if she could whip our asses.

"The only person who I remotely feel sorry for is Trinity, and that's because she really is in a dangerous situation with Pooch, but still, all you have to do is leave that nigga. All three of you are sitting up here, acting like the world is on your shoulders when it ain't," she said and turned to Trinity. "If you love Dreads, leave with his ass. You got your own ass caught up following up Pooch's lame-ass promises when you knew he wasn't nothing but a dope boy."

Next, she directed her attention to Lucinda. "And you, give that damn man a chance. How many of us can say that a man like that would even be interested in us? He got you a job and all. Please miss me with that drama, Lu. For the first time since Raul, you have a chance at something special. Stop being stupid."

Then, she faced me. "But you are the worst of all, Charice. I watched you nearly break down when Ryan left you with three kids and having to abort a fourth. Of all of us, you graduated and went to college with three kids. I've seen you struggle with those kids and push your dreams to the side just to get a decent-paying job, and I admired that. You were the encouragement for every teenage mother and single parent around. Now you up here trippin' off the fact that the media has put your fucking relationship with a multimillionaire on blast. Hiding behind your five-hundred-dollar shades and tinting the windows of your eighty-thousand-dollar SUV. For what? You fucking made it! You got a baby daddy who now loves his kids and takes damn good care of them, and a rich man who loves you regardless of the fact that he was dead-ass wrong for hooking up with your ass! Please. Your only decision these days is whether or not you want diamonds or pearls on your Vera Wang original wedding dress, and you worried about looking bad on the news? Oh, whatever shall the fuck you do? You wasn't worried about the news or Ryan when you was flying your ass in and out of Dallas and to Paradise Island! Don't even act like that shit bothers you now. Some of us have real shit to worry about," LaMeka spewed at me.

Lucinda and Trinity stared at her with their mouths wide open, unable to believe that LaMeka just said that. Of all of us, LaMeka was the quiet one, the super-sensitive one, the one who always encouraged people and gave out empathy. Now she all but accused us of being self-absorbed. Granted, my situation may not have been the hellacious situation that Trinity was in or that Lucinda had to face, but it was still a situation to me, and nobody had the right to discount it regardless of what they were going through.

"Now hold the fuck up, LaMeka," I started. "You are the one who needs a fucking reality check! I will admit that of all our situations, I'd rather be in my own. You're right. My baby daddy is rich, and so is my man, but money ain't everything. All of us are after the same thing, peace of

mind, and right now, none of us have that. Now I'm sorry
you had to endure the hell you did behind Tony's raggedy
ass, but let's be real. The Tony Light we knew in high
school ain't the same Tony he is now. You've been out of
high school for years, LaMeka. You should've been woke
up on that shit! None of us made you stick around while
Tony tagged on your ass, and I do remember that both
Trinity and I begged you to leave. We both had the funds
to help you get set up, but you chose to stick around
hoping and wishing. Now I'm not knocking that, because
I've been there. We all know Ryan was my heart long
after everybody had given up on him, but what I'm telling
you is I won't knock the fork out of your hand if you don't
snatch the spoon out of mine. We all made fucked-up
decisions behind a nigga, and we all deserve happiness.
So pour out your little fucking cup of haterade, put your
big-girl drawers on, and handle that shit with Tony," I
said sternly with a finger point and an eye roll.

"*Ay, mami!*" Lucinda said, high-fiving me. "I couldn't
have said that shit better myself." She looked over at
LaMeka. "The fact still remains that I have to deal with
Raul, and you speaking up on Aldris as if it's certain he's
the one. I haven't even gone out with the man yet," she
said, rolling her eyes.

"And you talking about just leaving Pooch as if his ass
ain't one of the most notorious kingpins around. This
nigga got judges and police on payroll, and I'm supposed to what? Trust in the legal system if he flips and
tries to hurt me or my family? You trippin', LaMeka.
Tony done knocked the fucking sense out of yo' head
and shit," Trinity countered with plenty of attitude.

Tears welled up, and suddenly, LaMeka began to cry
again. "But I'll bet Aldris, Pooch, Terrence, Lincoln, nor
Ryan may have brought y'all back the package."

My heart dropped to my toes, and I instantly grabbed LaMeka and hugged her. For the next few minutes, all any of us could do was cry silent tears. Talk about news that could change your entire perspective in an instant. I didn't think emotions had ever taken over any of us so fast. But hearing that my bestie—scratch that, my sister—may have the package was enough to bring down my emotions like the Berlin Wall. We may have had to deal with a lot of things, but the possibility of death from an incurable disease wasn't one of them. *Forget all that mess I just said.* Immediately, I wanted to do whatever I could for her.

"Are you sure?" I finally asked. "How do you know this?"

"I saw that bitch Kwanzie at the hospital. I was going to fire up on her ass, but she looked like death. Then she told me that she had it. She was getting help for her addictions and HIV. She says she got it sharing dirty needles with some junkie," she explained to us.

"You're not sure if you have it?" Trinity asked with a worried expression on her face.

She shrugged. "No, I'm not sure if I have it. Hell, I'm not sure if he has it. I got tested three months ago, and I spoke with the nurse, and she said a positive normally doesn't show up for six months. I took another test, and it was inconclusive, so right now I'm in limbo. The sad part is I still haven't told my sister. I guess now is probably the time to tell you all that I caught Misha and Tony screwing in my bed, raw." We all gasped. "She was blazed, and so was he. That's how everything came to a head. We had a confrontation, and I busted him in the face with his gun. Fearful that he'd kill me, Misha, the kids, and I ran and jumped in the car to leave. And he tried. He busted my car window out and nearly choked the life out of me, but I escaped. I dumped Misha off at our mom's house, and after I left the hospital, I ended up at a shelter that

Pastor Gaines recommended. Afterward, Pastor Gaines got me set up at this transitional house. I haven't seen Tony since," she explained.

"I have to get Misha tested, but I'm so scared to do that. If she's positive, then that means that Tony definitely is, unless she got it from Joe or some other knucklehead, which I doubt. But if Tony has it, then there is a strong possibility that I do too." She broke down in tears again. "Y'all, I don't want to die. I want to live. I want to find my soul mate and go to school and be somebody one day. I want to be a good mother and grow old watching my grandchildren play. I don't want to go out like that. Not with the package."

We all sat there silently for what seemed like forever, holding hands and crying. Who knew when we all were playing hopscotch and double Dutch in the neighborhood that our lives would be so complicated? Who knew we'd meet boys who'd promise us everything under the heavens and put us through hell? Who knew that one night of youthful pleasure could lead to a lifetime of heartache and pain? We certainly didn't, but here we were. In LaMeka's case, that lifetime could be cut real short. For the first time since Ryan found out about Lincoln and me, I was thankful for my problems, because at least HIV was not on my list of them.

Chapter Nine

Lucinda

"How many more dresses are you going to try on?" Nadia whined.

"Just this last one," I said, modeling another dress. "What about this one?"

"I like it," Nadia said plainly.

"You've said you liked all five of them. I need a decision. Mom, please help me here. This date is important to me." I threw my hands up.

My nerves were a wreck as I prepared for my first date with Aldris. For the past few weeks, he'd been a constant factor in my life as he helped me prepare for my new job opportunity. No lie, Aldris had been absolutely amazing the last few weeks. He'd been more than amazing. He'd been a godsend.

Everything was just as he'd stated when I called Suzette, and I interviewed the next day. After the interview, she hired me on the spot and at $18.50 per hour just as Aldris had said. First things first, after securing the new bag, he went shopping with me to ensure I had all the proper equipment needed to work from home. He helped me pick out the perfect PC in my price range, a Dell Inspiron with a twenty-inch flat-screen monitor, and he even sprang for an ergonomic keyboard for me. Of course, I didn't want to accept it, but he insisted. Afterward, he came to my apartment and hooked the computer up for me and made sure the medical software was installed correctly. What I loved most was that I never asked him to do any of it. He just did it. This dude was truly a man, and I liked that about him above all else.

The work hours totally worked out, because my classes were from 8:00 to 10:00 a.m., so I was able to drop Nadia off at school in the mornings, go to class, and then come home to cook and do my homework before I had to pick her up at three. Once she was home, I helped her with her homework and fed her, and then she read her books, watched TV, or played with her dolls until I could take a break to bathe her and send her to bed. After that, I worked usually until about one in the morning. Thankfully, Ms. Ana helped me out on Saturday mornings by picking up Nadia so that I could get some rest.

After only two weeks on the job, I already had the game on lock. Once I found my groove and set my routine, I was able to finish my designated paperwork, do a little extra work, and still rest before it was time to clock out. Suzette and the doctors could only sing praises about me. I was doing—as they could say—the damn thang!

What I was most excited about was that pay. I had to wait a paycheck in the hole, but ooh wee! My first paycheck was $1,480 for two weeks, and even after Uncle Sam and benefits, I still cleared $1,140. The doctors even decided to award me with a sign-on bonus of $500 because their claims processing had improved 3 percent just in the two weeks I'd worked for them. It felt good to pay all my bills and still have a whole paycheck left. Not only that, I still had $1,500 left in my account between my stripping money and my unemployment checks. Hell, I wasn't Donald Trump rich, but a *chica* was sitting pretty and looking lovely. For the first time, in forever, I could breathe. Ahhh, didn't that feel good? Yep! And that's all I ever wanted.

Now back to the next best thing—Aldris. We talked on the phone all the time. We were constantly making each other laugh, and he'd met Nadia, who thought he was "sooo" cute. He was such a gentleman, even postponing our date to give me time to settle into my new job and routine. I was in such awe of his patience that when he asked me if I would be free this Saturday night to go out to dinner and then to see the play *A Raisin in the Sun,* I easily accepted. Now my only issue was my attire.

"Well, *Mami,* I said I like all five because I think you're pretty in all five," Nadia said to me.

"Aww, sweetie, thank you," I said, kissing her on the forehead.

"She's right, you know. You are smoking hot in all of them," my mom agreed. "But if you must have a decision, I'd go with the classic black dress. The halter style accentuates your soft shoulders and your cleavage. It also accentuates your waistline, and the ankle length makes you look regal. And those silver stilettos are to die for!"

My eyebrows jogged, and I pointed my index finger in agreement. "You're right. And I don't know what color he's wearing, so I don't want to be mismatched or loud."

"Do you want me to pin your hair up for you?" my mom asked.

"Yes, would you please?"

"Of course."

Since my mother was going to assist with my hair, I hurriedly bounded to the shower. Once I was out, I moisturized my body, put on my undergarments, then tossed on a button-down shirt so that she could begin on my hair.

"You really like this Aldris fellow, huh?" my mom asked as she brushed my hair.

Releasing a deep breath, I hoped to mask my inner feelings. "He's nice."

My mother paused, and her lips curled at the corners. "You're going through all this trouble for someone you think is just nice?" She eyed me, unconvinced, in the mirror.

When I blushed, she poked my cheek. "Stop, Mama!"
She laughed. "That's the look I want to see! You like
him, Lucinda. There's nothing wrong with that. You
made a mistake with Raul, but that doesn't mean you
can't find someone."

No offense, but this advice from her was shocking to
me. Of all people, my mother should have been the first
one to denounce love. "How can you say that when your
marriage ended in shambles?"

"I haven't given up hope that the man for me is still out
there. What your father did discouraged me, of course.
I thought Emilio and I would be together forever, but
look at your *abuelo* and *abuela*. My parents have been
together for fifty years. That is proof positive that real
love, everlasting love, exists."

She finished pinning my hair, and I turned around.
She lifted my chin up so that I was looking in her eyes. "If
Mr. Aldris is worth it, then don't let Raul or your father
hold you back. Step out on faith that God will show you
if Aldris is the man for you," she schooled me as I fanned
tears out of my eyes. "You look beautiful."

I hugged her. "Thank you. I love you, *Mami*."

"Oh, *hija*, I love you too."

My mom left my room so that I could put on my makeup
and clothes. I thought about what she'd said and realized
that she was right, but so much weighed on me. Our
different upbringings, the whole strip club thing, and to
top it off, LaMeka's whole confession about the possibility
of being HIV positive had me on edge. I had to make sure
that Aldris wasn't on some bullshit, because my girl was
proof that shit was real. However, I promised myself that I
wouldn't ruin this night.

As I finished dressing, I heard my mom open the
door for Aldris. He introduced himself to my mom, or
rather Nadia introduced him, and all three of them were
chatting it up like they were old friends.

"Ay, Lucinda! The man is going to fall asleep out here," my mom yelled.

Laughing, he said, "It's okay, Ms. Rosa. I was a little early."

"She's just ragging on me," I said, making my grand entrance.

Aldris's eyes nearly popped out of his head, and his mouth hung agape. "Oh my God," he said as he stood up. "You look . . . I mean, you are . . . My God," he said, looking mesmerized.

"I look that bad?" I giggled.

"No, you look that stunningly amazing," he said with a kiss on my cheek.

My mom laughed. "Oh, I like him."

"Me too, *Abuela*," Nadia giggled before facing Aldris. "Mr. Aldris, I'm glad you like it, because my *mami* spent all day trying on dresses, and she got so mad because we couldn't decide which—" My mom closed Nadia's mouth with her hand.

"Sweetheart, we don't tell our menfolk all of our secrets," my mom whispered as Aldris and I laughed.

"Thank you, Mama."

Aldris turned to face me again. "It's nice to know that you put so much effort and care into tonight. More importantly, it shows."

This man and his words! My face reddened as I bent my head, slightly embarrassed of my schoolgirl response. Fanning myself, I gathered myself and offered him a compliment as well. "Thank you. I'm so rude. You look very handsome." He was very debonair in his designer suit.

"Thank you." He winked at me, and I felt my cheeks flush yet again. "I hope I still look twenty-eight in it."

I laughed, grateful for the comic relief. "Yes, you do!"

"We better be getting out of here," my mom said, picking up Nadia's suitcase for her weekend stay.

"Allow me, Ms. Rosa." Aldris reached for the suitcase, but my mom fanned him away.

"No, no, I have it, but I like that," she said, looking over her shoulder at me. "I really like him. Yes, I do," she said with a grin on her face on her way to the door. I couldn't do anything but snicker and shake my head.

"See you on Sunday, *Mami,*" Nadia said as we hugged tightly.

"I love you, kiddo."

"Back at you, Mom," she said playfully. She was so amusing.

My mom hugged me and Aldris, then Nadia and Aldris exchanged a handshake he'd taught her, before we all left.

Dinner was simply amazing. Not wanting to embarrass him, I made sure to learn even the small things, such as using proper table etiquette so I knew my salad fork from my dinner fork. We looked great together, and our conversation was refreshing and light. Unaccustomed to this lifestyle, I sat there in childlike wonderment. Aldris glanced over at me and just smiled. He had to know he'd introduced this *chica* to some of the finer things in life.

The play was so inspirational. During intermissions, I splurged on a glass of wine more than anything to relax my nerves. That wine was so sweet and smooth that I wanted to toss that shit back, but remembering to be classy, I sipped it. Granted, they were some big sips, but I sipped to showcase my best behavior.

Being a true gentleman, as he'd been throughout the night, Aldris opened my car door for me, and I climbed into his black pearl BMW 750i to leave the play.

"Did you have a good time?" he asked as we got on the road.

A shy smile graced my face as I turned my head toward him. "I did! The food was awesome, and the play was fantastic. Thank you for taking me. You have been quite the gentleman and a wonderful date."

A hearty baritone chuckle escaped him as he flashed his award-winning smile toward me. "Good, good. I'm glad. You've been an amazing date as well. I've thoroughly enjoyed myself with you, Lucinda."

There was a slight pause after his compliment, which created a slightly awkward silence. Perhaps it was my nerves kicking in, because I could feel the butterflies fluttering in the pit of my stomach again. Deflecting, I looked at my watch and saw it was 11:30. "I guess we're calling it a night, huh?" I asked nervously. I didn't want to, but I didn't know what else he had planned, and I didn't want to assume anything.

Gripping the steering wheel with his left hand, his right fell to the console gingerly as he flicked his wrist. "We don't have to unless you want to." He looked over at me as if silently pleading with me to say no.

Calm down, nerves, I coaxed in my mind as I nodded. "Sure, I can hang out. I'm used to the vampire hours."

"What would you like to do?" His smile beamed brightly even under the darkness of the night.

I figured that I'd play it safe and go someplace quiet but not romantic, so we went to this park that I used to go to when I was a kid. He didn't protest at all. He simply asked me to plug in the directions to his car's GPS system. I was grateful that he hadn't thought the idea was lame and attempt to change the plans. My aim was to talk and keep the evening nice and light rather than find myself back at his place or him at mine. That dynamic was far too enticing, and I didn't trust myself with that type of alone time with Aldris.

Once there, we exited his vehicle, and then he pulled off his suit jacket, placed it on the trunk of his car, and sat down. I stood off to the side, eyeing him as he took his seat on his car.

"Come here," he said to me, motioning with his index finger.

Slowly, I walked over to him, taking him in with each step. His muscles bulged through his dress shirt as he sat there waiting for me to come close to him. Damn, he was so fucking fine.

"What's up?" I asked, trying to seem nonchalant to mask the nervousness coursing through my body.

Gently, he grabbed my hands and then pulled me close to him. "You are," he said, giving me those damn eyes. Those eyes had definitely changed from puppy-dog eyes to bedroom eyes. Those eyes were trouble.

"Me?" I pointed to myself and dropped my head, avoiding his sexy gaze.

"You know you are," he said, holding me close and tight. His cologne infiltrated my nostrils, and I swore I damn near creamed myself as he cocooned me in his arms. *Ay Dios mio!* This man! Using one hand, he lifted my chin to capture my gaze again. "Lucinda, since we've been around each other these past few weeks, I've loved being with you. At this point, I hope it's obvious to you that I'm really feeling you a lot. But if not, I want to let you know that I like you—"

Suddenly, I was fearful of what he was about to tell me, so I spun around with my back to him and pointed to the sky. "Aren't the stars beautiful?" I interrupted.

Not bothering to respond to my question, he released a small sigh, then turned me back around to face him again. "The only star I'm focused on is you. Why are you running from me?"

"Huh?" I asked, biting my lip. It was a nervous habit.

Cupping my face, Aldris licked his lips sexily, and his gaze was intentional. "You don't have to run from me. I'm not Raul."

Truth be told, he'd hit one of my major concerns right on the head. Having to go through the bullshit with

Raul scorned me and kept me from feeling comfortable enough to pursue another relationship. But when it came to Aldris, that was a secondary concern. "It's not just that," I admitted.

"What else is there? Why else are you afraid of the possibility of us? Let's get it all out there so there is no question left unanswered."

He was right. As great as this moment felt, I needed to know Aldris's true intentions with me. Even though I trusted that he was a good guy, a part of me still had my reservations, especially after Club Moet. I pulled away from him and placed my hands on my hips. "Okay. Why me?"

He shrugged as if he were confused as to why I'd asked. "Because I'm attracted to you, and I like you." He smiled demurely and bit his lip. "You make me laugh. We have great conversations. We are interested in the same things professionally—"

"You saw my ass in your face at Club Moet," I added as I turned and walked a few steps away.

I could hear that he'd climbed down off the car, and the next thing I knew, he stood in front of me. "I've never brought that up to you. Not even once. That's not fair to me, Lucinda."

Now my attitude was slightly on go. Club Moet was the biggest elephant in the room. We both knew that. I couldn't believe that he was really going to stand here and act like seeing my tits and ass on full display had no bearing on his sudden interest in me. I didn't believe that shit for one minute. "But it's the truth. Please just admit it, Aldris. Please. The only reason you're wining and dining me is because you want to see a little Spanish Fly."

He shook his head, obviously irritated. He swiped his hand down his face before he lifted his wallet out of his back pocket. "You want me to treat you like Spanish Fly?" He pulled a $50 bill from his wallet. "Go ahead.

Shake that ass. Rake it up." He tossed the bill, and it floated between us to the ground.

Did this nigga just toss some fucking money at me? My mouth dropped open. "Hell no. Are you crazy? I can't believe you said and did that!" I was completely pissed off.

"No, I didn't. You did," he said angrily. "I'm over here on my real-man shit. I'm trying to get to know Lucinda, but you seem to be stuck on introducing me to Spanish Fly, so go ahead and let me see her so we can get this shit over with. Maybe then I can finally get back to getting to know Lucinda."

Stun took over my body at the realization that he was serious about truly wanting to know me. All this time, I believed his interest had been sparked by Spanish Fly when he was honestly interested in me. Me. Lucinda. That thought alone scared me even more than feeling as though he wanted a little of the Spanish Fly. Releasing a deep groan, I shook my head. "I'm sorry. No dude—I mean, man—has ever been like you. Aldris, I don't know how to handle this. You're so nice and respectful. I'm not the woman for you. I'm not your type."

He glanced at me sideways. Anger danced in his eyes. "And how the hell do you know what my type is?"

To prove my point, I counted on my fingers the reasons why I was not a good fit for him. "You come from a good home. You've experienced things in life. You're intelligent and educated. You need to be with someone of your . . . your caliber. I'm not that chick . . . I mean, woman. I come from a broken home with uneducated parents. I'm just trying to get my life together, and I already have a ready-made family. We're different, Aldris. I'm not who you need in your life!"

With his jaw clenched, he remained quiet as he placed his hands in his pockets and paced back and forth. After a few moments, he turned to face me and shrugged his shoulders. "That's it? You're going to pass judgment on me and kick me to the curb without even knowing or trying to understand how I feel about you?"

Frustrated beyond belief, I tried to further explain. "I just don't want you to waste your time. You—"

He picked up his jacket and put it on. "Get in the car, Lucinda," he said sternly.

"Huh?" The harshness of his tone stopping further protests.

"Get in the car. I'm taking you home."

His words were searing now. He was so upset that I could almost feel the heat radiating off of him. To prevent a major blowup between us, I said nothing further and instead walked to the passenger side of his car. I waited for him to open the door, but instead of opening my door as he'd done every time we were together, he walked to his side, got in, and slammed the door. Realizing that I'd truly pissed him off, I hit myself on the forehead before slowly easing inside of the car. I hadn't meant to anger him. I simply wanted to save him from my drama. I thought I was looking out for him. Once I nestled inside and buckled up, I glanced over at him, but he didn't even look in my direction, and I didn't know what to say. Obviously, everything I'd already said had been wrong, so I just shut the hell up. I thought he needed a moment to collect himself, but Aldris wouldn't even look at or speak to me for the entire ride back to my house.

Once he parked beside my car, I turned to face him, but he still kept his face forward. Regardless, I spoke to him. I didn't want him to think that I was unappreciative of everything he'd done from the job recommendation through our date tonight. I was extremely grateful for him and all he'd done. I just felt that I wasn't the woman for him. He was a perfect ten, and he needed a ten. Hell, he deserved a woman who was a hundred. And that wasn't me. Even if I wanted to be, I wasn't. I couldn't drag him down with me.

Swallowing the lump in my throat, I spoke softly. "Aldris, I had a great time. I'm sorry it ended on a bad note. I hope that we can still be friends."

For the first time since the park, he turned and looked at me as if I were crazy. "Friends?" he asked in disbelief. *Ay Dios mio.* I'd said the wrong thing again. "I better go," I said, opening the door and turning to get out.

"For the record, Lucinda, I liked you before I even saw you at the club. I just wasn't allowed to fraternize with my employees. I've been attracted to you since the first day you walked into National Cross, and I always felt like there was something special about you," he admitted while my back was turned.

What? His words were like daggers to my back. I didn't realize that he'd liked me all along. This revelation stung me to the core. How could I have misjudged him so badly? Instantly, I felt horrible. I still didn't feel on his level, but those words provided a change in my heart. *Shit. I should've shut my mouth and heard him out.* The urge to apologize and the need to discuss things immediately tugged at my heart. I turned to face him. "Aldris—"

Before I could say another word, he glared at me. "Good night, Lucinda," he said with finality.

The finality in his words indicated that he was done. Done with the argument. Done with the conversation. And done with me. There was nothing that I could say, and my face went flush as hot tears threatened to fall. Out of respect for his hurt feelings, I didn't attempt further conversation. I felt so awful as I exited the car and headed to my apartment. Aldris may have been pissed, but he did wait until I was in the house before he pulled off. Even in his anger, he was still a man. I had messed up bad. I knew it. I promised myself that I wouldn't do that, but I did.

After I showered, I sat on my sofa, worrying about how things ended with Aldris. Over and over again, my mind replayed what he'd said: *"I liked you before I even saw you at the club."* After about thirty minutes, I couldn't take it. I wasn't going to be able to lay my head down to rest until I cleared the air between us.

I called Aldris, but he didn't answer. I even called again for good measure, but he still didn't answer. *Fuck that.* Any normal person would chuck it up and count it as a loss. Hell, I would've done it. But something about the thought of Aldris being angry with me and, worse yet, never speaking to me again bothered me. I couldn't allow things to end on that note. Even if he never wanted another thing to do with me, I wanted to talk, to give him the opportunity to talk, and to apologize for my actions. I had to find a way to make things right between us, even if there was never anything else between us. He'd been too good to me to end that way.

Without hesitation, I got up, slid on my flip-flops, and drove to his condo. I was happy that I had paid attention to the directions when we'd stopped there briefly after I got my computer. When I arrived, his car was in the parking space. Good. He was home. Quickly, I approached his apartment and knocked on his door.

"Who is it?" he asked.

"Aldris, it's me. Lucinda. Please let me in."

He partially opened the door and stood there in a fitted white tee that defined all of his muscles, some gray cotton sweatpants, and socks. "What do you want?" he snapped.

I looked at him with pleading eyes. "Please, can I come inside? Please."

He bit his lip and shook his head before he opened the door. I came inside then turned to face him. "I called you. Twice," I said softly.

"I got it. Twice," he countered. "What is that you want with me?"

"I'm sorry. I didn't give you the opportunity to express yourself. I just made a bunch of assumptions because of my insecurities, and for that, I owe you a huge apology. I am sorry."

He huffed and rubbed his forehead. "How I feel didn't start because I saw your ass in Club Moet. It didn't start because I felt ill over you getting fired either. Like I said, I've liked you since the moment I laid eyes on you. I prayed to God that if you were the one, He'd make an opportunity for me to able to approach you, which is why I gave you my business card when they terminated you. I was hoping that you'd call, but you didn't.

"When I saw you at the club, I was hurt because that wasn't you and because my boys had seen you intimately. I started to give up on you, but when I saw you leave the club, it felt as if God Himself were telling me to follow you. I was happy I did, because it showed me that I was right and that girl in the club wasn't you. It also led to blessings for you and made a way for us to become friends, and I knew then that this was what I'd prayed for. But I guess I was wrong. You are so hung up on the situation at the club, how I was raised, and the things I've done in my life to give us any type of chance.

"Then you further insult me by asking if we could remain friends. I've got news for you, Lucinda. I don't date friends, and I damn sure don't feel for them how I feel for you. I'm not trying to be your friend. I'm trying to be your man, and I wanted you to be my woman."

Talk about floored. Aldris pulled the trigger and unloaded the clip on me. It left me leaking with a huge hole in my heart. Here, this amazingly amazing man poured out his innermost secrets to me about his feelings, and I questioned him. He'd done all of this because he sincerely wanted to be with me. I was wrong all along. I felt like an idiot. Scratch that. I was an idiot.

Easing up to him, I grabbed his hands. "I had no idea, and it wasn't for me to know at the time. I should have trusted you, but please understand that it's hard for me to do that. No man in my life, not even my father, has been trustworthy. I can't judge you by that, but it makes it hard for me to trust because of that. I'm a rough *chica,* but I'm crazy about you. I was afraid of those feelings. I understand if you don't want to deal with me anymore. I messed up, and I have to live with that. I just wanted to give you the opportunity that I didn't before. Again, I'm sorry." I let his hands go, and I turned to leave.

"You're just going to walk out on me again?" he asked.

"But I thought—" I turned back toward him.

"You overthink sometimes."

He pulled me close to him and kissed me. When he pulled back, I brought his ass right back for some more of that kiss. That shit was good, and I wanted more.

"Girl, you better stop," he laughed, causing me to blush.

"I'm sorry," I said, getting serious for a moment.

"Me too," he said and pecked me on the lips. "You still leaving?"

"Not unless you kick me out."

He laughed. "Good. You can stay. But we have to get something clear. I am a man, Lucinda, so you're going to have to work on treating me as such. 'Cause I am damn sure going to treat you like a woman, not some chick or damn Spanish Fly."

Damn. I'd never had a real man put me in my place before, and surprisingly, it turned me on! We'd only just begun, and he knew how to handle my ass. I threw my hands up in surrender. "You got it. But I have a question," I said as we held each other and gazed into each other's eyes.

"What's that, baby?"

"I'm your baby now?"

"Yes, damn it, woman. You're my baby. Didn't we just straighten all that out? If not, allow me to make it clear for you. You are now in a relationship with Aldris

Sharper. You are officially my baby, and I'm yours," he laughed.

"Good." I smiled. "But I do still have a question."

"What is it?" he asked me.

I stood on my tiptoes and whispered in his ear. "Are you ready to get caught in the Spanish Fly trap?"

He burst out laughing and sat on the sofa. "As long as Spanish Fly only surfaces for me."

I laughed. "Only for you, baby. But I thought you weren't attracted to Spanish Fly," I teased as I slowly began swaying my hips from side to side as I stood in front of him.

"Shit, bullshit," he said, gazing at me with lust in his eyes as he rubbed his hands up and down my thighs. "I just didn't want my boys to see it. I am a man. So please go ahead and introduce me again to the fly trap, because I have someone to introduce you to as well."

"Who is that?" I giggled.

"Mandingo," he chuckled. "The blacker the berry, the sweeter the juice, and you know what they say. Once you go black—"

"You don't go back," I hollered, straddling his lap and kissing him. "Thank you for bearing with me."

He held the sides of my face in the palms of his hands. "Thank you for giving us a chance. I know it took a lot for you to come over here tonight, and I promise you, you will never regret it." And with that, we shared another intimate kiss.

I didn't know what I did to deserve a man like Aldris, but I wasn't going to question it anymore. Thank God I had him. With every touch and kiss, I knew this is where I wanted to be. I also knew I wasn't going to make it back to my place. As of tonight I was forgetting all of my fears and giving my all to Aldris . . . in more ways than one!

Chapter Ten

LaMeka

I'd been stressed out to the max ever since Kwanzie's confession, and I'd lost about ten pounds in one week because of it. I wasn't eating right, sleeping right, and I could barely think right. All that consumed me was worrying about whether I had the package. I'd even been let go from my job at the day care because I called in three days straight. Now I had no job, and I had to worry about paying Pooch's car payments on top of that. One thing I wasn't crazy enough to do was miss those payments. If I had to starve first, I would give that fool back his money. If he could fuck Trinity up for being around Dreads, imagine what he would do to me. Even the threat of HIV seemed a little better than pissing Pooch off. At least HIV was treatable. You couldn't treat crazy. Not his kind of crazy anyway.

Who was I kidding? As much as I would want to believe facing Pooch would be worse, it wasn't. One thing I desperately needed to do, though, was get my sister and take her down to the clinic. I may have been pissed about what she did, but she was my sister. She was only 17. I remembered being 17 and making dumb-ass decisions, but my decisions gave me Tony Jr. Misha's might have given her HIV. More fucked up than anything, the same man could potentially ruin both our lives, and I didn't know if I could live with that pain.

"Hi, Mom." I greeted her with a hug and came through the door.

"Hey, baby. I'm glad that you wanted to come over and visit. Misha misses you." I nodded in response as we sat down on the sofa. "Misha is only seventeen. She's just making mistakes like we both did at that age. One thing we can both agree on is that a man is gonna always be a man, but you only have one sister," my mom said.

I didn't know this woman who had invaded my mother's body. I wasn't trippin', because I was happy for the change in her, and with this news I was about to drop on both of them, this change came just in time. 'Cause right now, Misha and I needed our mother more than ever.

"Yeah, I know, Mama. I was just pissed off with her. I went through a lot to try to make it better for her. It wasn't even about Tony. It was about Misha hurting me. I'd never do anything in the world to hurt her. Not even now."

She lovingly squeezed my hand. The expression she gave was one of hurt and sadness. The heartbreak felt as if it oozed from her soul. "I know you wouldn't, and that's one reason— well, one of many reasons—I owe you an apology. I took advantage of you. Growing up, you were always more of a parent to Misha than I was. It was wrong of me to put that burden on you. I never stopped to think about what I was doing to you because I just assumed you'd always be there for her. But that was my job, and I apologize to you for making it yours."

Touched by her words, silent tears flowed down my cheeks. I swiped them away in the hopes of stopping a complete emotional breakdown. My entire life, I'd waited for some type of remorse, a morsel even, from my mother, and the time had finally come. It meant so much to me to get that one apology. This was the mother I'd prayed for, for many years, and for the first time in my life, I felt like

I truly had just that—a mother. That feeling alone was enough to erase her past indiscretions.

"Thanks, Mama. You don't know how much that means to me."

She hugged me. "You don't know how much you mean to me."

The little girl in me soared at those words. However, the grown women in me fought against the genuineness of them. I wanted desperately to take everything she'd said at face value, but a small part of me wondered if it could truly be trusted. The only answer to that would be the "why." Why after all these years had she changed?

"Can I ask you a question, though?"

"Sure, Meka."

"What changed? Not that I'm not happy about it or accepting of it. It just all seems so, I don't know, sudden."

Nodding, she sat back and sighed. "I understand that, and it's only fair. Actually, Joe did. Believe it or not. I can't give his raggedy ass credit for anything else, but he did make me realize that I needed to change."

Now I was intrigued for real. *Joe? Child-molesting, abusive, using-ass Joe?* I had to hear how that bastard was responsible for anything remotely positive, especially life-changing positive. "How?"

"The day I kicked him out, he was mad because I didn't want to have . . . relations with him. He got so mad, in fact, that in the heat of the moment, he admitted sleeping with Misha," she confided.

I gasped, covering my mouth. "You know?"

"Yes, I know."

"Does she—"

"No, she doesn't know that I know, and I don't want her to. He's not even worth the argument. Besides, Misha is my blood. Joe wasn't nothing but some dick. I can get dick anywhere," my mom said as we shared a laugh.

"True," I agreed.

"After he admitted that, I went berserk on him, and do you know that fucker had the nerve to blame me? He said if I had been handling my business, he wouldn't have turned to Misha. Bullshit. He was a rotten, child-molesting asshole. If it hadn't been Misha, it would've been somebody else's underage daughter. I might've made stupid decisions, but I wasn't dumb enough to believe that Misha was his first or would be his last. After I kicked him out over that, I realized in a major way he was right. Not about the handling my business part, but for blaming me in general. If I had made better choices, been a better mom to you girls, and made wiser selections in the men I chose, then I wouldn't have been stuck with a man who beat me, degraded me, or had the audacity to sleep with my child. How fucking nasty was that? I vowed to do better. With the help of the Lord, I pray that I can."

It's crazy that after all those years of running from man to man, and us being scared that those men would take advantage of us, the defining moment of our mother's change came from exactly that. The one time one of the men she brought home decided to have an inappropriate relationship with one of her daughters sparked her to become a better mother. Not to say that I wish things had been worse, because I'd come to understand that people also come into change at different points in their life. I was just happy to know that somewhere deep down, regardless of how much she loved men, she had a line in her heart that she wasn't comfortable crossing. It meant the world to know that we at least meant that much to her, after years of feeling like we never mattered. But we did. We mattered to her. And that was a freeing feeling.

"You will be better, Mama. You have us. Now just have faith."

Just as I said that, Misha came through the front door. "Sorry I'm late. I was just studying with my friends. I have exams next week," she said as she shut the door and set her book bag down. Her gaze finally caught me, and her words stopped just as sudden as she stopped dead in her tracks. Timidly, she waved her hand. "Oh, umm, hi, Meka," she said sheepishly.

"Hi, Misha," I responded coolly.

Her eyes were cast downward, and I could see the heartbreak all over her face from my lack of emotion. It wasn't that I was trying to be mean. It was just awkward conversing after what had happened.

"Well, I guess I better go—" Misha tried to say.

She stopped speaking again when she saw that I stood up and walked toward her. Like my mom said, I only had one sister. No Joes or Tonys could separate us. I may not have trusted her in this moment, but I'd never stop loving her. This kid was like my kid. More importantly, we all made mistakes, so I had to allow her the opportunity to grow and learn from what she'd done. We may not have been all the way there, but if my mother could try for us, then I was willing to try for Misha.

"No. We cool, Misha."

She looked at me as if she wasn't sure I was telling the truth.

"Look, what you did was fucked up, but at the end of the day, you gon' always be my sister. I'm gon' love you no matter what and no matter who comes or goes 'cause you my family. Ain't nobody gon' take care of family like family," I explained.

She gripped me so fast and pulled me so close we nearly tumbled over. No matter what, this crazy little chick had my heart. I hugged her back just as tightly. "I love you so much," she cried.

"I love you too, baby girl. I love you too."

My mom joined us. "This is how it's supposed to be. We are all we got. We have to be there for Tony Jr. and LaMichael."

This was what I'd always wanted, for us to be a real family. It felt so good to be here in this moment together. This moment solidified our bond forever and gave me the strength that I needed to face anything, even the unfortunate news that I was about to deliver to them.

Misha was the first one to pull away, and when she looked at us, she began crying. It split my heart in two to see her so emotional. Our mom and I tried to console her as best we could, but she only broke down more. She appeared on the verge of a nervous breakdown, and at this point, I was terrified because I didn't know what was wrong with her.

Finally, we coaxed her to take a seat, and she did. Gathering herself, she finally spoke through a quivering voice and teary eyes. "Actually, there is something I have to tell you all. I did something to both of you. I figured that if you all knew your men were foul, you all wouldn't mess with them no more—"

"I already know you were with Joe, and I couldn't bring myself to go behind my own daughter," my mom interrupted, figuring that Misha was about to admit about Joe and saving her the trouble.

However, something in what Misha had said stood out to me. "You slept with them to get us away from them?" I asked.

"Yep, and to get back at them," Misha continued. "Meka, I need you to know that I had never slept with Tony before that night, and I knew you'd be back home because the pastor had already left you a message that Bible study was canceled—"

"Why would you intentionally hurt me?" I interrupted.

"I didn't do it to hurt you. I did it to help you. You and Mama," she said. "Remember the dude I used to date, Vince?"

My mom and I looked at each other and nodded. "I thought you'd be together forever," Mom said.

Misha scoffed. "Me too. Until I found out he'd been sleeping with his mama's best friend," Misha confessed. "Only thing is I found out when I went to the clinic six months ago that Vince, who was the only boy I'd been with at the time, had given me, umm . . . I have . . . I contracted HIV." She broke down.

Thank God we were all sitting down already. If not, I would have to be scooped off the damn floor. My heart sank in my chest, yet I could hear the thump in my ears. My sister was already HIV positive. *OMG!* I couldn't believe this shit. How could she not tell us? How did we not know?

My mom burst into tears. "Are you sure? How did you know? How come you didn't say nothing?" my mom rattled off.

"Right! Not to mention you didn't think that we may have slept with them ourselves. We could've forgiven them, gone back to these men, and ended up with HIV ourselves, Misha." I was in total shock and disbelief of her reckless behavior. "What were you thinking, Misha? Come on. You played with all of our lives."

Misha shrugged with aggravation. "Don't you think I realize that—now? I don't know what I was thinking, Meka. I was pissed off with the world. Pissed with men. Hurt. Alone. Confused. I just wanted revenge on any man who wasn't about shit. I won't lie, part of me didn't even care about you, Mama," she said, gazing over at our mother. "I thought you'd choose Joe over me regardless. But it was mainly to give him a dose of his own medicine. He'd been mean to me, and he used to hit me when you weren't around, and I felt like I couldn't say shit. He even flirted with me a few times, but I think he was afraid to really try me because I was so rebellious. So when I offered it, he took it. And for that, I'm sorry. I really am." She cried before continuing. "To be honest, my head wasn't on straight with any of this. I found out that not only had my first love cheated, but he'd given me the package, and I had no one. No mom. Not even you, Meka." She pointed at me. "Not that you wouldn't have been there, but you have your hands full with the boys, and Tony had you so fucked up in the head that I didn't want to add to your stress. Most of all, I was scared. Hell, I still am. The clinic has been helping me. I've been going to counseling, but my life is over, so yeah, I figured I would take some muthafuckas along the way. Vince's dirty ass already got it, so since I couldn't pay him back, I decided to pay back y'all's men. A low-down, dirty bastard ain't nothing but a low-down, dirty bastard. Joe and Tony don't deserve y'all. They are a waste of God's air. So I gave them some of this PYT with a loaded package. Thanks to me, Joe and Tony finally gonna get theirs, so y'all don't have to hurt no more. Find some men who love y'all so I won't die in vain," Misha cried.

Her revelation took away what was left of my soul. Her actions were fucked up for sure, but they weren't entirely selfish. Besides, I couldn't even imagine being 17 years old and learning that type of information. It wasn't like finding out she had the flu. Hell, it wasn't even like she found out she was pregnant. That you could deal with or even resolve if that was her choice, but HIV didn't give that option. She had to feel lonely and despondent. I felt horrible that I hadn't pried and been there for her. No matter what, I would've been there for her. I wished she knew she never had to face that alone.

My mom's trembling voice broke my thoughts. "I'm so sorry, Misha. I'm sorry for what he did and how I treated you. I'm so sorry that I didn't look out for you and put Joe before you. But it's okay. You only wanted to hurt me, and I deserved that." We shook our heads, and she nodded. "No, I did," she argued. "But thank goodness we didn't sleep with those bastards after you. I don't care about Tony, Joe, or Vince. I care about you, Misha. I care about making sure that you live, because you ain't dying. I'm gonna get you the best care," my mom said between sniffles. "Do you hear me? You're getting the best care. You ain't dying on us!"

All we could do was sit on the sofa, all three of us, and hold each other as we cried. But if both Misha and Kwanzie had it, that still left the question, which one gave it to Tony? Sadly, that was the only question in mind, because at this point, I knew without a shadow of a doubt that Tony was HIV positive.

Chapter Eleven

Charice

When it rained, it poured. Ryan had been battling with me as much as he could over my relationship with Lincoln, and it was wearing me down. I caught flak from the boys, who wanted me to be with their daddy, and Ryan's parents, who begged me to give him a chance. I understood their position, but I loved Lincoln. I couldn't change that. Lincoln and I continued to get into little spats over the phone because he was stressed over the strain of his professional relationship with Ryan and the team. Having gotten into more physical confrontations with Ryan, it had begun to be an unpleasant situation. To add to the stress, we hadn't seen each other since the weekend Ryan found out about us, and I couldn't wait to see him. We needed this time to build our relationship and deal with this hurdle in our lives. It seemed like we were losing our bond with each other because of all the bullshit, but I refused to give up on him. Yet ever since I stepped foot in the house, it had been filled with petty arguments and awkward silence. This was not the trip I'd hoped for.

"I'll have dinner ready for you when you get home," I told Lincoln before he left to go work out and condition.

"I'm on a strict diet—"

"You don't trust my cooking?" I asked, interrupting him.

He shook his head. "It ain't that. You shouldn't be cooking. You're visiting."

Put off by his visitor remark, I frowned. "I'm your fiancée and a nutritionist, and I resent that comment about me being a visitor. This is my home and kitchen too."

Irritated, he groaned. "You know what I mean, Charice. Damn."

"No, I don't. Make it clear for me," I said, folding my arms.

"Whatever. I'm out."

"Why are you taking out your frustrations on me?"

"I'm not," he said in an attitudinal way.

"Whatever, man." I threw my hands up. "You know what? Grab something. I'm going to take a damn nap."

I made my way upstairs and lay across the bed. Lincoln and I exchanged no further words before he left. Hearing the door close without an attempt to make things right between us bothered me. We'd had another argument, and I didn't even understand why. Where our relationship had been so smooth and welcoming, it now had somehow become a drain.

Despite my attempt to rest and relax, I couldn't sleep, so I got up, cleaned, and then watched television as I lay in our bed to clear my mind, but I still couldn't help but worry if we could weather this storm. My attitude concerning others' opinions about our relationship was that everyone would get over it. Lincoln, however, took it to heart. That scared me because I felt as if he thought that he bit off more than he could chew, but our love was so worth it.

Somewhere along the way, I'd fallen asleep on the bed, and when I woke up, I saw that it was ten o'clock at night. Lincoln wasn't home. He had left at three o'clock this afternoon. Instantly, I was worried. I grabbed my cell phone, and the only missed calls I had were from my mom and LaMeka. Listening to their messages, I knew it had nothing to do with Lincoln, so I called him. The call went straight to his voicemail, so I tried again with the same result. I called the office of his nonprofit and of course got no answer. Then I called a couple of his teammates, who hadn't seen him since about six, so I made the call that I dreaded.

"Hey, Ricey, what's good?" Ryan asked me.

In a panic, I asked, "Ryan, have you seen Lincoln?"

"Gee, thanks. I'm doing all right, and you?" he replied sarcastically.

"Gawd damn it, Ryan! This is not the time to be fucking playing. He should've been home hours ago. I can't reach him by cell, and no one has seen him since earlier today," I said frantically.

"With any luck, he jumped off a bridge and killed himself."

A gasp escaped me. Even though he was pissed with Lincoln, I never would've suspected something so vile to spew from his mouth. "How dare you? You may be angry, but wishing death on someone is extreme, even for you."

There was a brief pause before Ryan spoke again. "Ricey, I'd kill for you, so why wouldn't I wish death on him if it meant I could have you?" Ryan asked nonchalantly.

Whoa. Ryan had done some cruel things in his lifetime. Despicable things. Unforgivable things. But even with all that, those words were a new all-time low. "Okay, now you're scaring me. Where's Lincoln, and what have you done to him?"

His laugh came out sinisterly. "Pipe down. I ain't done shit to that nigga. But if he's lost, I damn sure ain't trying to find him. If you're worried, call the police. They get paid to search for muthafuckas. I don't."

"He was your best friend. How could you?"

"He stopped being my friend the moment he pushed up on you, so forgive me if I don't have no sympathy or empathy for him. I don't know where he is, but I'll be

more than happy to keep you company while you wait,"
he said slyly.

Unbelievable. My brow furrowed at the audacity of his
actions. "You are so wrong. I have to go so I can find my
man."

Ryan chuckled. "Fine. Suit yourself."

Rather than continue this back-and-forth, I hung up
on him and kept calling Lincoln. I didn't know if I should
be pissed or worried, so I stayed in limbo between the
two. By midnight, I was fully clothed and about to head
out of the door to the police station when the front door
opened and Lincoln walked inside.

The sight of him caused me to lash out before I knew it.
"Where the hell have you been?"

His eyes were red. He seemed like he'd been drinking.
"Man, I just got home. Can you please stop fussing? Is
that any way to greet your man?" he said.

*This man did not just walk his ass up in this house
hours late and ask me if this was any way to treat my
man.* My hands flew on my hips, and my attitude was
on go. "And is this any way to treat your woman? You've
been gone all day. You're not answering your phone.
You had me worried sick! Do you see me right now? I'm
trembling and scared. I was on my way out of the house
to the police station, and all you can say is 'stop fussing'?
You must be out of your mind!"

Lincoln put his gym bag down and sauntered past me
into the kitchen. "It's been a long day, and I just want to
be left alone."

Thinking back to my conversation with Ryan, concern
overtook me. "What happened?"

"Nothing. I went to work out and condition."

"From three in the afternoon until midnight?" I hollered. "And you have liquor on your breath, just so you
know. I mean, unless you always exercise drunk." I
followed him into the kitchen.

He drank a bottle of water and threw it in the trash. "I'm about to shower and go to bed. You coming?"

"Hell no! And you're not going anywhere until you give me an answer," I said, gripping him by his forearm.

"I got drunk and got some ass," he said sarcastically.

Without warning, I slapped his ass. "You bastard!"

"That's what you want to hear, right? You want to hear that I was out being trifling to give you a reason to leave. Ain't that right?" Lincoln said harshly.

Something was not right. I was in a state of shock at his behavior, but I could sense his pain. "No! I don't want to leave, but I do want to know what's wrong," I pleaded. "Baby, this isn't you. Talk to me."

"You don't know me, Charice."

"Yes, I do. You're the man I love. How could I not know you?" I protested.

"Let's just go—"

With a huff, I belted, "I love you. Please be straight with me. That's all I ask."

His face was a mix of emotions as he tried to rub out the creases of worry in his forehead. "I don't know how to say this."

"Say what?" I asked nervously.

He groaned out his frustrations and placed both of his hands atop his head. With his eyes closed, he gritted his teeth and mumbled, "I've done some deep thinking, and I realized that this isn't what I really want."

The temperature in my body played tricks on me, because a coolness ran through my veins, causing my hands and feet to feel clammy, but my skin felt as if it were on fire. My system seemed just as confused as my heart and my mind. What the fuck was he saying? "What are you talking about?" I asked nervously. "Lincoln, you're scaring me."

Lincoln lifted his head, and the most sorrowful expression was trapped in his eyes. The pain that emanated from him was enough to level the entire city. His shoulders deflated as he began to explain. "I'm sorry. I am. I wish I had never seen you at the Westin. I never should've let this go this far. Look, what I'm saying is . . . I don't want this anymore."

Tears fell from my eyes. "I can't . . . What are you—"

"We need to end this," Lincoln boomed, cutting me off midsentence.

Panic set in as I began to ramble. "Okay, umm, so you don't want to get married right now. I get that. Let's just hold off on that. We'll work on us—"

"Charice," he yelled, throwing his hands up. "I don't want to be married. I don't want to be in a relationship. I don't want to be with you!"

The air immediately left my lungs, and my chest heaved up and down as his words hit me like bricks in the face. I would've preferred being shot to death than what he was telling me. There was no way this could be happening. No way. I loved him, and he loved me. Why would he do this to us? Why?

"No, no, no. You don't mean that. You can't," I cried. "Please." I rushed to him, grabbed his waist, and hugged him. "I love you. Don't do this. Don't!"

"Go home." He pulled away from my embrace. "Go back to Atlanta, and leave me alone."

"Lincoln!"

"Go!"

Tears rushed down my face as I stared up at him through pleading eyes. "You promised you'd never hurt me. I gave you all of me. I chose you over Ryan."

His nose flared as he spat, "Well, you should've chosen Ryan. I'm not built for this. I feel smothered and . . . please, let's just end this amicably."

The sting I felt couldn't have felt stronger if he'd actually laid hands on me. Not only had he just shredded my heart into pieces, but he also had the nerve, the unmitigated gall, to want to end things on a friendly note. We weren't friends. We were lovers. Then out of left field, with no rhyme or reason, we suddenly weren't lovers anymore?

My emotions welled up inside of me, causing me to combust. "Amicably!" I ran up to him and began continuously punching him in the chest. "You promised me," I screamed. "On Paradise Island, you promised me you'd never give me a reason to run. You told me this was what you wanted. You said you'd stand by me. What about that?"

He grabbed my hands to stop the pounding blows. As he held my hands in his, he drew in his bottom lip and stared intently into my eyes. "I know what I said, and at the time, I thought that's what I really wanted. I'm sorry, Charice. I am. Isn't it better that you know now rather than after we get married and tie ourselves down together?"

The foolishness just didn't stop. What kind of fuckery was he on? "Tie ourselves down? I'm already tied to you. What the hell? Better to know now? It would've been better if you told me this shit six months ago or, hell, even a month ago! If this isn't really what you wanted, why didn't you let me leave when I started to after the benefit dinner?"

He flailed his hand and fanned it to cease my questions. "Listen, I know it's hard, but this is for the best. I didn't say anything, but I was hesitant on Paradise Island to ask you to marry me for a reason. I was second-guessing this whole thing. I thought at the time it was what I wanted, and I realize now that it was the wrong decision. I wanted to wait until the morning to tell you all of this, but you wanted to know now, and I felt I owed you enough to tell you. I'm so sorry," Lincoln apologized. "I'll help you make your flight arrangements in the morning," he said, and without another word or even a bit of comfort, he began to walk away.

As he walked away, I stood in place, dazed for a moment. That's when the reality of this situation really hit me. This moment was really real. He left me, and there was nothing I could say that could change his mind. I loved him. I couldn't lose him. I just couldn't. Desperation caused me to run and jump in front of him. "Please, please don't leave me. I'll do anything. Please," I begged him as a fury of tears streamed down my face.

"Please stop," he said quietly, trying to maneuver past me.

Overcome with fear, I fell to my knees and grabbed his legs. "No, wait, please stop, baby. No. I love you. You can't leave me. Please don't leave me!"

"Charice, get up," Lincoln begged.

I shook my head fiercely. Pure and utter desperation had settled in, and I was terrified of losing Lincoln. At this point, I had lost myself. Without Lincoln, I was nothing. Something came over me, and I pulled at his shorts.

"What are you doing?" he asked, confused.

"Making you remember how good we are. Is this what you want me to do?" I asked as I took his manhood in my hands and started massaging it. Before he could protest, I placed his wood in my warm mouth and worked it like I never had before.

"Mmm," he moaned as his head fell backward. "You have to . . . oh, Lord . . . you have to stop." He gripped me by my shoulders and forced me back off of him. Glaring down at me, he roared harshly, "Stop this. Stop it right now."

My heart split in two as I looked into Lincoln's eyes. He was serious. Suddenly, I was no longer the grown and mature Charice I had worked so hard to become. I was automatically 19 years old again when Ryan had walked out on me for good. I was that same scared, timid, desperate, naive, confused, and worthless teenage girl who'd begged a man to love me the same way I loved him. I slid away from him as he fixed his shorts, and I curled up in a ball with my back against the kitchen island. I buried my face in my lap and cried from the aching pain. I couldn't think. I couldn't breathe. I couldn't do anything but wish someone could put the shattered pieces of my heart back together again.

Suddenly, I thought of how good I had been to Lincoln, and all the things I'd done for him flooded my memory. It was I who'd started Lincoln's Little Ones for him: a foundation that taught inner-city youths who were below grade level how to read. It was I who gave him the idea to extend Camp Lincoln into a mentoring program. Camp Lincoln was geared toward boys between the ages of 6 and 16 who excelled in football. They were shown proper techniques and went through training and conditioning so they could continue to excel in the sport, and I introduced learning other social skills such as chivalry and etiquette, and I was in talks to start the same type of program called Lincoln's Little Princesses.

I helped him choose the best endorsement deals to seek and accept. It was I who encouraged him and stood by him during the season. I was the one who paid his bills and kept his money in line by overseeing the protection of his investments and retirement plans. I was the one who gave him nutritional tips and medical advice when he refused to consult his doctor or the team physicians. I was the other daughter his mom and dad never had and a sister to Leo and Krista.

I even got along well with his baby mama, Lauren. His daughter, London, loved me, and it was because of me that Lauren and he had actually established a friendship for the sake of London. I put plenty of work into this so-called relationship, and now he was tossing me like I was yesterday's trash?

Suddenly, I was no longer hurt or upset. I was mad as hell! I jumped up from the floor and dusted myself off. If Lincoln didn't want me, fuck it. I didn't want his trifling ass either. From now on, it was all about me and my children. I dried my eyes and began to walk away to gather my things.

"Charice, I'm sorry that it had to be this way. I—"

I spun back around and put my hand up. "It is what it is. Excuse me." With that, I headed out of the kitchen and back up the stairs. My first stop was his bedroom. I pulled out my luggage and began to pack, not realizing he'd followed me.

"You don't have to leave now. I told you in the morning we—"

Continuing to stuff my bags, I bellowed, "I'm a grown-ass woman, Lincoln. I don't need *we* to do anything for me. I got me. I can take care of myself."

"I'm not letting you go out after midnight—"

"That's not your choice. You made your choice when you chose not to be with me. I'm choosing not to be here with you. I don't need you." I went to the bathroom to collect my toiletries.

Lincoln followed me. "I didn't want us to end like this. I don't want you to storm out of here like this."

The side-eye glare I tossed at him was searing. "Save it. You made it perfectly clear that you don't want this relationship, so stop trying to smooth shit over now. It's obvious to me that I'm not wanted here, and I refuse to stay anywhere I'm not wanted. I played that role with Ryan for too many years. I'm not doing it again for anybody else. I don't want your sympathy. I don't need your empathy, and I damn sure ain't feeling your feeble attempts at friendship. As far as I'm concerned, you never met me, and I never met you," I spewed as I shoved the rest of my things into my suitcase.

I zipped up the two pieces of luggage and began to roll them out of the bedroom.

"Here, let me help," he said, attempting to grab one.

"I got it!" I snatched it away. "Don't touch my shit!"

Once downstairs, I grabbed my purse and my cell. I pressed my home button and connected to Siri. "Courtyard Marriott, Dallas, Texas," I said into the phone. Siri supplied the nearest locations, and I pressed the first one to dial the hotel.

"Do you have any available rooms for immediate check-in? I only need single occupancy," I asked the reservationist once I was connected. "That's fine. Here is my card." After I reserved my room, I called a cab, and I told them I'd pay them double if they made it here quickly.

"You shouldn't leave here at night like this. Just because we're not together doesn't mean I'm not concerned about your well-being. Come on now," Lincoln pleaded once I was done.

I chuckled in disbelief. "You have some king-size balls." I shook my head as tears found their way to my eyes again. "How the hell can you break off an engagement and a relationship, then with a straight face have the nerve to tell me you're concerned about my well-being? News flash! My well-being is no longer your concern. In fact, don't even act as if you're concerned now." My heart fought between loving him and hating him, and I couldn't wait to get away from him.

Lincoln sat on the stairs. "Please stay until the morning."

I scoffed. "For what? You want some exit cutty? Sorry, I don't give out farewell fucks, nor do I want any. Please leave me the hell alone. I want to go in peace."

"You'll have a clearer mind, and what if you forget something?"

"If I have some shit here, mail it to me. You can even COD it," I said angrily. "Oh yeah, by the way, here are your house keys, car keys, and foundation keys." I threw them at him one by one, then reached into my wallet and snatched out his credit cards. "Here is your money," I said as the cab pulled up.

As I began to leave, I thought about one last thing and snapped my fingers. I pulled off my engagement ring and held it out for him.

"You can keep that." Lincoln held up his hands, refusing it.

"I don't need any reminders of you. Since you don't want to take my hand in marriage, I don't need the symbol of something that was never meant to be," I said, throwing his ring to the floor. "I will send you a check to pay for the Range Rover so I don't owe you shit."

"That's a gift. I'd never charge you—"

"I don't care. I don't need it or you. Go to hell. Don't call me, worry about me, or ask about me. If I never see your face again, it still won't be long enough." I swung the door open to leave.

My exit was suddenly halted by the strength of Lincoln's grasp on my arm. I faced him, ready to knock his block off for putting his deceitful hands on me, but the tears that streamed down his face briefly stopped me. "Charice, I'm so sorry things didn't work out for us."

"Don't be. I'm not," I said, seething.

With that, I snatched my arm out of his grasp and stalked away to my cab. Even as I settled in the cab, Lincoln stood watching in the doorway, but I refused to acknowledge his presence. The bottom line was that Lincoln had ripped my heart out and stomped on it, so now I had to take care of Charice.

As soon as the cab driver pulled off, though, the floodgates opened, and tears began to pour again.

"Are you okay, ma'am?" the cabbie asked.

"I'm fine. Just get me to the Courtyard Marriott as fast as possible. Thank you."

As soon as I said that, my cell rang. It was Ryan. "Did you find your fiancé?" he asked with a blasé attitude. All I could do was break down even more. "Wait. Charice, what's wrong? Did something really happen to Lincoln?" he asked, panicked.

"No. I wish it had though," I said as I cried. "Let's just say everything you ever wanted happened."

He paused. "He broke up with you?" he asked slowly.

"Yep, so you and all the other critics should be happy now."

"Charice—"

"I don't want to hear it."

"No, I was just gonna say that I'm sorry. I don't like to see you hurt." He sighed. "Where are you now?"

"Heading to the Courtyard Marriott downtown."

"Just come over here."

"No, I'm going to the hotel," I said bluntly. "I want to be alone."

"Fine, go, but I refuse to let you be alone. I'll meet you there."

Once I got to the hotel, I left a message at the front desk to give Ryan my room number. There was no fighting him coming, and I didn't have the energy to argue about it. In my room, I fell onto the bed and cried my eyes out. A little while later, Ryan arrived armed with a box of Kleenex, a bottle of Moscato, and some ice cream.

"I figured I'd bring the works," he said, showing the items.

Though my eyes were bloodshot, my nose puffy and runny, and my lips quivering, I cracked a little smile as I let him in. He set the items on the table, and when he turned back to face me, I fell into his embrace and released a gut-wrenching wail.

"He left me. I can't believe he left me," I repeated. "Oh God, it hurts so bad."

Ryan walked me over to the bed and rocked me as he stroked my hair. "Shh, it's okay. I know you love him. You're going to be fine. He's a fool just like I was. You'll bounce back. Just wait."

"I thought you'd hate me," I whimpered. "I thought you'd be happy to see my pain."

Ryan cupped my face, forcing me to stare into his eyes. "First off, I could never hate you. You're the mother of my three beautiful children and still the greatest love of my life. Secondly, I never want to see you in pain. I'll admit that part of me is happy, but that happiness is only because of the breakup and not the pain behind it. I wish I could say I wasn't happy about any of it, but I can't deny that. But whatever happiness I feel is overshadowed by your pain. The last thing on earth I want to see is you like this," he said sweetly, gently wiping away my tears.

"Please hold me and don't let me go."

As we lay back on the bed, I continued to cry while he held me. Soon all that could be heard were the sounds of raindrops as they fell. They matched my tears. Even when I had cried all I could cry, I just lay there and let Ryan hold me. I needed his strength to get me through this turmoil. Listening to one another's heartbeat and the rise and fall of our breathing, we didn't say a word as he continued to console me. After having a glass of Moscato, my body relaxed, and sleep invaded me despite myself. As I faded off, the smell of Ryan's cologne reminded me that I wasn't alone. For once, I had someone to help me pull the pieces back together.

Chapter Twelve

Trinity

Life as I knew it had suddenly become a cake walk. Pooch was really on a mission to prove he could be a good man and father. He'd stayed true to his word and tried to change. When he was at home, he helped with the kids and even cooked dinner for us one night. Granted, it was only fried egg and bologna sandwiches with French fries, but it was a meal. And boy, did I ever laugh at this fool's attempt to wash his own clothes. He ruined a slew of white tees and designer shirts by mixing colors and whites. With my direction, he got it right the next time, but I kept his crazy ass away from my designer duds.

The funniest thing of all came when he changed Princess's diaper for the first time. She had a slight case of diarrhea, so her diaper was fully loaded, and he got some poop on his hand. Then as he tried to change her, my baby knocked everything off the changing table, and by the time Pooch got it together, boom, she exploded another stinky load all over his shirt. That was one time when I volunteered to relieve him. I could tell he was happy, because he nearly threw her in my lap.

It was such a shame that it took this pregnancy for him to try to act right. Even with all he did, my feelings remained the same. I loved Terrence. Though I knew Terrence was being low-key so as not to draw suspicion from Pooch, I was beyond ready for him to make good on his plan to get me away from this muthasucka for more reasons than one.

And one of those reasons, which was beginning to get on my last damn nerve, was Pooch's need for sex. I'd managed not to give it up, claiming the illness from the pregnancy was what hindered us. The truth of the matter was that I wasn't going to have sex with him while I carried another man's baby. To me, that was beyond fucking nasty. He bought into it for a minute, but that was getting old real quick.

"Babe," Pooch said, rubbing on my ass in the bed. "You up?"

"No," I lied. Even though I wasn't in a deep sleep, I had drifted before he started calling me.

"Then how you answer me if you ain't up?" he asked.

I rolled my eyes. "'Cause you woke me up by calling me."

"Well, since you up now, let me g'on and hit that shit right quick. I'm hurting like a sumbitch over here," he whined.

"Pooch, I was asleep," I whined back.

"Man, I'ma get the fuckin' blue balls and shit," he fussed. "Come on. I promise it's gonna be quick. I'm so fuckin' backed up right now I'll explode fast."

"We got some Vaseline in the bathroom. I'm not stopping you from handling ya business."

"I need to feel some of that gushy stuff. This fuckin' jacking off ain't working. It's only releasing pressure. It ain't killing the urge. Come on, babe," he whined, kissing my neck. "I need to feel you."

"You already know I'm battling with my blood pressure. All this increased activity is not going to be good for me or the baby." I flipped to my back and looked over at him.

"Let me get on top. You don't have to move or nothing."

"So just let you put your weight on me and the baby?"

He rubbed on his dick. "Well, ride it like only you can." Pursing my lips, I smarted off, "Hello? Increased heart rate and high blood pressure do not go hand in hand." Pooch fell back on the bed in frustration. Then he snapped his fingers. "Let me eat you out. I can pull on myself as I do it, and then we both can get off. Maybe that will dead some of this urge," he said, smiling over at me as if he'd made an offer I couldn't refuse. "I know how much you like that tongue action."

"I'm really not in the mood. I don't know if it's the medication or what. I wish I were, though," I lied.

Shiiiiiit. I loved tongue action, and this pregnancy had me in the mood every other day. But the only person who gave me tongue action was Terrence, every chance I got. I refrained from intercourse since I still lived with Pooch, but trust me when I say I was getting so much tongue action my pussy probably smelled like Terrence's breath. As a matter of fact, I had a 9:00 a.m. appointment for that when I went over to comb Brittany's hair in the morning.

"Can you suck on it or something?" he begged.

"You know these iron pills make me sick. You really want me to shove your dong down my throat?"

"Please, babe." He paused and looked around strangely. "Wait a minute. Why am I begging for my own woman to please me?" he asked himself. "I've been real patient with you, Trin, but you gon' have to do something around here. Now we was supposed to be working on us and shit, and I'm trying real fuckin' hard not to lose it. So I'ma try this again. Just suck on it a little bit so I can get the fuck off," Pooch said tensely.

I scoffed. "What you saying? You gon' make me suck it, or are you going out there and be dirty if I don't?"

"Dirty is as dirty does, meeting ma'fuckas in the park and shit," Pooch said cynically.

"Nice way to work on us, Pooch."

"A'ight then," he said, and I could tell he was upset. The next thing I knew, he grabbed his cell phone and dialed a number. "What's up, Chocolate Flava? I'm cool. Nah, this ain't no business call. I wanted to see if you was free to roll by my house right about now."

Now I knew this muthasucka wasn't inviting one of his strippers to our house. I couldn't care less if he went out in the street and did dirt, but to my house in front of my baby? Hell to the no!

"What the fuck is you doing?" I asked angrily as I sat up.

"Hold up a minute, sweetie," he said into the phone before placing the phone on mute. "Doing my dirt. That's what you want me to do, right?"

"Not at this house with the baby in here, you ain't."

"It's my house, and it ain't gon' be in front of the baby. It's gon' be in here with the door locked. I'ma let her suck the rock right quick while you sleep and send her on her way," he said as if I were gonna sit by while some bitch rolled through here and got him off in front of me.

"Nigga, please. Have you lost your damn mind? I know damn well you ain't 'bout to disrespect me like that. And you ain't 'bout to disrespect Princess either," I said angrily.

He shrugged. "So what you gonna do?"

I rolled my eyes. Even though I knew he was doing this shit to get next to me, I didn't have a choice. I wasn't going to let him do some nasty shit like that to me. I wished that Terrence would hurry up with his plan to get me away from this rotten bastard. In the meantime, I had to do what I had to do to survive, even if that meant sucking his pipe.

I nodded. "A'ight," I conceded.

He smiled and unmuted the phone. "Yo, Chocolate. Sorry to keep you up. You ain't got to roll through. Yeah, I'm positive. Yeah, I know you don't mind being down for me, but you know I'm a one-woman man, so we can kill this noise for real yo, 'cause my lady is waiting. Make sure y'all catch that party tomorrow. A'ight. Peace."

Pouting with my arms crossed, I asked, "Are you done talking to your hoes?"

He slid his cell back onto the nightstand before looking over at me. "Them bitches don't mean shit to me, and I'on even fuck wit' none of 'em like that, and you know it, but you better quit trippin' around this bitch. 'Cause as you can see, not one of them hoes gives a damn about replacing yo' ass," he said matter-of-factly.

"Not one of them gave you a baby or will be loyal to your ass like me either. They just looking for a fucking come-up," I shot back.

"Oh, and you wasn't?" he asked.

"I didn't come looking for you. You brought your ass where I was, so miss me with that shit for real, yo." I fanned him off.

He brought me to him so fast I didn't know what was happening. He held my face in his hands. "Don't be talking to me foolish like that. Do you hear me?"

"A'ight," I said nervously.

He had the nerve to smile at me after that with his evil ass. "Don't be nervous. I ain't gon' hurt you. That shit is kinda sexy though." He rubbed my cheek with one hand and eased his boxers down with the other. "Handle that shit, babe."

That sadistic muthasucka. Who does shit like that? Only a crazy-ass nigga like Pooch. Who would want to have any type of sexual intimacy after the stunt he just pulled? Not just with calling Chocolate Flava's thirsty ass, but also snatching me as if he'd never laid hands on me before while I was pregnant. *I should bite his shit clean off.* But as long as I was stuck here in this ruse of a relationship, I had to put up my pretenses. That meant I had to pleasure my so-called man. Holding his dick in my hands, I lowered my head and went to work.

"Ooh shit, babe. That's it right there," he moaned, stroking my hair. "Get at him."

Fortunately, it didn't take long. I was only down there for two minutes tops before his toes curled and balls tightened up. I pulled up just in time as he erupted like a volcano. He gripped the hell out of the headboard and convulsed.

"Ooh yeah. That's that good-good," he said after he relaxed. "I told you it wasn't gon' be but a minute," he added before we got up to clean ourselves.

I finished up in the bathroom before him and hurriedly jumped into bed to go to sleep before he had the bright idea to ask me for some more sexual favors. That one horrendous experience was enough.

However, when he snuggled against me, he woke me again. "I'm sleepy now—"

"Nah, I'm good. Believe me, I'm real good. But I was just holding you and shit. I thought you might like that," he whispered.

I did, but not from his ass.

"Before you go to sleep, I just wanted to tell you I'll be gone most of the day tomorrow. Tot got these brothers he want me to meet with so I can begin expanding my organization."

"Oh yeah?" I said nonchalantly. "Who?"

"Umm, some cats from out West. I think he said they name was the Crown brothers. One of the top connections."

"Crown brothers, huh?" I said. For some reason, the name sounded familiar to me. "You heard of 'em?"

"I heard of some of their clients, and them niggas is big time for real. When you start fuckin' wit' cats who keep they name off the grid, that's when you really on some king shit," Pooch confided in me.

Not that I should have cared, but I did. I wasn't heartless, and he was still Princess's father. I faced him and questioned, "Don't you be scared of doing this shit sometimes?"

In a rare sweet move, he lifted my chin so that we were looking directly into each other's eyes. Surprisingly, he gave me a soft and tender kiss on the lips. "No. You know what scares me the most?"

"What?" I asked him as we continued to lock eyes.

"Losing you," he said nervously. "Real talk. I'd go insane without you."

I guessed it was the pregnancy that had my emotions all over the place, but I felt giddy on the inside when he said that to me. It reminded me of the Pooch I fell in love with a few years ago, back when he was always so sweet to me. For the first time in a long time, I saw the old Pooch from when we were teenagers, the sweet and vulnerable Pooch.

"Aww, baby," I said, pulling him into a passionate kiss. My reaction to him shocked me.

He smiled lovingly at me after the kiss. "Yeah, that's the Trin I remember." He lightly brushed my hair, then caressed my face. The stare he donned for me made my heart flutter in a way that it hadn't in years. "It feels good to be back here at this place. I love you, girl. I love you for real," he said tenderly and hugged me.

Pooch had touched my soft spot, and it was the first time I questioned my true feelings for him. That was, until he said the one infamous thing that reminded me that the flash of the old him was only temporary.

"And as long as you remember that shit, we all good."

Same old Pooch, different day. How could I even get sucked up into his bullshit for even a moment? I'll tell you why, because I was still living with his ass, pretending to be his lady. Pooch officially made me remember that no matter how much good game he talked, being with him was not where I was trying to be. I bid his ass goodnight and had sweet dreams about Terrence. Now that's the shit I was remembering.

Chapter Thirteen

Lucinda

I know damn well I didn't let Aldris talk me into this, I thought, changing outfits for the tenth time.

Everything had come along well for me. I enjoyed my classes, did wonderful on my new job, and Aldris and I were good. Then he decided he wanted me to meet his mother because she'd begun questioning him about missing his Sunday visits with her. He was usually with me on Sundays since that was my official rest day. Having Aldris at the house with Nadia and me had become routine, and our relationship had flourished. I loved the way he just completed me. Even the simple things, like our corny-ass inside jokes, solidified our relationship. Got a chick like me feeling that Ella Mai for real. Yeah, "Boo'd Up" was definitely in heavy rotation on my Spotify playlist.

Still, I didn't think I was ready to meet his mother. What if she was pissed because I was Hispanic? Let's face the facts on this one. I may have been from the hood and had all black friends, but the only thing that granted me was a ghetto pass. It in no way "entitled" me to have a black woman's most precious commodity— a black man. Black friends or not, I realized that most black women are offended when a black man dates outside of his race, especially if they have someone like Aldris on their arm.

You don't think so? Let me just state the facts one more time. What if she thought I was too low-class for her son because of my lack of education and upbringing? What if she didn't appreciate that I had a ready-made family? And heaven forbid she find out about Spanish Fly! Now all of that may have been cool if the chick were black, but let her be of another ethnicity and the first thing that came to mind was that timeless comment, "A good-looking, successful black man wouldn't dare date a sista with all those issues."

I'd heard the comments in my own neighborhood from people I grew up around. They've seen Aldris pull up in his BMW 750i, with his fresh-to-death outfits and killer good looks, and instantly I was public enemy number one. Fuck that I grew up in the hood right along with them. I was used to the hate. If it weren't because of Aldris, it would be for another reason, so I embraced my relationship despite my insecurities. However, meeting his mom was some next-level shit, and all those same insecurities came raging back.

"*Mami,* are you and Mr. Aldris going on another fancy date?" Nadia asked me as she sat on the bed looking at me.

"No, it's not really a date at all," I said, looking in the mirror.

"So why are you trying on all those clothes?"

I turned to face her and smiled. "I'm meeting Aldris's mom today, and I want to look presentable."

"What is presidual?"

I giggled. "It's 'presentable,' and it means to look appropriate. Or you could say to dress the part."

"Oh, like on Halloween when I have to put on costumes or we won't get any candy," Nadia related.

Kids say the darnedest things! "Yes," I laughed. "There's a time and a place for everything. You wouldn't wear your Halloween costume at Christmas, right?" She giggled at that. "What do you think?" I asked her, settling on the jeans and a short-sleeved batwing top.

"I think you looked prettier in the dress," Nadia told me.

"You may be right," I said. I snapped my fingers and changed into the spaghetti-strap sundress. "Now what do you think?"

"I like it! Don't worry, *Mami*. Mr. Aldris's *mami* is going to like it too."

I hugged her. *From your lips to God's ears.*

About five minutes later, Aldris knocked on the door. "Hey, two of my favorite women in the whole wide world. Are you ready?" he asked, placing a soft kiss on my forehead.

Nadia sighed. "Not me. Peter gets on my nerves. He thinks he's my daddy. I know he's my uncle, but we're almost the same age."

I leaned on Aldris's shoulder. "Ay. The woes of having a younger brother and a daughter."

Looking at me with admiration, he smiled. "You look beautiful," Aldris complimented me. "We could just bring her with us."

I shook my head. "I want to make it through this initial visit myself. Next time we'll bring Nadia."

"Are you nervous?" he asked in shock.

"As a whore in church who screwed the pastor last night."

"*Mami,* what's a whore?" Nadia asked me.

"None of your beeswax. Go get your bag," I scolded her. She pouted and walked away, and Aldris laughed.

He could tell by my expression that I was not amused. "Hey, you said it in front of her, not me. You know Nadia has a supersonic ear."

"And a big mouth," I added, grabbing my purse.

"She's just inquisitive," Aldris defended her.

"Mr. Aldris, what's inquisify?" Nadia asked, emerging again.

"It's 'inquisitive,' and that is exactly what you are," I chimed in.

"What am I if I'm inquistafive?" Nadia asked again.

"It means you ask a lot of questions," Aldris explained.

"And that means you're nosy," I added. "Now, let's go."

Nadia looked at Aldris as if to ask what my problem was, and he just shrugged his shoulders, and we left.

At my mom's, Nadia and Peter started up their arguments before they could get in the house good. We waved goodbye, and I told my brother Jose to look out for them.

"You really are on edge about meeting my mom?" Aldris asked.

"Kinda," I replied, staring out of the window.

"Only kinda?"

Turning my nervous face to him, I confessed, "Okay, I'm petrified. How did you know?"

"Well, you were a little snappy with Nadia back at the house, and you haven't said two words to me since we left your mom's."

Exhaling the nervous energy, I admitted, "Yeah, I know. I just don't think I'm ready for this."

"So you tell me. When would be a good time?" he asked.

Leave it to him to hit me with a question that I had not considered an answer for. "I really do not know, Aldris."

"That makes today as good a day as any." He rubbed my knee with his hand for encouragement. "My mom's a sweetheart. She will love you."

"So you say."

"Have I ever lied to you before?"

With an eye roll, I had to admit, "No, you haven't."

"So trust me now. You'll be fine," he assured me.

With my fake smile plastered on my face, I gave him a flash of my dazzling whites so that he wouldn't see that, regardless of what he said, I was utterly and completely terrified. "Have you told your mom anything about me?"

He shrugged. "Only that I've been dating a beautiful woman who used to work for me. She knows your name is Lucinda, and she knows that you must keep me happy since I'm staying away from her cooking," he joked.

"You haven't told her any major details?"

"Major details? She's my mother, not a detective." He laughed. "No. My mom knows she raised me to make good decisions in that area of my life. She's not a snoop. I mean really, baby, we're just having Sunday dinner with my mom. It's not a federal investigation."

"I sure as hell feel indicted," I mumbled.

"Huh?" he asked since he was unable to interpret what I'd said.

"Nothing," I answered, opting to leave the conversation alone, and we rode the last fifteen minutes in silence.

We pulled up to a beautiful home that sat on a freshly cut, manicured green lawn. The house had amazing curb appeal with its elegant circular driveway, where a C-class Mercedes was parked. She may not have been rich, but from the house, the car, and the neighborhood, she damn sure wasn't hurting. I could totally see Aldris fitting right into this type of environment. He was born into success and bred to be nothing less. Now I was officially freaked out.

"Hey yo, Mama," Aldris yelled as we came through the front door. "Where you at? Company in the house!"

Soon a gorgeous, caramel-complexioned woman with almond-shaped brown eyes and long brown hair came around the corner. She appeared to be in her fifties, and Aldris looked just like her. There was no mistaking it: this was his mother.

"I'm right here, Al, so stop yelling through the house." She grinned and hugged him tightly.

"Yeah, Al," I joked because I knew he hated that nickname.

"You know I hate that name, Mama."

"And you know I don't care. Shut up and let me bask in my hug," his mother said. Then she stepped back and looked at me. "And you must be Miss Lucinda."

"Yes, Mom. This is Lucinda Rojas. Lucinda, this is my mother, Lily Sharper," he introduced us.

I extended my hand for a handshake and greeted her. "It's a pleasure to meet you, Mrs. Sharper. Aldris has told me such great things about you."

Sweetly, she waved my extended hand away. "We don't shake hands in this household. We hug," she said and embraced me. "It's a pleasure to meet you too, Lucinda, and please call me Lily."

"What's for dinner?" Aldris asked, cutting our introduction short.

His mom laughed. "No 'How are you doing?' or anything. Just straight to the food. Can you believe this son of mine?" she asked.

"I'm sorry, Mama. How are you? How's everything going—"

"We're having fried chicken, macaroni and cheese, collard greens, black-eyed peas, white rice, cornbread, and banana pudding, and it's not finished yet," his mom said, cutting him off.

"Oooh weeee! That's what I'm talking about," he exclaimed and planted a kiss on her forehead.

"Lucinda, I hope you're not one of those salad-eating girls, because we eat soul food in this household."

His mother's comic relief tickled and calmed me, causing me to release a chuckle. "No, ma'am. I love soul food."

"Do you cook?" she asked me.

Now I was getting nervous. I cooked, but mostly Hispanic dishes. Although I could make some mean fried chicken and macaroni and cheese, I usually got all of the other stuff from my girls' houses. Still, I decided to be honest instead of claiming to be a jack-of-all-trades.

"Um, I dabble with soul food. I must say fried chicken and macaroni and cheese are about as deep as I can get. My specialties are arroz a la cubana, frittatas, and escabeche."

His mom looked at me and then at Aldris and smiled. "I'm sorry. I don't know anything about arrow and escape. Oh Lord, child, come with me. We're going to have to teach you, and then you can maybe teach me your dishes and how to pronounce them."

Aldris rubbed my shoulders. "Don't knock it until you try it, Mama. Frittatas are the bomb!"

We all went into the kitchen to help finish up dinner, and that's when the questions began. Of course, she wanted to know my exact nationality, and she asked a lot about my heritage. Realizing it was my nerves and not any disrespect, I tried not to let it get the best of me.

"I'm going to run to the ladies' room really quick. You all can go ahead and set the table in the dining room," Ms. Lily said to us.

"Quick question," I said as soon as his mom was out of earshot.

"What's up, baby?" Aldris asked, handing me three plates.

"Have you ever dated outside of your race before?"

"Why does that matter?" He scoffed.

"Does everything have to be a sidebar with you? Can you just answer the question?" I asked, getting a little frustrated.

"When I was in the tenth grade, I dated a girl for three months who was half black and half Dominican, but other than that, all of my girlfriends have been black."

"Did you tell your mother before today that I'm Hispanic?"

He shrugged. "No, because it doesn't matter."

Setting down the plates, I reared back and crossed my arms. "Oh, since when does it not matter to a black woman that a black man is dating outside of his race?"

"Does it matter to you?" he shot at me.

"Of course not."

"And it doesn't to me either, so that's all that matters." He removed the remaining saucers from the curio, set them on the table, and walked to stand beside me. Lifting my hand into his, he gently urged me to face him. "I can't help who I am attracted to, and I certainly am not trying to live up to anyone's standards but my own."

Still filled with uncertainty, I quizzed him again. "So it's cool with your mother that I'm not black. Is that what you're telling me?"

His head fell back as he groaned from my continued line of questioning. His gaze returned to me, and he shrugged. "I haven't really asked her about it. I guess I've never had to, but my mom is cool. She doesn't care who her kids date as long as they are happy." He glided his thumbs across the tops of my hands. "And I am happy," he said, kissing me on the lips. "So stop worrying, okay, beautiful?"

I nodded in agreement, and we continued to set the table without any further questions from me about the subject. Aldris was a chatterbox, and I remained silent, content that it was better for me to be quiet than to keep drilling him for something that appeared to be more an issue for me than him. I only prayed it wasn't an underlying issue for his mother.

When his mom returned, we all made our plates. After saying grace, his mother lightened the mood by offering plenty of stories of her family. I listened to several different stories about Aldris's dad and found out a lot about Aldris's childhood. I even got to see some old photos that I was sure he wished had gotten lost over the years. It felt good watching him and his mom reminisce about the good times. This was the kind of family I wanted so badly, and since I couldn't have it, I desperately wanted it for Nadia. Aldris seemed to be right about his mom, because she was so welcoming and inviting that I let my guard down and began to feel at home. That was, until she started questioning me on my life.

"How did you and Aldris meet again?" she asked as we ate.

"He actually used to be my supervisor at National Cross."

"Yes, she was my top employee," he chuckled.

"You don't work there any longer?" his mother asked.

"No, I work from home for a group of orthopedic surgeons. Essentially, I do the same job but make a lot more money. It gives me the opportunity to finish college," I explained.

She flashed a beautiful smile. "Oh, great! What are you working on? Your master's?"

Here we go. This is what I was afraid of. The expectation. She'd already assumed that I was college educated and was simply furthering that education. This was what I meant by major details. People can act like they don't matter, but they do. They always matter. I gave Aldris an "I told you so" glare and drank a swig of my lemonade.

"Umm, actually I'm in technical college. I'm earning my associate's."

"Okay. That's wonderful," his mother said, but it seemed far less enthusiastic than when she thought I was working toward a master's degree.

"But I'm considering getting my bachelor's. It just depends on how things go in the household," I explained, trying to make up for the fact that I really didn't have anything under my belt.

That's when she raised her own eyebrow in curiosity. "You aren't still living with your parents, are you?"

I waved my hands, happy to be able not to disappoint in that area of my life at least. "No, I have my own apartment."

"I was about to say. I thought you were twenty-one. There are plenty of young people who still live at home, but I always told my sons you have to learn to be independent," she said with a chuckle.

"Oh yes, I've been independent since I was nineteen. It's just my daughter is getting older now—"

"Daughter?" she asked, shocked. "Well, where is she?"

Open mouth, insert foot. I just knew Aldris didn't have me up in his mother's house and had not revealed that I had a child. If I could've slid up under the table, I would've. There was absolutely no way I would make it out of this dinner unscathed at this point.

Nervously, I answered, "Um, yes, I have a five-year-old daughter named Nadia. She's at my mother's house right now, but she lives with me." I swallowed the lump in my throat.

"So, you had her in high school?" Ms. Lily asked, quickly tabulating her age against mine.

Damn it! My reckless mouth again. Of course, if she didn't know I had a child, she clearly wouldn't know that I had her in high school. This night got worse by the second. "Yes, ma'am."

Aldris reached over and gently gripped my hand. "Lucinda is a great mother and a hard worker. I'm so proud of her for accomplishing everything she has on her own," Aldris said encouragingly when he noticed the shift in my comfort zone.

"That is wonderful to be able to rise above your obstacles." She nodded her agreement. "Is Nadia's father in her life?"

Yep, worse on the way to worst. It was all downhill from here, so why not pour on the remaining bad news? "He's ordered to pay support, but he's not a good father to her," I admitted without going into details.

"It's such a shame when men don't take care of their responsibilities," she remarked, shaking her head.

"I agree," I said, drinking more of my lemonade, which I wished was wine at this point.

Just then, her doorbell rang. Hell, I was happy for the relief, but Aldris furrowed his brow.

"Who could that be, Mama?" he asked.

She snapped her fingers. "Oh, your friend Mike stopped by here asking about you. He said you hadn't returned any of his calls. I told him that you had begun dating a young lady, so you were probably just on hiatus. I told him that you and Lucinda were stopping by for dinner today, so he said he'd try to stop by and speak to you. Excuse me. Let me grab that," she said and backed her chair away from the table.

"Mama, why did you tell him that? This is our time," Aldris asked, and I noted the irritation in his voice.

She looked at him strangely and scoffed. "Nonsense. You and Mike have been friends since you were in grade school. He's practically a member of this family." With that, she rushed off to answer the door.

"Who is Mike?" I asked Aldris, noting his tense demeanor.

He smoothed his hand over the top of his head as he sat back in his chair. A look of uncertainty graced his face as he reached over and caressed my hand. "Don't freak out, but he's the one who set me up to see you dance at Club Moet that night."

Instantly, my palms got sweaty, and my bottom lip began to quiver. There was no way in hell I was going to be able to sit here staring at this dude who knew me as

Spanish Fly while I tried to win over Aldris's mom. She'd already confirmed that Mike was basically an honorary member of the Sharper clan, so there was no battling that. I'd been happy for the break, not realizing I was welcoming the "worst" that I'd been expecting all night. At this point, we were beyond worst. We were at a wreck, a whole-ass train wreck.

"What? Does he know about us?"

Aldris continued grudgingly, "The reason I haven't talked to him is because I told him about how we knew each other. I had already told him about my crush on you, but after the whole club fiasco, he told me not to get involved with you. I told him that I made my own decisions and that you were more than just a stripper at a club. We exchanged a few words, and that's the last I spoke to him and the reason I haven't called him back," he confessed to me.

My stomach did monkey flips as I could literally hear the steps that his mom and Mike took toward the dining room. Thinking quickly, I tried frantically to plan my escape, but the only way out was the same way in. I bit my bottom lip to quell the wave of nausea that threatened to spew from my mouth and wiped my hands on the handkerchief.

"Don't be nervous. I got your back," Aldris whispered to me as if that was supposed to make me feel any better.

Lo and damn behold, not only was it Mike but the other dude who had rained money on me too! I could've crawled up somewhere and straight died!

"We are eating in here," Ms. Lily said as she ushered Mike and the other guy inside.

"Hey, man," the two guys greeted Aldris.

"Sup, y'all," he responded unenthusiastically.

"Long time no hear from, Dri baby," Mike said, patting his shoulder.

"Yeah, you went from not hanging with the fellas to not talking to us either," the other one added.

"It's probably because of this beautiful young woman. Stop being rude, and introduce Lucinda to your friends," Ms. Lily insisted.

"Um, Mike Johnson and Rod Campbell, this is my girlfriend, Lucinda Rojas. Lucinda, this is Mike and Rod."

"Hello. It's nice to meet you both," I said softly.

"It's nice to formally meet you," Mike said as he smiled at Rod.

"Yeah, it is," Rod agreed.

"Do you guys want to sit and eat?" Ms. Lily asked.

"No, Mama. I'm sure they just wanted to speak and leave. Ain't that right, fellas?" Aldris asked as more of a command.

"Actually, I'm pretty hungry. How about you, Rod?" Mike said.

"I could use a helping of your mom's good fried chicken and collards," Rod added.

"Then it's settled. Have a seat," Ms. Lily said and got up to set two more plates.

Once Mike and Rod had a place at the table, the phone rang. "I'll get it. You boys help yourselves," she said, dashing out to the living room.

"Why are you two here?" Aldris demanded quietly.

"What is she doing here?" Mike retorted, pointing at me.

My mouth flew open at that blow. I had to check and make sure I was still sitting in the seat and awake because I nearly fainted. Torn between embarrassment and anger, I tried to reason with Aldris's so-called friends. "Look, fellas. I don't want any problems. I understand this is a weird situation for all of us, but I really do like Aldris," I said, erring on the side of caution, but I really wanted to fuck up these two *hijos de putos*.

"And like I told you, Mike, I like Lucinda. There is a lot more to her than you know. This is my choice, and I'm proud of it," Aldris said sternly to them.

"Oh, so your mom knows your little girlfriend here was the number-one hot show at Club Moet? Are you proud of that?" Rod countered.

"Man, we've known you and your family a long time. I don't know if it was the booty or the *español,* but you can do so much better," Mike said, smirking at me.

"Oh, and have two different kids by two different baby mamas like you, Rod? Both of whom didn't graduate high school and collect welfare for a living? Or would it be like you, Mike, tied down to the same woman for the past five years with three kids and not looking for anything long term because she's put on some weight and works a minimum-wage job?"

"My point exactly. They were mistakes. The same kind we're trying to bail you out from, college boy," Mike fumed.

At this point, my head throbbed, and I rubbed my temples to relieve the ache. "I knew this wasn't a good idea."

"See, even she knows." Mike pointed at me.

"Shut the fuck up," Aldris said to him. He turned to face me and lifted my chin so that we were eye to eye. "This is me and you. I don't care what they say or what they think. I know your heart. I know you," Then he looked at them. "I promise you both gon' get dealt with later."

Just then, Aldris's mom walked back in and noticed the tension. "Is everything all right?" she asked.

"Actually, I really need to go. Ms. Lily, everything was great, but I can't stay," I said and scooted my chair back.

"But you haven't even had dessert yet," she said to me.

"I thought she was the dessert menu," Mike laughed, and he and Rod high-fived.

"You know what? Y'all two clowns need to fucking bounce. Now!" Aldris hollered and jumped up.

"What the hell is going on in here?" Ms. Lily asked tensely.

Out of nowhere, tears sprang to my eyes, and I had to get out of there. "Ms. Lily, I'm sorry," I apologized and ran out of the house.

Inside of Aldris's car, I cried my eyes out. This was why I didn't want to date Aldris. This was why I should've stuck to my guns on our first date and continued to run for the hills. It was too good to be true. Nothing good ever followed me, and if it did, it never lasted. I had to be a complete idiot to believe I could go from deadbeat-ass Raul to dapper Aldris. But Aldris made me feel as if I were fucking Princess Diana knowing damn well I was more like Cardi B. Hell, and broke Cardi at that. I couldn't wait for him to bring his ass out of that house so I could go home to my baby, cut my losses, and stay the fuck in my lane.

Although I sat in Aldris's car for what seemed like forever, I refused to get out and snatch his ass. But if he didn't come on in the next five minutes, I was calling an Uber. I had my escape mapped out until a knock at the window scared the hell out of me. It was too late to pretend I was asleep since I'd jumped and looked to see who it was. Reluctantly, I rolled down the window.

"Get out of the car," Ms. Lily commanded. "Let's take a walk."

Though I had no desire to do as she'd commanded, I obeyed and got out of the vehicle. We walked into her backyard. She didn't speak a word, and neither did I. I didn't know what to say or do. Finally, we stopped at a plant. She watered it, checked the soil, and repositioned it in the sunlight.

The silence was torture, and I needed to get things off my chest before she put me out of her house. "Ms. Lily, I'm sorry—"

"You see this plant?" she asked, pointing to the one she'd finished nurturing.

"Yes," I replied, halting my previous statement.

"You know, my husband bought this plant. I've always had a green thumb. He, on the other hand, killed things that were nonliving," she joked. "One day, he decided he wanted his own plant. He tried, but God rest his soul, he was awful at it, and the plant slowly wilted and began to die. Daniel was a proud old man. I don't know if it was the years in the corps or a man thing, but he never wanted-ed to be defeated and refused to ask for my help. Finally, when the plant was on its last leg, he asked me for help, and I gave him advice. At first, I didn't believe he'd be able to turn it around, but he did. Heaven help me, it's the biggest and most beautiful plant out here still, to this very day, and all it needed was a little time, guidance, patience, and love."

She turned to face me before she continued. "Plants are much like people, you know. We may think we know all there is to know about them based on the things we see on the outside, but when we get down on the inside, that's when we see their full potential. That's when we realize that if we had just taken the time to guide them, love them, and be patient with them, they would grow to be the biggest and prettiest of them all."

Her words were so refreshing and soothing that I couldn't stop the tears from flowing as I tried relentlessly to wipe them away.

Gently, she placed her hand on my arm in a motherly way. "I haven't lived on this earth for fifty-four years for nothing. I learned a little along the way. I learned that you judge people by who they are on the inside and not their circumstances."

"Aldris told you," I said, downhearted.

She looked at me and cradled my face. "Let me ask you this: do you care about Aldris?"

I smiled brightly and nodded. "Yes, I really do."

"Then, to me, that's all that matters. I know that Aldris truly cares for you, and if you give it a little time, guidance, patience, and love, you'll see how much he cares for you too. That's the way Aldris is. He measures the heart of a person. He's a good son. We raised him well. He's strong enough to carry the burden for both of you because he's a man. That's why I don't worry about him. What you've done in your past to sustain a life for you and your daughter is no one else's concern because it doesn't matter that you fall down. It matters that you got up."

Overcome with emotion and grateful for her kind words that penetrated my heart, I hugged her tightly. "Thank you,"

"You're welcome." She patted my back before pulling back and looking at me confidently. "I believe we've yet to see how big and beautiful you will become, and if you know you are more than what they claim, why would you let two people who don't know you tell you any different? Now, dry your eyes, go inside, and handle your business. Mike and Rod are like sons to me, but they have their own issues, and they can't throw stones living in a glass house."

Her words were like a healing balm to my soul. Now I understood what Aldris had tried to preach to me this entire time. How could I doubt the genuineness of Ms. Lily when Aldris was a product of her? And she was absolutely correct. I tried so hard to gain approval, but the only thing I really needed to do was be me. I laughed to myself. Mike and Rod wanted to see Lucinda. They asked for it.

Now confident of my place and acceptance in the Sharper clan, I bossed up to go and give those two in there a piece of my whole mind. "Are you coming?" I asked.

"No, I'll be out here for a bit to give you all some time to clear the house. I'd love it if you would get Nadia and bring her over here, though, so I can meet her."

I smiled. "I can arrange that."

"And, Lucinda, if you plan on staying with my son, I need you to do some things for me. First, you've got to teach me those recipes so we can have cook-offs, and second, I wouldn't mind learning a few of those Spanish Fly dances either." She winked at me.

"Ms. Lily!" I gasped.

She moved toward me and leaned close to my ear. "Between you and me, I'm dating a man too, and if you were able to clinch Aldris—who I swore would be a rolling stone—then, honey, you are one bad mutha shut yo' mouth! So I need some tips," she joked.

"I got you covered." We shared the laugh before I hugged her again, and I strutted into the house where Aldris and Mike were going back and forth.

"And you're back again? Ms. Lily didn't run you off?" Mike sneered.

I put my hand on my hips. "As a matter of fact, she didn't. Regardless of what you think of me, I'm with Aldris, so you better get used to the fact that I am around."

Aldris pulled me to him by my waist. "Baby, you don't have to argue with these fools."

"It's no argument, baby," I corrected him, turning to face Mike and Rod with one hand on my hip and the other pointed at them. "You know what I think? I think you both wish you had a little Spanish Fly in your lives. Your babies' mamas ain't putting it down, and you mad because your boy gets all the perks without having to go deep in his pockets. Well, guess what? You may have had your little fun at Club Moet, but the only person reaping the benefits from this point on is Aldris. And trust me, I am just fly enough to keep him. So you two *putos* can kiss my entire Hispanic Spanish butterfly ass!"

Aldris laughed hysterically. "I guess now you can leave, bruhs."

"Whatever, man. You gon' wish you listened," Mike said as he motioned for Rod to leave before storming out.

Rod looked at me and shrugged. "I'm man enough to admit it. Yeah, I am jealous. Can't you just break up long enough for me to get one private dance?"

"Nigga, if you don't get the hell out of my mama's house . . ." Aldris yelled.

"My bad. Take care of it, bro, 'cause I'm honest when I say if you slip, I'm right there," he said, grabbing some cornbread before he left.

"Can you believe those two?"

"Can I believe you is the question," he said, turning me to kiss him. "I love the way that hood chick, as you can say, handled that. Got me feeling kinda horny."

"I guess that means you're ready to get caught in the Spanish Fly trap."

"I'm always ready," he laughed. "You and my mom straight?"

"Me and Ms. Lily are cool," I said, hoping it stayed that way.

Just then, his mom came into the dining room. "When are you going to get Nadia?"

Aldris looked at me.

"She wants to meet her," I told him.

"Mom, let's make it next Sunday. I've got to get Lucinda home," he said hurriedly.

"What's the rush?" she asked.

"Nothing. Just gotta get things ready for tomorrow," he answered, taking our plates to the sink in the kitchen.

She looked at me and winked. "Mm-hmm."

I laughed. "Stop it, Ms. Lily."

"You ready, Lucinda?" Aldris asked, pulling out his keys as I nodded. "Why are you two smiling?" he asked us.

"Nothing," we laughed.

He shrugged. "All right, Mama. I'll call you tomorrow."

"You call me too, Lucinda, so we can hook up on those . . . recipes." She hugged me then Aldris.

"Will do." I winked at her. "Again, it was a pleasure to meet you."

"Likewise, sweetheart."

Once in the car, Aldris lightly grabbed my hand. "You cool?"

"I'm just upset about your boys, but you can't please everyone."

"Exactly, and the only one you need to worry about pleasing is me. Trust me, you handled that so proper." He lifted my hand and kissed it.

It wasn't the perfect dinner as I'd hoped, but confession is good for the soul. I just hoped Aldris didn't get the notion to listen to his friends' warnings. I put on a good front like I was past the outcome because Ms. Lily and I were in a good space. But with his friends' negativity, how long could we really last? And in the back of my mind, I wondered, was I really right for Aldris?

Chapter Fourteen

Charice

The past couple of months had been hell trying to get over Lincoln, but I was getting better with it. I refused to answer any of his calls, and I deleted every text, voicemail, and email I received from him. It was hard enough dealing with my emotions, let alone to have them continuously stirred up by following up Lincoln's bullshit. He'd broken up with me, so I was done. It was time for him to be done too.

Part of the reason I was doing better was because thus far, I'd had an amazing summer with my kids. We'd been to different water and amusement parks, museums, and shopping outlets. The other part of it was because of Ryan. He'd been with us for a few of the trips, and he was really keeping my spirits lifted. He'd done so much for me that it was unreal. He'd even given Lincoln a cashier's check to pay for the Range Rover. He'd been my friend and listened to me when I wanted, comforted me when I needed, and gave me advice only when I asked.

He paid all of my bills, since I'd quit my job thinking I was going to be a housewife for Lincoln, and he told me not to worry about working. He liked that I was at home and able to tend to the children. We'd grown really close, and I could honestly say he had turned into one of my very best friends. We'd really become a true family. So much so that we'd decided to have a family barbeque at Ryan's parents' house so we could all spend some quality time with Ryan before he headed to training camp.

My dad and Ryan's dad, Jimmie, were manning the grill while the women threw down in the kitchen.

"I already took the hamburgers out there to my dad," I told Ryan's mom and my mother. "You know he and Mr. Jimmie ain't doing nothing but shooting shit to each other while they cook on the grill." I laughed.

"Those two are a mess," Ryan's mother said.

Ryan walked into the house from the back double doors. "Those kids were going to beat me down if I didn't get that inflatable waterslide up and operating. Finally, I have that huge contraption together!"

I giggled playfully. "Ooh, sounds like fun."

He walked up behind me. "I can always put you in my lap, and we could slide down together," he said in my ear.

"Boy, quit fooling around," I laughed at him as I slightly turned and slapped him playfully on the shoulder.

Glancing back, I noticed our mothers soaking up the banter between Ryan and me, and I knew the interrogation was about to begin.

"Charice, are you ever gonna give my baby a chance?" Ryan's mom asked.

Right on schedule. "Dang, Ms. Debra, you ain't waste no time asking me that question," I joked.

"Hell, I want to know. I don't know what's wrong with y'all young people," she fussed.

"I just prefer to get over one thing before I jump into something else," I said sadly.

"Ma, don't pressure her. She's been through a lot," Ryan insisted.

"And that 'lot' has to do with Lincoln Harper, and if I get my hands on him, I'm gonna make him pay," my dad said, bringing in a tray of hot dogs.

Consoling my dad, I rubbed my hand on his arm. "Daddy, don't get upset. This is a fun day."

"Yeah, Mr. Taylor. You don't need to get worked up over that clown. Besides, I just want us to enjoy our family before the season kicks in," Ryan added.

"Don't worry, we will. Go ahead and enjoy your family, baby," my mom said. "The rest of us are going to stay out of y'all's business." She glared at my dad and Ryan's mom.

They both silently consented even though I knew they didn't want to. With that, I went with my mom and dad to play outside with the kids. After being damn near soaked from being on the waterslide with the kids, I came back in to get a towel. On my way to the bathroom, I heard Ms. Debra's voice coming from the living room.

"When are you going to tell her?" she asked Ryan.

"Ma, I don't know how. Charice is still going through a lot, and I don't know if I can just dump this on her right now," Ryan explained.

I walked into the living room. "Tell me what?"

Ryan and his mom looked up in shock. "Uh, Charice. I didn't see you standing there."

"I gathered that by your comments. Tell me what?" I asked in confusion as I wrapped the towel around my waist.

Ms. Debra put her hand on Ryan's arm as if to encourage him. "I'm sorry. I should've waited to discuss this," she said to him.

Patting her hand, he forgave her for opening an obviously closed conversation. "It's all right, Mama."

"Okay, I'd really appreciate it if someone would get to talking around here. I'm getting a little nervous, and I've come to the point in my life where I do not like surprises," I said, slightly irritated.

"Ma, will you excuse Charice and me for a moment? I should talk to her," he asked.

His mom excused herself, and Ryan waved me into the room. "Come over and sit down."

"I think I'd rather stand."

Ryan came over, grabbed my hand, and walked me back over to the sofa. "It's not that terrible. Just have a seat." We both sat, and he leaned forward, clasping his hands together.

"Ryan, you're scaring me a little bit."

He put his hand on my knee. "Don't worry, Ricey. It's just difficult for me to come out with this."

"Come out with what?" I asked him. "You know you can tell me anything," I coaxed, gently rubbing the top of his hand.

He smiled, raised my hand, and kissed it. "That's why I love you even to this day." He exhaled as he prepared to tell me what was on his mind. "I, uh, I got an offer from the New York Giants. If I take it, I'd be the highest-paid running back in the league. It's good for my career, and the Giants are in a good position for the playoffs this season."

Not being one for this whole buildup, I forced him to get to the point. "What are you telling me?"

"I took the deal. I'm moving to New York to be a Giant."

My eyes nearly popped out of my head. I was completely blown away by his news. "New York is so far away. Dallas was too, but at least the kids and I have gotten to know the city, and I was looking at moving there eventually. The kids have gotten so close to you, and you're going to New York? Wow."

"That's what's got me. The kids, you, and I are so close now. We're like a real family, and I hate to break us up, so I was thinking and hoping that maybe you would consider moving with me to New York," he asked sheepishly.

Was he serious? He'd just knocked me in the head with the news that he was moving, and now he wanted me to pick up and move from one end of the country to the other? My mind scrambled as I tried to take in exactly what he was asking. "Move? All the way to New York? With you?" I repeated in shock. "That'd mean uprooting the kids from the only place they know to a place they know nothing about. What about our parents?"

"No shade, Ricey, but I've literally been away from my parents for eight years. So my moving from state to state isn't an adjustment for me or them. Besides, there isn't a place on earth that our parents wouldn't travel to see their grandkids. You know that as well as I do. I'm sure they will miss them, but distance isn't going to stop them," he countered. "You can even keep the house you have here in Atlanta. I'll pay it off, and I'll buy you one up in New York," Ryan coaxed.

"I don't have any friends or family in New York."

"But you'll have me and the kids."

"And I'm supposed to live in that city by myself?"

"Then move in with me, and let's be a family," he pleaded. "Damn it, Ricey. I love you. I'm not Lincoln, but I do love you. Haven't I shown you how much? You and I could start over, and you could learn to love me again. I'm patient. We could start slow, but I really want you to be with me in New York."

Silence trapped my voice. It was all too much for me. I was still reeling over the foolishness with Lincoln, and I didn't want to be unfair to Ryan. Part of me loved him, but partial love was not complete love, and I felt strange thinking of living with Ryan when I knew I wasn't giving him my all.

Suddenly, there was a knock on the front door. "Do you want to get that?" I asked him.

"No, Leilene will get it," he said, referring to his parents' maid. "Charice—" he began, but we heard a commotion coming from down the hall as Ryan's parents and my parents came rushing in from the backyard. "What the hell?" Ryan stood to see what was happening.

Suddenly, Lincoln appeared in the living room and jacked Ryan up. "You son of a bitch," he yelled angrily and punched Ryan square in the face as all the ladies screamed in horror.

As if someone unleashed caged animals, my dad and Ryan's dad instantly ran in to jump on Lincoln. "You bastard! You think you're gonna beat up on my son?" Ryan's dad yelled as he grabbed Lincoln.

"Oh, and you definitely catching it for my daughter," my dad yelled and punched Lincoln in the stomach.

"Stop it! Stop it right now," all the ladies yelled as we tried to maneuver around the three-on-one melee.

As if in slow motion, my attention turned to Ryan Jr., who'd run in from outside with a panicked expression. "Mom!" he yelled.

"Stay back, Ryan," I screamed at my son.

"Something's wrong with Charity," he cried out.

Without question or a second thought, I ran toward the backyard with everyone else in tow behind me. I couldn't move fast enough as I ran outside and saw Charity unconscious in the grass.

"Oh my God! What happened?" I asked Ray, who was crying as he sat by his sister.

"We don't know, Mama. We were just playing and running, and she just fell down. She didn't run into nothing, and she didn't hit her head. She just fell down, and she won't wake up," he said between sobs.

I picked up her head and elevated it. "Come on, baby. Wake up. Sweetie, please," I screamed as Ryan kneeled down next to me.

"Charity," he hollered. "Come on, princess. Get up," he said frantically with tears streaming down his face.

"I'm calling 911," I heard Lincoln say. "Yes, please send an ambulance quickly. There is a six-year-old little girl. She's passed out, and we don't know why. . . ." His voice trailed off as he walked away

"Oh God! Charity!" My body was numb as I sat there, holding my baby's lifeless body. She had to be okay. She had to.

It seemed as if time ticked on forever. For the past hour, I stared at the time on the wall. My lips were parched, and my throat was dry from screaming. I didn't even have tears left to cry. I was weak in my body and in my mind. Nobody spoke a word, breathing was all to be heard, and I was numb. Everything happened so fast. When the paramedics arrived, Charity had a faint pulse and was barely breathing, but she was alive thanks to Ryan's split-second decision to start mouth-to-mouth resuscitation. A whole hour later, I knew about as much as I did when we got there. Nothing. Just that my only daughter was in the hospital at the mercy of doctors we didn't know, ailing from an unknown sickness. The only refuge I had was Ryan's powerful arms wrapped around me and the fact that my family and my girls were waiting with me.

"Mr. Westmore and Ms. Taylor," the doctor called out, walking into the waiting area. Everybody stood. "Can I please talk to you two in private?"

Scared yet hopeful, we walked over to the nurse's station with him. "What's going on with our daughter?" Ryan asked point-blank.

"I'm Dr. Wellington, and for now, your daughter is conscious and doing all right considering her ordeal.

After consulting with cardiology, we've discovered that she has a condition known as congestive heart failure, which basically means that her heart can't pump enough blood to meet the needs of her body," he said, explaining the diagnosis.

"Oh my God," I wailed, falling into Ryan's embrace.

"How come this wasn't detected sooner? She goes to doctor's appointments," Ryan asked angrily. "What does all this mean? What's going on with her?"

"Well, the symptoms of CHF are very common and present as other illnesses. Has she had any cases of shortness of breath or anemia?" Dr. Wellington asked.

Lifting up from Ryan's embrace, I nodded. "Yes, she takes iron tablets for anemia. She's been anemic since birth. Sometimes when she plays, she gets short of breath, but it was never anything severe."

"See, that's what I mean. The onset of the disease seems sudden because she appeared to be a normal, healthy child."

"Does this mean she's going to be all right?" Ryan asked.

"For now she is. In her case, her heart has become enlarged in order to try to increase its pumping power, but her heart just couldn't take the added stress anymore," the doctor explained.

"Why did you say for now? Do you know who I am? Tell us what we need to know and what I have to do," Ryan demanded angrily.

"I really shouldn't go into details because we have our head pediatric cardiac surgeon coming to explain more in-depth," he whispered and pulled us to the side out of the earshot of hospital staff. "But I'll tell you this. She needs what's called an intra-aortic balloon pump placed inside of her heart to help circulate the blood, but this solution may only be temporary. Please do not quote me on this, because cardiology would need to do a final confirmation, but I want to be completely transparent with you. Depending on the severity of her condition, the balloon pump may be it or just the beginning. The most extensive scenario would be that your daughter may need a heart transplant," Dr. Wellington confided in us.

At that moment, my heart shattered in a million pieces. This news was beyond devastating. It was downright sadistic. The only question in my mind was why. One minute we were having a celebration as a family and the next, tragedy. This had to be a nightmare, but as I pinched myself, the pain let me know that it was indeed real.

Ryan held me close and tight as I collapsed against him again and cried, "Oh my God, Ryan."

I was wrapped in his powerful embrace, and he kissed the top of my head as I felt the wetness from his tears dampen my hair. "It's okay, Ricey. I've got you. I've got us. She's going to be just fine. She's a trooper. We're going to make it through this. Just be strong for her, okay?" Ryan consoled me, then refocused his attention on the doctor. "Look, you get that surgeon down here immediately, and if she needs a heart, you get her on the top of that transplant list. Spare no expense. I will pay for it out of pocket, because I'm walking my little girl out of this hospital, do you hear me?"

"He'll be down right away, Mr. Westmore. But let's try to be optimistic. Hopefully, a transplant will be a null conversation. We'll take it one step at a time to ensure that Charity receives the best viable solution we have to offer. If you'd like to see your daughter, you can, but she's very weak, and she's connected to several machines to help stabilize her. Try to be as calm as possible so as not to alarm her and potentially cause more damage to her heart," Dr. Wellington said.

"Yes, please take us to our baby," I managed to say between sobs.

It was like nothing I'd ever seen. Charity was hooked up to every gadget imaginable. She looked pale, frail, and lifeless. She wasn't the 6-year-old little girl I saw this morning, and that made it real to me. I felt myself on the edge of a nervous breakdown. I couldn't lose my daughter after all I'd been through, but as much as I wanted to break down, I had to be strong for her.

As Ryan and I sat down beside her, she opened her eyes, and I held her hand. "Charity, Mommy and Daddy are right here, baby, and we're not going anywhere."

"I was so scared," she whispered hoarsely.

"Don't be, princess. Daddy is here to protect you," Ryan assured her.

"I love you, Mommy and Daddy."

"We love you too," we said in unison.

After about ten minutes, Charity dozed off, and Ryan went to explain everything to our family and friends, who'd been waiting patiently in the lobby. Everyone came by to see her and console Ryan and me. Lincoln stopped by to see her as well. He apologized for the commotion he caused and vowed to give us our space to tend to our daughter. We'd all called an unspoken truce for the sake of Charity.

Over the course of the week, Ryan and I spoke numerous times with the head pediatric cardiac surgeon, Dr. Nichols, about the severity of Charity's condition. Based on the results from the tests they'd run, it was deemed that it was imperative that she have a transplant as quickly as possible. As upset as I was about her condition, the blessing in it was that her medical case was being sent to the review boards, and she had a very good chance of being placed at the top of the list. Hopefully she wouldn't have to suffer long, especially with her life hanging in the balance. The transplant surgery was going to cost us a small fortune, but that was nothing compared to her life. I was just thankful that we were in a position in our lives to foot the bill.

Meanwhile, I'd completely immersed myself in taking care of my daughter. Ryan tended to the boys, and he was there every day, taking care of me. With her illness, every day that passed was an uphill or downhill battle. It seemed every time she appeared to take one step forward, something would happen to push us two steps back. It felt as if I were going to suffocate, but at long last, we got the news we had been waiting for—Charity was at the top of the transplant list. That joy was short-lived, though, because while she was at the top of the list, she still needed a donor who was a match to her. I tried to be the optimistic one since I was constantly around Charity, but it was so hard to do when it seemed as if I was just watching my daughter's life slip away without being able to do a damn thing about it. On top of everything else, Ryan was preparing to leave for training camp, and while he had to go, I needed him with me so badly.

"What about camp? When does it start?" I asked him as we ate in the hospital cafeteria.

"I'm leaving the week after it starts so I can be here for you and Charity," Ryan informed me before placing his half-eaten apple back on his plate and leaning back. He wiped his hands on his napkin before placing the crumpled-up paper onto his plate and clasping his hands together atop his head. "I feel so bad and so fucking helpless right now, Ricey."

"You're doing great. You've held this family together beautifully. If it weren't for you, I would be no good to Charity. Just keep holding on." I grabbed his hand to re-assure him of how wonderful he'd been.

Ryan looked at me through his tears. "Her condition is getting worse."

"We have to think positive—"

"She needs a transplant soon," Ryan interrupted.

"I know!" I belted. "I know," I said more calmly as tears found their way to my eyelids.

Ryan grabbed my hand. "I'm scared to leave you all here alone. If anything happens and I'm not here, I'd never forgive myself."

I scooted my chair over to him. "Nothing is going to happen. We'll talk to you every day, and I have Skype on my phone. You already have permission to leave when they find a donor. But I need you to be strong for me. Play and train like you never have before, for us." I leaned my head on his shoulder.

He kissed the top of my head. "I needed that so much."

"When you get back, I hope you have enough energy to pack boxes." I glanced up to find him staring down at me in confusion. I grabbed his hand and turned sideways in my chair to face him. "I thought about it, and I've decided I want to move to New York with you. But if I move with you, we move as a couple and not separated. Life is too short, and I'm not going to spend my life looking for what I already have in you."

Excitement burst through him, and he jumped for joy like a lit firecracker and pulled me out of the chair and hugged me tightly. "I love you, Charice. I love you so much."

"I love you too, Ryan," I said, and we kissed passionately.

When we broke our kiss, the few people in the hospital cafeteria clapped and cheered, and we left to get on the elevator to go check on our daughter. Once inside the elevator, Ryan dropped to one knee.

"What are you doing?"

"I don't need to wait and go through this dating process to know that you're supposed to be my wife. When you move to New York, please move as my fiancée. Charice, will you marry me?"

Without a moment of hesitation, I whispered, "Yes."

My immediate answer must've thrown him for a loop. He repeated my answer for clarity. "Yes?" he asked for reassurance.

"Yes!" I exclaimed.

He stood up and hugged me. "Um, I'm going to say goodbye to Charity for just a little bit because I have to go ring shopping," Ryan said excitedly as the elevator doors opened.

Everyone was ecstatic about our engagement, from our parents to our children. I won't lie. Even though I loved Ryan, I still had lingering feelings for Lincoln, but life is about making tough decisions. Never again, no more would I be any man's doormat. The father of my children had proven he was a fully grown man capable of loving me the way I needed and wanted. He wasn't faking it, and he wasn't doing anything for show. He stood by me through my ordeal with Lincoln, and he'd been beside me through our ordeal with Charity every step of the way. He did his dirt in the past, but he'd more than made up for any wrongdoings. I figured if he could still love me after I was blinded by Lincoln, then I could do the same. We were a family, and now it would finally be official.

Chapter Fifteen

Trinity

It was beyond time for Terrence to figure out what he planned on doing about us being together, because I sure as hell couldn't take no more of Pooch. It figured that now that he acted the way a real man was supposed to, I would loathe him. Like right now, I was trying to leave the house, and he kept rubbing and kissing on my belly as if I were even showing. All I had was a firm little pouch, and he acted as if I was ready to give birth. *Negro, please.* Part of me wanted to yell right in his face that the baby he worshipped wasn't his.

"What's up, little man?" Pooch said, breaking my thoughts.

"It could be a girl," I said plainly.

Pooch shook his head. "Nah, babe, he is definitely a boy. I can feel it," he said, gliding his hand across my belly.

"Can you please leave me alone so I can go and get Brit and Terry?"

Pooch pulled back hands in the air. "A'ight. Dang. I was just trying to bond with our baby and shit."

Feeling bad about my rough outburst, I softened my tone. "I know, but I just want to get there so I can come back."

Hearing that I was in a rush to leave Terrence's and get back to our house brought out all thirty-two of his pearly whites. "Yeah, do that, because I need some of that special attention," he said, rubbing on his dick.

That was another thing I was tired of: giving hand and blow jobs. "I thought you had some things to get together for the Crown brothers," I said, hoping he'd be too busy to remember.

"I do, but I always have time for you." He kissed my cheek.

"A'ight." I turned, rolling my eyes as I grabbed my purse and phone. "I'll be back."

This sentimental Pooch was on my last nerves. It's funny how I would've welcomed this just a few short months ago. Now I loathed everything about him. I swore it pained me to see him breathe in my direction.

My soul literally felt lifted the moment I parked beside Terrence's truck. I wished I were coming home over here every day. As I made my way to his apartment, I noticed right beside Terrence's truck was a tight-ass black pearl Cadillac Escalade sitting on at least twenty-sixes. I wondered who the hell had rolled up in this area in some shit like that. *Dope boys,* I thought, shaking my head. I swore them types of niggas were everywhere. I swore on my life I was gonna teach Brittany and Princess not to get caught up with niggas like Pooch.

"Hey, baby. What's up?" Terrence greeted me as soon as I stepped into his apartment. We kissed, and then he kissed my belly.

"Same ol' shit, different day. I was meaning to ask you . . ." My conversation stalled when I saw some dude I'd never seen before standing in the kitchen. "I'm sorry. I didn't know you had company."

"He was getting ready to leave. This is my cousin Thomas from Illinois. Thomas, this is my babies' mother, Trinity. He's the one I was telling you about who wanted our kids to go up to Illinois and spend some time with his kids."

Thomas eased from his seat on the barstool in the kitchen, came over, and shook my hand. "It's nice to finally meet you. I've heard so many good things about you."

"Oh yeah, that's right." It finally dawned on me who he was from a previous conversation with Terrence. We shook hands. "Now I remember. Please forgive me for being rude. I didn't know Terrence had family visiting. However, it is good to finally meet some of his kinfolk from Illinois who he brags so much about."

He stretched his arm out with the palm of his hand raised, letting me know that it was cool. "You're fine. I was just passing through and stopped by to check on my big cuz." He turned back to Dreads. "Well, bruh, I'm about to head back to my side of the country."

"A'ight, man. I appreciate the love." Terrence hugged him.

"That's what family is for. To make sure everybody is straight."

Terrence and he moved back from their one-armed embrace, nodded at each other, and slapped hands together, forming a fist. "Be easy out there."

"No doubt," he said as they walked to the door. "See you later, Miss Trinity."

I waved my goodbye as Terrence saw him out the door. He stepped out with him, and a few moments later, Terrence returned inside, then walked back over to me as he packed up the kids' overnight bag. "I'm almost done getting their things together."

"You planning a trip or something?" I asked, getting upset.

"I'm thinking about planning one for the kids."

Frustrated, I threw my hands up. "What happened to what we got going on here? You're supposed to be making a way for us. How you gon' do all that and you jet setting around the country?"

"I got that under control. Don't worry."

"That's easy for you to say. You don't live with Pooch," I whined, crossing my arms.

He wrapped his hands around my waist and pulled me close. "Don't I always come through?"

I nodded. "Yes, but—"

"But don't worry. When I say I got you, I got you. Just hold out a little while longer, and I promise you that everything you want is going to happen." Terrence palmed my cheek.

"What's your plan?"

"Baby, let me worry about the plan. You worry about taking care of yourself, the baby inside your womb, and our other children. That's all you need to worry about. But I will tell you this: the day I call you on your cell and tell you it's time to make moves, don't question it. Don't drag your ass. Just get moving."

Suddenly, my stomach lurched, and I sat down. "Okay, you're making me nervous."

"Don't be nervous. Just keep Pooch thinking everything is everything between you two, and when that time comes, just do exactly as I've told you," Terrence said as he finished packing the bags. "Okay?"

"Okay," I agreed, unsure of what the hell was really going on.

"I've got to go down the street and grab the kids from Skeet's house. They are playing with his kids."

Grabbing his hand, I gently pulled him back with a seductive grin. "Well, wait a minute before you do that."

Returning my gaze, he whispered huskily, "I know that tone in your voice."

"Uh-huh. It's feeding time."

He patted his stomach and licked his lips. "Daddy is kinda hungry," he said as I lay on his sofa and spread my legs.

I didn't know what the hell Terrence had up his sleeve, but for some reason, regardless of the fact that I had no clue what was going on, I felt everything was truly going to be all right. I figured that I was probably better off the less I knew. As of now, I was going to lie back and enjoy the hell out of my Dread's head game.

Chapter Sixteen

Lucinda

I'd never thought I'd see the day that I was financially stable, in college, and had the man of my dreams all at the same time. But I did, and it still didn't seem real to me. I'd watched the movie *The Pursuit of Happyness,* and I had to admit I felt when Will said, "Maybe happiness is something that we can only pursue, and maybe we can actually never have it. No matter what."

After the catastrophe at Aldris's mom's house, he tried to reassure me that everything was kosher, but how can you reassure someone who'd always fallen short of having all the things they wanted? It wasn't from lack of trying, because besides being my man, he was my best friend. He made me want to be an all-around better person, and we fit hand in glove, but I still had difficulty believing that all of this was completely mine. It was like I was in a dream, waiting to wake up to my reality.

All of this was on my mind as I sat up in my bed, trying to do my homework. Obviously unfocused, I decided to take a break. Checking my mail, I nearly pissed my pants when I opened a letter with regard to Raul's child support. After a three-month stint, he'd been released, and a total amount of $2,950 had been deposited into my child support account, which included his arrearage and the last three months' pay.

"What are you smiling about?" Aldris asked me as he put down his copy of *Black Enterprise* magazine.

"Raul is out of jail, and I am $2,950 richer," I laughed.

"What? For real?"

"Yep," I confirmed.

"Well, it's about time that fool made a move. He honestly thought he was getting out of jail without taking care of his responsibilities. He is a damn fool. I just don't understand it. Nadia is a beautiful little girl, inside and out, and I would love the honor of calling her my daughter," Aldris said.

His warm words immediately tugged at my heartstrings. "Aww, baby. You know just how to melt me." I kissed him.

Still with his lips grazing mine, he spoke, and his lust was evident. "Are you done with your homework yet? Because I don't know how much longer Mandingo and I can wait with you looking all sexy in those shorts and kissing me like this."

"And I can't wait for Mandingo either, *papi*. He whips me good every time. But if I don't finish this homework, my professor is going to whip me too," I joked.

He groaned and kissed my neck. "I love it when you call me daddy. I guess I can hold out a little while longer. I don't want to interfere. I remember how it was when I was in college."

"So, that's why you won't do my assignments for me?"

"Uh, yeah. Once was good enough for me," he joked.

"Oh, you got jokes," I laughed. "Yeah, but seriously, I better hurry up. It won't be too long before I have to get Nadia from Ms. Ana's house. I'm going to the kitchen to get a bottle of water. Do you want anything, baby?"

"Just you," he said, kissing my shoulder.

This man knew just how to make me blush. "You'll definitely have that. Just give me about thirty minutes,"

I teased before I got out of the bed and headed for the kitchen.

On my way back, there was a knock on my front door. Doubling back, I answered it, and lo and behold, it was Raul. "I hope you got what the fuck you wanted," he spat.

"Yes, I did. Just like you got what the fuck you deserved," I spat back, crossing my arms. "Why are you here?"

"The court said I couldn't apply for a reduction of child support right now. Seeing as how I don't have no job, I don't see myself paying child support until I get one, so you need to work something out with me," he said boldly.

No, the fuck he did not. I was flabbergasted for a moment as he stood there looking like the epitome of "if 'you got a nerve' had a face."

"You ballsy muthafucka. You got yourself fired for that bullshit you pulled at my job, and you know what? You got me fired too, so on the real, I ain't hearing nothing you saying!"

"You better hear me, or you won't get nothing," he mouthed off.

"Oh, so you looking for more jail time, huh? That can be arranged. You must like being Pedro's *puto* because that's where you're headed if you don't pay me. You better get it the same way you came up with it the first time. 'Cause you gon' run me my coins," I fussed with one hand on my hip and the other in his face.

"Shanaya got her moms to cop it for me. She is a real chick. She's down for me like four flat tires. I should've left you alone and dealt with her from the start. She knows how to be a good woman," Raul blasted.

"And just how does a no-good-ass man know when to recognize a good woman?" I laughed at him. "You need to get yourself together, but as far as the child support goes, I want every penny of my $350 next month and right on time."

Raul grabbed my arm. *"Dios maldita!* Now, you listen here, you bitch—"

Suddenly, I was pulled backward. "What the fuck do you think you're doing?" Aldris yelled in Raul's face. The next thing I saw was Raul flying backward. Aldris had knocked the hell out of him.

"Who the fuck are you?" Raul asked, stumbling to his feet as he held his eye from the blow.

"Don't worry about who the fuck I am. Just know this— your days of harassing Lucinda are over. The only contact you need with her about Nadia can be done through the courts," Aldris said to him.

Raul laughed. "Who the hell died and made you God?"

"Nobody, but I suggest that if you don't want to see God before your time, you leave Lucinda alone."

"Is that a threat?"

"No, muthafucka, that's a guaranteed promise."

Raul laughed. "Oh, I get it. You're supposed to be her new man. Lucinda wants to run into some nigga's arms now like that shit is supposed to help. Let me put you up on game, nigga. I don't give a fuck who you are—"

"No! Let me put yo' ass up on game," Aldris boomed, and Raul shut his mouth. "Lucinda is my lady, and I ride for mine. You don't know me, and I don't really give a fuck about you. But what I do need you to know is that I have connections everywhere. Your child support judge, Judge Cutliff, he's my cousin, and I have plenty of friends down at the jail, including your arresting officer."

Raul got extremely quiet and swallowed the lump in his throat.

Aldris scoffed and clapped his hands one time. "Yeah, I thought that'd shut you up. So this is what I'm saying to you, pa'ner. Make your payments, be on time, and most importantly, leave Lucinda alone, or that bid you did in county will be a cakewalk compared to what will be done to you if you have to go back. So, nigga, are we clear?"

Raul looked at him nervously and then back at me. "Yeah, whatever, man."

"Good. Now get the hell away from here," Aldris said.

"Fine. But there is something I think Lucinda should know."

"No, you should know that you gon' need something to put on the shiner that my man just blessed you with," I snapped, standing beside Aldris with my arms crossed.

Raul huffed loudly and felt his eye, then looked at me with a smirk on his face. "When I go back in a few months for my reduction, I'm adding all of my children. Expect to get your money reduced."

"You're stupid. Judge Cutliff already accounted for Doodlebug and Raulina."

Raul's sinister laugh told me that I was about to be hit with some news I wasn't expecting, and he most definitely delivered it.

"Well, the joke is on all of you, because I have two more kids. I have another five-year-old and one on the way. I plan on including them too and taking care of them."

"Shanaya is pregnant?"

"Nope, the new baby and the five-year-old in question have the same mama, but it ain't Shanaya, and it ain't Boop." He smirked. "Oh, and the next time you talk to your pops, tell him I said congratulations. Y'all be easy," he said and walked away.

Aldris shut the door. "Can you believe that fool?"

Before he could turn around good enough, I was in his arms kissing him. "What's that for?" he asked, staring down at me.

"For being my man. The way you handled Raul was so, so . . . sexy. I loved it, *papi*," I said, holding him about his waist.

"I told you that you'll never have to worry about a thing anymore. I'm going to take care of you because you're my baby."

"I see. I'm just wondering where this thug came from. I'm so loving your gangsta right now."

"Don't let the degrees, the *GQ* outfits, or the sex appeal fool you. I'm a man, Lucinda, and if anybody tries me on that, they get dealt with. You're my lady, and it's my duty to protect you and Nadia. And that, my baby, is exactly what I'm gonna do." Immediately, I slid out of my shorts. He rubbed his hands together. "What are you doing?"

"Saying fuck homework. I got some other kind of work to put in," I said while I slid his boxers down.

"*Ay, mamacita,*" he moaned as I began to massage him down below.

We kissed passionately. Then, Aldris said the one thing to me that made our relationship complete. "I love you, Lucinda."

Instantly, I melted. *Confirmation.* For the first time, I knew without a shadow of a doubt that this was where I was supposed to be. Regardless of Raul, our different upbringings, or his friends' opinions, this was where I was supposed to be. All I could think about was Will Smith's line in *The Pursuit of Happyness:* "This part of my life . . . this part right here? This is called 'happyness.'"

Chapter Seventeen

LaMeka

Ever since Misha confessed that she knew she was HIV positive, I had been a nervous wreck. I still didn't know if I had the virus. I hadn't slept or eaten right over the past couple of months, but I knew I had to pull myself together for her and my kids' sakes. In order to keep my mind off of it, I plunged headfirst into bettering myself, helping Misha, and raising my boys. You'd think that by being around my sister, it would further remind me that I may be suffering the same fate, but actually, it didn't. My concern was so much for her and learning how to battle this disease that I didn't have time to worry about myself.

In fact, we were bettering ourselves as a family unit. With the help of Pastor Gaines, my mother, sister, and I formed a tight bond, and I had to say my mama was doing her damn thing. Well, both of us actually. We'd both taken the GED test, so not only did Misha get her high school diploma, my mom and I got our GEDs too.

Pastor Gaines's counseling had begun to transform our mom into the mother we'd always wanted as well as the mother we needed. We went to church together, we ate dinner together, and we prayed together. We did everything together. Pastor Gaines even helped my mother land a job as the manager for this consignment shop, which she loved, while Misha was set to start Piedmont Tech in the fall. She took a page out of Lucinda's book and wanted to be a medical coder, but I thought she was more hooked on the bank that Lucinda was making than the job. Using a scholarship from the church and a grant, I enrolled in college to start my nursing program, and I was overjoyed about it. Despite my situation, not everything was all bad in my life.

I still hadn't heard from or seen Tony since that fateful night, and I was happy about that. Word on the street was that he was bouncing from crackhouse to crackhouse straight zooted up. He was so far gone at this point, I doubted he even remembered me or his kids. The sad part was I wanted him to forget he ever knew me, and maybe somehow the hurt, anguish, and yes, even love I still had in my heart for him would somehow disappear. I found it completely crazy that after all he'd put me through—the verbal, mental, and physical abuse—and possibly giving me a potentially deadly disease, I still loved him. I guessed if you truly loved someone, you never really stopped. That's not to say that I would ever take him back—that was a guaranteed hell no—it just meant that one day I hoped he was able to get his life together before it was too late for him. Regardless of our differences, he had two sons who needed a man in their lives.

Pastor Gaines was a perfect example. I admired him and looked up to him as a father figure for myself, but little boys need their daddies just as much as they need their mommies. I did a great job as a mother, but I couldn't train my sons to be men. A real man could teach their sons how to be men, and that's real talk. There was just some shit about men that I would never get, and if I didn't get it, then on some level, my sons would not get me. That's why they needed Tony, and if Tony could get clean just long enough to see that truth, I bet he'd realize he needed them just as much.

That was, if he lived to raise them. I wasn't just speaking about the risks of his drug abuse. I was talking about if I didn't kill him myself if these results came up positive.

"Are you nervous?" my mom asked me.

"Did I not throw up twice before we left?"

She gripped my hand. "Don't be nervous. God will sustain you."

"So says the woman whose HIV test came up negative." I rolled my eyes at her.

"LaMeka, how can you be a positive force on your sister, who already has this disease, if you can't even be positive for yourself? There is a fifty percent chance that you could walk out of here free and clear, and instead of you holding on to that, you're acting as if you've already been condemned to die. I understand you're frustrated and anxious, but please try to remember those who no longer have that glimmer of hope, like your sister," she huffed as we sat there waiting for the results.

She was right. Here I was throwing my own pity party, and my sister— God bless her soul—was already living with it. She absolutely amazed me. You'd think she'd give up hope and be miserable, but she hadn't. She was so happy about the positive changes in my life and in our mom's life that it kept her going. She even volunteered to do advocate work for local groups about HIV/AIDS awareness. I was proud of her. I was proud of my mom. Hell, I was proud of me. So regardless of what I heard today, good or bad, I was going to walk out of here with my head held high and live my life. My life was not going to end just because of my circumstances. I made up my mind that from that moment on, if I had it, HIV would be living with me and not me with it. Point blank period.

"Are you ready for your results, LaMeka? They are conclusive," the doctor said as she entered the room and broke my train of thought.

I looked at my mom, clasped her hand, and nodded. "Yes."

She opened the report and scanned over it. "Ms. LaMeka, you are negative," she announced.

A gasp of relief belted out from me as my mother yelled out in joy and hugged me tight. Tears of joy slid down my face. "Are you sure? I'm negative?"

The doctor smiled at me and nodded. "Yes, I'm sure. You do not have HIV," she repeated gladly.

I didn't know what else she was trying to tell me, because I fell straight to my knees and began praising God as if I were in Sunday morning worship service. My mom joined in right along with me as we just thanked and praised Him. I wasn't sure if the doctor thought we were crazy, but she just let us continue to get our worship on. She didn't have a choice, because I was just like old shoutin' John at this point. Hold my mule! I had too much to be thankful for to not recognize Him for His blessing. I literally danced on death's doorstep, so for this, He was more than worthy to be praised. Once I finished, she gave us some tissues and finished discussing preventive measures. She gave me a copy of my results and sent us on our way. No sooner than we got in the car, Misha called me.

"What was the result?" she asked as soon as I answered.

"Negative."

She hollered with joy. "Thank you, Jesus!" she yelled. "I knew you were okay. I just knew it!"

"How are my boys?" I asked, immediately thinking of them.

"They are fine. LaMichael just lay down for his nap, and Tony Jr. is watching cartoons in here with me."

"Good. I just want to come home and be right up under my boys, you, and Mom," I said as my mom looked over at me and smiled.

"Yeah, we have to celebrate. Oh, and you got some mail that looks really important. I think it's from the State of Georgia," Misha said.

"What in the world could that be?"

"I'm not sure," Misha answered.

"Oh well, I'll see when we get there. We'll be there in like ten minutes."

My mom and I talked all the way to the house about what we wanted to do to celebrate. When I got there, I immediately hugged Tony Jr. and Misha. We all sat there laughing and talking until I remembered the mail. Misha handed me an envelope from the Social Security Administration, and I nearly fell off the sofa when I read it.

"What is it?" my mom asked me.

"Yeah, Meka, what's wrong?" Misha asked with a worried expression on her face.

I looked up with joy in my heart. "Not a damn thing."

I turned the paper around so they could see the source of my happiness. The state had revisited Tony Jr.'s autism case and had awarded him another lump sum disability payment. I wasn't rich by any means, but this money meant three surefire things for me. One—Pooch was getting paid in full immediately. Two—I was taking a page out of Charice's book and investing. Without Tony pulling me down, I would make this money work for me so that by the time I moved out of the transitional house, I could pay cash for my own house for my boys, my mom, my sister, and me to live in. Three—having this money and investing it meant guaranteed health coverage for Tony Jr. and Misha.

Misha and my mom jumped up and down and celebrated, and I just relished their joy. Never again, no more did I have to worry about my family's well-being. For once, everything was all right. Everything was all right.

Chapter Eighteen

Charice

Since Ryan's departure, I rotated my time away from the hospital with my mom and Ryan's mom so that I could spend some time with my boys. I realized through this ordeal that I'd kind of abandoned them, and I didn't want them to think I loved them any less because of Charity's condition. However, I'd underestimated my boys, because they truly understood. Hell, they wanted to spend the night with their sister too. There's just something about life-threatening situations that change everyone. Even the children matured suddenly.

Being in the hospital had taken a toll on me, though. I was tired all the time, and I was in desperate need of some R and R. One day, the ladies got together and gave me a huge surprise. We did a half a day at the spa, and then they treated me to lunch and purchased me an outfit and a pair of shoes.

"Hey, lady," they greeted me as they came into the hospital room.

"What's up, y'all?" I hugged each one of them, happy to see them, and then they all hugged Charity and played with her for a little bit.

"How are things?" I asked them.

"Aldris and I are wonderful—" Lucinda started out quickly.

"Oh, please, don't nobody want to hear about Aldris today. That's all I ever hear anymore is Aldris this and Aldris that. Let it go, Lu," Trinity said to her.

"Well, forgive me, *por favor*. I'd think you'd be happy for me, but I guess you're just hatin' on my situation because you're still stuck in yours," Lucinda shot at Trinity.

"Come on, you guys. This is not the place for petty arguments," LaMeka said to them.

Charity giggled softly. "My aunties are so funny, Mama."

"Pay them no attention." I rubbed her forehead.

"Anyway, we came by because we have a surprise for you, cuz," Trinity said.

"And just what might that be?" I asked them.

"Since we haven't officially celebrated your engagement and you need a little break, we figured we'd take you out," LaMeka answered.

"Oh, thanks, but I can't. I have to stay here with—"

"Oh no, you do not have to stay. I'm going to be here. You go and get some 'me' time," my mom said, coming into the room.

"See, Ms. Charlene says so. You know we were going to come prepared. So let's go, and let me see the size of the rock on your finger," Lucinda said, staring down at the two-carat diamond set in a platinum band. "Ryan did good."

As they gushed over the rock, I blushed before I bragged, "Yeah, I love it too, but it's a temporary ring. My boo is getting a ring custom made. It's going to be called the Charice Original."

"Damn!" they all said in unison, including my mother.

"Shit, if that's only temporary, then he should've just given you a Cracker Jack box ring," Trinity said smartly.

"You're right, Lu. She is a hater," I agreed.

"See," Lucinda said, pointing at Trinity. "Stop hatin'."

"Heck! He has the money, so why not?" LaMeka added. "He can do what he wants."

"This new 'Christian' LaMeka is so aggravating," Trinity said.

"We should've left your pregnant, whiny, fussy ass at the house. How's that for my Christianity?" LaMeka took a dig at Trinity.

Everyone burst out laughing, including Trinity, who put her hands up in surrender. "I'm sorry. You guys are right. My issues, coupled with this pregnancy, are really bugging me lately. I promise to be on my best behavior," Trinity apologized.

"Good. Now let's go," LaMeka said.

I hugged my mom and Charity and left to enjoy my day with them. When I returned, I was so refreshed and relaxed. I didn't realize how much I needed that "me" time, if for nothing else but to restore my energy for Charity.

Reminiscing on that day, I realized that little bit of R and R came just in time. Within a few days, we finally got the call we had been waiting for. Ryan was in the middle of training camp when the good news came. To say we were overjoyed was an understatement.

"Baby! They have one!" I yelled into the phone. "They have a heart for Charity!"

"I'll be on a plane today. Oh God! Thank you! Hey fellas, we have a donor," he yelled to his teammates. Afterward, all I could hear were thunderous applause, hollers, and well wishes.

"When is the surgery?" he asked.

"The transplant team and Dr. Nichols want to run some more tests to be sure Charity is still a good candidate for the transplant. The heart is being airlifted here as we speak."

"I'm on my way out of the stadium. Once I get some things together, I'm outta here on the jet, but I will be there before the heart does. I promise you that," Ryan guaranteed.

"Okay, baby, be careful."

"I will. I love you, baby."

"Me too," I said and blew a kiss into the phone.

Finally, all of this madness was coming to an end so that Charity could be on the road to recovery. Ryan made it home just in time for the doctors to discuss her risks of surgery and after-surgery care. We were so excited but nervous at the same time because there were so many risk factors involved, but I refused to worry about that part. I just wanted the surgery to go well so that I could bring my baby home and we could live our lives as a family in New York.

"Everything is going to be fine," I told Charity. "Daddy and I will be right behind this window, and we'll be waiting for you when you come out, okay, sweetie?"

She nodded. "Yes, ma'am."

"I love you, Charity. I love you so much. Be strong, princess," Ryan said as he held her in his arms.

"I love you too, Daddy," she said. "I love you too, Mommy."

"I love you, too." I kissed her forehead.

"I'm happy you're getting married," she said out of the blue.

Ryan and I looked at each other, surprised to hear her mention anything about our nuptials. "Thank you, sweetie," I said to her.

Ryan Jr. and Ray came and played with her, and then our parents came in. Everyone got their chance to visit with Charity before the surgery, and then it was time. Ryan and I gave her one last hug, and then we headed into the observation room as they rolled her into surgery. I could hardly contain my tears as I watched them crack open my daughter's chest like she was a damn egg about to be fried for Sunday breakfast. The scene before us was graphic, but after fighting the administration to allow us to view the surgery, Ryan and I endured for Charity's sake.

The surgery was going fine, and then all of a sudden, after the team disconnected the bypass machine, the donor heart wouldn't beat, and she began to flatline.

"Oh my God, Ryan! What's happening to our baby?" I screamed while he held me.

"It's okay. She'll come back. She will," he said as if trying to will her to pull through from behind the glass.

Soon, a nurse ran into our observation room and told us to wait outside, and a massive curtain began closing, blocking our view of anything going on in the operating room.

"Why? What's going on?" I asked frantically.

"Ms. Taylor, please just wait—"

"What the hell is wrong with my baby?" I screamed, interrupting her.

"Please, Ms. Taylor, I have to get back inside," she practically begged me. "I'm not doing Charity any good being in here. Please."

"Come on, baby," Ryan conceded as he lightly tugged at me, and we left the room.

Ryan and I waited for about thirty minutes before Dr. Nichols and Dr. Wellington came inside the waiting area where we were located. By the time he got there, I was a nervous wreck. My eyes were red, and my hands were trembling.

"Dr. Nichols," I shouted and rushed up to him. "What's going on?" I asked frantically as Ryan put his hands on my shoulders.

"Please tell us what's going on with our princess," Ryan asked more calmly.

"Ms. Taylor, Mr. Westmore, I'm so sorry. The surgery went as planned. However, once we disconnected the bypass machine, we were initially unsuccessful at getting the heart to start—"

"What are you saying to us?" I screamed.

Dr. Wellington took over and grabbed my hands, moving me to sit down beside him. With tears in his eyes, he said, "Charice, I'm so sorry. We were able to resuscitate Charity. However, she went into cardiac arrest. After the second attempt, she was gone for a long time—"

"What the hell are you saying to us, Dr. Wellington?" Ryan urged, his voice cracking from emotion.

Dr. Wellington took a deep breath. "We were able to bring her back, but she's suffered a lot of trauma due to the lack of oxygen going to her brain during that time. She's fallen into a coma, and she's on life support. She's in a very unstable condition, and right now, all we can do is watch and wait. I am so very sorry."

"Nooo! Not my baby. You're lying to me! Not my little girl! She fought so hard. You can't be telling the truth," I screamed at him as a river of tears slid down my face.

Ryan tried to console me between his own sobs. "Can we see her?"

"We're wrapping everything up and preparing to take her back to ICU. You can see her then," Dr. Nichols said. "I have to go back in to assist, but I want you to be prepared. The donor heart is beating, and right now, there aren't any signs of rejection, but she's very weak, and her condition doesn't look promising. I truly hope that she can pull through, but it's all in God's hands at this point," he explained before leaving.

"There will be no loss! Charity will not die! I refuse to believe that! No way," I screamed on the brink of hysteria.

"At this point, it is out of our control. All we can do is wait," Dr. Wellington said, trying to bring a sense of calm. "Perhaps I can prescribe a sedative for you," he said, patting my hand in a feeble attempt to console me.

"I don't need a damn sedative. I need to see my daughter and know that she is all right. That's it. She will not die. Do you hear me? Nope, not my daughter," I said belligerently.

Dr. Wellington looked sadly between Ryan and me. Ryan placed a hand on Dr. Wellington's shoulder and nodded to him. "I'll talk to her, Dr. Wellington." Ryan excused him. Dr. Wellington gently rubbed my back and shook Ryan's hand before exiting.

"Don't tell me you believe them," I said to Ryan.

"What I believe is neither here nor there, but we have to face this together, Charice. There is a possibility that Charity isn't coming back—"

"She'll come out of the coma. You'll see. You'll all see," I wailed as I rocked back and forth.

Ryan nodded. "Okay, baby. She will," he said and kissed my forehead. "I'm going to talk to our parents and friends."

It'd been a week since the surgery, and I was sitting at Charity's bed, holding her lifeless hand and praying for a miracle. I hadn't eaten solid foods because everything came back up. The only thing that I'd taken for sustenance was broth and water to keep me going. But I stayed right there, only moving to use the bathroom or shower. *Jesus, if you rose Lazarus, why can't you wake up my daughter?* Even though she was on life support, her other organs were beginning to fail. The doctors said she had very little brain function, and with her failing organs, they said she was most likely not going to wake up. I refused to believe that, though. Everyone had given up hope on Charity. My parents had made their peace with it. Ryan's parents, our kids, our friends, and even our reverend had said a prayer giving her spirit back to the Lord, but not me. She had to wake up. If she didn't wake up, then I'd surely die right behind her.

I looked up as Ryan came into the hospital room immediately following an interview he'd done. Despite the obvious stress on his face, he looked good in his crisp Tom Ford suit. His Rolex and Super Bowl ring gleamed as he approached me, taking off his suit jacket.

"Hey, baby. I'm just sitting here waiting to see some kind of movement or something. It's going to happen. Just look at our miracle. We're together." Finally focusing in on him, I complimented him. "You look good. Did the interview go well?"

He smiled and kissed my forehead. "The interview was fine, and yes, our rekindling was indeed a miracle."

"Pull up a chair and sit with us. Maybe telling her stories will stir her so she can wake up and prove these airheaded doctors wrong," I said to Ryan, and he pulled up a chair.

He rubbed my hand between his. "You know I love you, don't you?"

"Yes," I replied confidently.

"And I hope you know how much I love Charity," he added.

I looked over at him. "Of course I do."

Ryan got quiet for a moment as he reached for and rubbed Charity's hand. He leaned back, and tears began to form in his eyes. "Maybe God is punishing me for being absent so my years by doing this. I don't know."

I hugged him for what seemed like forever. "No, God isn't that cruel. He sees the change in you."

Ryan was quiet for an extremely long time as he shed silent tears, gripping Charity's hand while holding me in his other arm. Afterward, he pulled away and wiped his eyes. "I guess you're right. Whatever He does, He does for a reason. He doesn't make mistakes."

"That's right," I concurred.

Ryan turned to face me and palmed my cheek. "If you believe that, if you truly do, then do you believe that He didn't make a mistake by taking Charity home to live with Him?" Ryan asked me. "I mean, she suffered so much in this world—"

"Don't say that to me." I snatched my hand away and pushed his other hand from my face. "I refuse to believe that."

"Ricey—"

I jumped up. "Don't Ricey me! How dare you! You're her father! You're supposed to fight for her until the end!"

Ryan jumped up. "And I did," he boomed and clasped my shoulders with his powerful hands. "This is the end—"

"No, it's not!"

He leaned over to her and pointed. "Look at her, Charice! Look!" he yelled tearfully, but I refused. By now, tears poured down both of our faces. "All of her organs have shut down. Is this what you want for her? To be sustained by a machine? Tubes hanging all over her body instead of letting her rest in peace?"

"I just want her to wake up," I yelled, beating against his chest repeatedly. "Just wake up," I cried.

Ryan held me, and I slid down into his arms, crying hysterically. He patiently rubbed my back while rocking me back and forth to comfort me. Once I'd finally calmed down and our tears were no more than whimpers, Ryan sat and placed me on his lap, cradling me in his arms as if I were a baby.

"She did wake up . . . in heaven," he whispered, his voice drenched in pain. "Our princess is now our angel, and we have to let her go, Charice. We have to let her go to her heavenly home."

The finality in his words pushed my heart and head into a reality that I'd struggled hard not to accept. An ugly cry unleashed from me and racked my body. Ryan held me tightly, rocking me back and forth in his power-ful arms until my tears subsided. Once I finally removed my tearstained face from his chest and looked up at him, he kissed me all about my face and head to comfort me as his eyes leaked tears and his lip quivered.

I could tell that this was shredding him into pieces. He'd been there for me, the boys, our family, and no one had been here for him. He'd had to suffer in silence while being the pillar for us all. All the while doing the one thing that I'd finally had to come to terms with. I moved out of his lap and sat down in the chair beside him, then looked at Charity. He was right. She was gone, and this was no life for her to live. The reality was that if Ryan was having this conversation with me, then he'd also been forced to have it. There was no way that he'd agree to broach this subject with me otherwise.

The time had come to let her go.

"How long do we have before we have to say goodbye?"

Ryan leaned forward with his elbows on his knees, his fingers pressed together, and his head bowed. He released a deep sigh as he wiped his tears. "I met with Dr. Wellington yesterday. Since Charity hasn't shown any signs of improvement and continues to get worse, they are giving us until midnight tonight to voluntarily remove the life support."

Hearing that our last day was tonight caused my eyes to drip again. There was no choice but to accept reality. It was time to say goodbye. "Did you gather the family? Is everyone outside?" I asked him. Unable to speak, he could only respond with a nod. "Then let them all come in and say goodbye," I permitted.

One by one, each family member and friend came in and hugged Charity. My girls had come with their kids. Even a few of Ryan's teammates and Lincoln had come down to say goodbye to her. Each one had tears in their eyes. They gave us hugs and condolences as they left to wait in the waiting area for that time.

"Sweetheart, do you want us to stay with you and Ryan when it's time?" my mom asked in tears.

"No, we need to do this alone."

After everyone cleared out, Dr. Wellington, Dr. Nichols, some nurses, and the reverend came in with Ryan and me. The reverend said a prayer first, and then Ryan and I said our goodbyes.

"You'll always be my princess warrior," Ryan said to her and kissed her forehead. "I'm so sorry I haven't always been there for you the way I should've been. That will forever be my greatest regret. But I thank God for the moments we had. I want you to know they are forever priceless to me. You're the light of my world, and I love you more than words can express. Baby, Daddy needs you to rest for a while until I can be with you again. Have a tea party and play with Barbie all day in the sun. And remember you're golden. And please put in a good word for your old man with the Man Upstairs. I love you for eternity and even past then." He kissed her again before turning away.

Before he walked to the side, I pulled him into an embrace to replenish a little of the strength that he'd given to me. His shoulders slumped, but he held it together just like the real man he was. He refused not to be strong in this moment for us.

Once we released each other, he moved to the side, and I made my way over to our baby girl. "Charity, please don't think you disappointed anyone. You fought so hard. Having you as my daughter was the greatest blessing that God ever gave me. You made me better, baby girl. Because of you, I'm a better mother and woman, and I thank you so much for all you added to me and to this world. But your time on this earth has come and gone, and you made every moment your best. I will always love you, and I will never forget you. You're always and forever my baby girl. Make sure you keep a spot in heaven open for me, your daddy, and your brothers. One day we'll be together again. I put that on everything I love. So, little Miss Charity McKenzie Westmore, I release you back to heaven, my angel, because God loves you best," I said full of tears as I hugged her.

Dr. Nichols went to move toward the machine to prepare to disconnect the life support as the nurse moved to escort Ryan and me out of the room, but Ryan stopped him. "Dr. Nichols, can we stay to observe? I mean, that's if you want to, Charice."

I agreed because I understood why he asked. Deep inside both of our hearts, we hoped she'd just pull through once it was removed. They granted us permission to stay, and with our consent, Dr. Nichols began shutting down the machines that kept our daughter alive. Soon the constant beep turned into a flatline tone.

"Time of death: 7:01 p.m.," the nurse called out, and all that could be heard was the bloodcurdling sound of my screams as I lost my child . . . my only little girl.

Chapter Nineteen

Trinity

How could you tell the measure of a man? How he acts when faced with adversity is a reaction from his soul. I pondered that a lot lately. It had seemed weird as hell that I went to church with LaMeka and heard Pastor Gaines preach those exact words, and the following week I watched as Ryan proved exactly what the pastor had spoken. No matter what beef any of us might've had with Ryan in the past, watching him be such a man for Charice at my little cousin's funeral was nothing short of amazing. It's funny that I hated him for the majority of the time I even knew him, but as I watched him hold up Charice and embrace her with such love and support, I had nothing but admiration for him. He not only held her together, but the boys as well. He was truly their rock.

It was the first time I actually felt that she made the right choice in choosing to marry him instead of trying to work it out with Lincoln, but I was shocked to see that Lincoln was also in attendance. He played his role and stayed in the background, never bothering Ryan or Charice but mourning Charity's life just the same. His face was drenched with tears, and I couldn't figure for the life of me how a man who claimed not to want this woman was still so dedicated to what was going on in her life.

As I looked around at all of our men when we were at the funeral, I knew exactly what Pastor Gaines meant. Pooch went out of town on "business" the day of Charity's funeral. How was that for a supposed boyfriend? But it didn't matter. I didn't want him to come, and I was sure Charice and Ryan appreciated his absence as well. No need for Ryan's rep to be ruined by saying he was affiliated with the local drug lords. Of course, Dreads was right beside me, supporting me the way a real man should.

If there was one thing I knew for certain, it was that Charity's death put a lot into perspective for me, and in a lot of ways, I guessed, it did for all of us. I was completely decided that come hell or high water, I was getting the fuck away from Pooch. This lifestyle was no way to raise a child. Hell, it was no way to live for a decent human being. I just wanted to finish school and raise my babies. I didn't want to have to worry about whether my man was going to one day end up in prison or, worse, dead.

As a matter of fact, I didn't want my kids or me to end up being a victim to somebody with a grudge or just trying to come up. Their lives meant more to me than what I gave them, so when Dreads asked me to let the kids stay with him for a little while, I let them. With Dreads, they were safe, and he had their best interest at heart.

He wanted them to visit his great aunt Beatrice in Illinois for the remainder of the summer just to get away. I didn't mind, because they needed to experience things besides this thug life. I just told Pooch the kids were staying with Terrence, and I didn't volunteer any further information. He was probably just happy not to have them around the house at all. Truth be told, I wished I were with them. At least I wouldn't have had to look at this fool and wish I were somewhere else. But what I did know was that if Terrence didn't make a move quickly, I would, whether or not it meant playing with fire.

I was enjoying one of the rare days when Pooch wasn't around by lying on the sofa and watching a good movie on Lifetime while Princess played in her playpen. When I thought about it, it was kinda odd that Pooch wasn't here, especially since on Friday nights he'd usually be at home up under me by now, and if not, he'd always tell me ahead of time why he wasn't. I wasn't even gonna question it, and I thanked God for the small favor, because I was having a peaceful time with no kids fighting, no upset stomach and sickness, and no Pooch.

"Aww, girl, go on and kiss him!" I shouted at the Lifetime movie while dabbing my eyes with a tissue. "Damn movies get me so emotional," I fussed as my cell phone rang. I hit ignore so I could keep watching my movie, but the damn thing rang again.

"Ah," I huffed. "Who the hell keeps calling?" I looked at the display and saw it was Dreads. "Oh, shoot. Hello?"

"What are you doing?" Dreads asked.

"Watching Lifetime, why?"

"Turn it off. Time to roll."

"Huh?" I asked in confusion.

"Pack a bag, quickly, Trinity. Enough clothes for a couple of days and fuck the rest. Grab Princess and anything of importance to you, and be by your front door in fifteen minutes," he instructed. "I have to go now, but I'll see you soon."

Without further conversation, he disconnected the line, and I did just what he said. I didn't ask a single damn question. I went to Princess's room and grabbed three packs of Pampers, a box of baby wipes, her travel kit, and about ten outfits. Then, I went to Brittany's and Terry's rooms but found out all of their favorite things were gone already. I remembered the kids asking me for them before they left, but I didn't think a thing of it at the time.

I went to my room and grabbed my Louis Vuitton luggage and packed as many of my favorite items as I could. I grabbed all my jewelry and my stash of fifty grand that I'd gathered from Pooch over time. I grabbed my little file box from the back of the closet that had all of my important papers like our birth certificates and my photo albums. Just as I was hauling everything down the stairs, my doorbell rang. Terrence's cousin, Thomas, stood at my doorstep when I answered.

"You ready?" he asked me.

"Where's Dreads?"

"Waiting on us."

"Grab this stuff while I get my baby and her sippy cup."

"Cool." He loaded the bags and was back by the time I got back to the door with Princess, along with her snacks and sippy cup.

"I'm ready," I told him.

"Good. I have a car seat already," he said.

"What's going on?" I asked as soon as we got in a Suburban. "Dreads told me this day was coming, but why the hell are we sneaking like thieves in the night?"

Thomas laughed. "That's a good one."

"Sure is," I heard a man's voice say, and I jumped. I saw Big Cal when I turned around.

"What the hell?" I asked, getting nervous.

"Sorry," Big Cal said. "Don't be afraid. I'm not gonna hurt you."

Thomas looked at me as I sat there, scared shitless. "I know you've got a lot of questions, and we're gonna answer them for you."

"You two know each other? Where is Terrence?" I asked, my voice full of fear.

Big Cal smiled at me. "Meet my brother, Thomas."

"Your brother? But I thought he was Dreads's cousin."

"I am," Thomas said.

"And so am I," Big Cal told me.

Confused, my face held a screw-faced expression. "This don't make no sense."

"You were introduced to me as Thomas, but you probably know me as Tot," Thomas said to me.

All of a sudden, I looked at them, and a slow smile crept onto my face. "Y'all muthasuckas been setting Pooch up!"

"'Setting up' is such an ugly phrase. We prefer the phrase 'serving justice,'" Big Cal laughed.

"I still don't get all of this," I said to them.

"You will," Thomas assured me. "Trust me, you will."

We drove into this nice neighborhood where the uptown condominiums were being built. Thomas pulled into a parking spot and blew the horn twice, and soon after, Dreads walked out, looking fly as hell with a duffel bag. He got in the back and kissed me.

"What the hell is going on, baby?" I asked him as we pulled off.

He gave Thomas and Big Cal pounds and then wrapped his arm around my shoulders. "I know you got a lot of questions, and I'm gon' answer them all, but first watch this," he said to me as he pulled up the monitor in the front seat and turned to the news.

A few stories passed on the evening news, and then they got to the major story of the day. "Today, Police Commissioner Bobby Franks, along with Police Chief William Settles, in a joint effort with the drug task force, have arrested thirty-five men in what is being called the biggest drug sting operation of the decade. Alleged members of the infamous drug organization known as DBC or the Dope Boy Clique were arrested and charged. The alleged head of the organization, Vernon 'Pooch' Smalls, was arrested and charged with a long list of allegations, including drug possession, distribution, and intent to distribute, and first-degree murder for the deaths of

LeVerneus Sims and five others. Several businesses, including Smalls Tires & Rimz and Club Moet, have been shut down and employees detained for questioning. Two police officers, Detective Lee Hines and Sergeant Calvin Rowe, along with one judge, the Honorable Madison Liable, have resigned due to allegations of connections with the Dope Boy Clique. Charges against these three are pending an ongoing investigation. We'll have more on this story tonight at eleven and updates as this story develops," the anchor said, and they moved on to the next story.

I covered my mouth in shock. "Dreads, what happened? That was your arresting officer and your judge."

"Sucks to be Pooch." Terrence shrugged. "See, you asked me a good question that I wasn't ready to answer one night. Actually, it was the night we conceived this little one," he said, reaching forward and rubbing my stomach. "On the way back, you asked me how I got caught being as good as I am at dodging trouble. Well, li'l mama, I didn't get caught. I got set up, and it was all because of you."

"Because of me?" I asked, pointing to myself.

"Yep. I was pushing my own weight and getting my shit from the best connects—"

"The Crown Brothers," I interrupted as it dawned on me where I'd finally heard that name from. The Crown Brothers used to be Terrence's connects.

He nodded. "Yep. Your boy Pooch got pissed that my game was tight. I didn't need all those soldiers, and I damn sure wasn't trying to rule the world. I was about gettin' that bread so you and my babies would always eat. And that bread I was gettin', I just didn't floss. I was stackin' my shit proper so I could get out of this shit and be straight, but Pooch was pissed about that and about the fact that I had you. Only thing is your boy wanted you a little more than I anticipated. Remember when he asked you to leave me after Terry was born?"

"Yeah, but I never took Pooch serious until after you got locked up."

"That was my one miscalculation too. He got me on some trumped-up charges and had my case padded so I'd take a serious fall," Terrence explained.

"That's where Sergeant Rowe and Judge Liable came in," I realized.

"Exactly," Terrence said. "I'll never forget that night in the warehouse. I knew some foul shit was going on when I met my contact and he called me by my real name. I rushed dude to confront him, and it all went so fast." Terrence zoned out as he began to reminisce over his story.

"'Freeze! APD! You're under arrest!' officers, DEA, and special enforcement agents from the narc squad yelled.

"There was a blaze of fire and smoke as police and both sides busted their cannons. Skeet had my back, fending off the Feds as they made their way through the warehouse while Rome cleared the way, picking off as many of the suppliers' henchmen as he could to get out.

"The back door was cleared as Rome made his way out, but the red dot on my chest caused Skeet to pause and both of us to look up. Visible was the drop-off's gun, which was aimed directly at me. Quick with the trigger finger, Skeet let off one round, instantly putting his ass to sleep.

"'Freeze!' Sgt. Rowe yelled out.

"'Fuck, man!' Skeet said to me.

"'Look, man, only one of us can make it to the back door. You go.'

"'Fuck that! You got kids—'

"'No time. You been in prison before, and you done caught at least three bodies. That's life, my nigga. Go,' I yelled. 'Go, muthafucka!'

"With regretful eyes, Skeet gave me a fist pound and ran for the door as I stood with my hands over my head. I had money saved up, and it would be my first offense. With my attorney, I just knew I could beat the case easily. At least, that's what I thought.

"When Sgt. Rowe walked up to me and said, 'Terrence Marsh, you're under arrest,' all I could do was zone out as the cop Mirandized me. All I could think about was getting home to you and my babies and praying that I could get out of that with little to no time at all. But Pooch had other plans for me."

The reality of what had actually happened hit me like a ton of bricks. "Oh my God. You mean to tell me the whole time I thought this bastard was trying to rescue me and my children, he was really the reason you were taken from us?"

"Yep, li'l mama. I'm afraid so." Terrence nodded.

A rage burned inside of me. As I viewed the news report, part of me wanted to feel sorry about the shit storm Pooch was in. But now knowing this bastard had plotted on me from the jump and set up my man, I was happy as fuck that he was going down.

"How did you find all this out?" I asked.

Thomas piped up then. "That came through me. See, Pooch contacted me because he thought I was Terrence's connect. That's how we kept it so niggas wouldn't be in our business. Thing was, he didn't know Terrence was my cousin, and I kept it like that. I knew that grimy bastard had something to do with him getting locked up, and it was a matter of time before I found out, which I did. So I hooked T up with the info."

"You were a part of the plan?" I said, turning to Big Cal.

"Yeah. My real name is Aaron, by the way. I came down and made my way up through Pooch's ranks to his right-hand man so I could get next to him to bring him down," Big Cal explained.

"Who y'all got on the police side to bring him down?" I asked. They looked at each other and laughed.

"Let's just say Big Cal is more than just my cousin," Terrence said as Big Cal showed me his shield. "He's undercover."

"Damn, y'all raw. That's how you got your sentence reduced," I said, looking at Dreads, and he nodded.

"And you got the missing bricks?" I asked Dreads as I finally put everything together. He pointed at me, indicating that I was correct.

"Not that he needed it. My cuz already has plenty," Thomas added. "And well, one setup deserves another," Thomas joked.

"You already have plenty?" I asked, looking to Terrence for clarification.

"Yes. I told you I was investing in proper shit for all of us."

"What you saying?"

Thomas laughed and interjected. "Let me just say that your man is straight, and so are all of us."

"Straight as in six-digits straight?" I asked, remembering that Pooch was sitting on at least a seven-digit operation by himself.

Dreads looked at Thomas and Big Cal and gave me that ever-sexy smirk. "Nah, baby. Straight as in eight-digits straight, and it's all for you and my babies."

I almost choked on my own spit. My Dreads, my baby daddy frontin' with the brick mason job and the old late-model truck was a fuckin' multimillionaire? It didn't seem possible, but I knew it was true. Dreads had been baiting Pooch since before he got out of prison, and not only did he take his shit, he brought down Pooch, his family, and his entire organization. Dreads was certified hell. Told you if that nigga had gone to college, he would've been hell to deal with.

"Where are we going?" I asked Terrence.

"We are going to Illinois. With all the heat in Atlanta, we can't go back there. I don't want Pooch putting shit together or finding out about us. He gonna be looking for you, so we gon' have to take on my dad's last name and take some other precautions that I'll explain later. In the meantime, you gotta get your contact list, but ditch that phone, and your contact with your girls needs to be limited and only through secured lines for a while," Terrence said.

"I got the police looking out for your mom," Big Cal told me.

"She gonna need to move," I told Dreads. I was scared for her and my siblings.

"Fo' sho. I got you covered. She knows we had to break and is already making headway to Illinois with your sister and brother. I told you, I got you," Terrence said, cupping my face.

"Dreads, I'm still a little nervous," I said to him.

"Don't be. Everything is going to be all right. Why don't you go ahead and back up your contacts on this chip and then take a nap? We have a good little drive ahead of us."

Without hesitation, I did what I was told. Then he took my battery out of my phone and threw it out the window. After a pit stop so Big Cal and Thomas could get some food, we got back on the road. I sat in the back seat with Dreads and lay across his lap, happy to be away from Pooch and to be starting my new life with him. Still, I was worrying my head off, because Pooch was slick as hell. I didn't want no demons in my past to invade my new life. It wasn't the things I knew that bothered me. It was what I didn't know. But for now, I was cool with the peace of mind I had knowing that Pooch finally got his and I got mine. I laughed to myself as I thought, *I bet you Pooch will definitely remember this shit.*

Epilogue

LaMeka

Six Months Later

"And that's it," I said as I removed the loosened band from the patient's arm and gently removed the needle.

"Nobody has ever been able to find a vein. You are good," Mr. Santiago said to me.

"Yeah, she is getting pretty good at this," Gavin, my instructor, complimented me.

"Thanks, Mr. Santiago and Gavin. I try."

"You're going to make one hell of a nurse, young lady. Best stick I've ever had," he laughed.

"Well, all right! You just wait right here. I'm going to get this blood work to the lab for you, and the doctor should be back in after that, okay?" I said, patting Mr. Santiago on his shoulder.

"All right, sweetheart. You can come back too, you know."

I laughed. "Are you getting fresh with me?"

"Is it working?"

"Absolutely," I joked. "You have a good one, Mr. Santiago, and I don't want to see you anytime soon. Stay out of the ER."

"Only if I can come back and visit you sometime."

"As long as we don't have to triage you, you're more than welcome to come," I giggled.

He laughed. "Have a good one, sweetie, and thanks for bearing with this old man."

Gavin and I walked out. "You really have a way with the patients, and your handiwork is fantastic. This is truly a gift for you," Gavin praised me.

"Thanks. I've always liked science and wanted to be a nurse. I finally feel like I'm in my mode, you know?"

"Yeah, you are definitely in your mode, but I wish you'd try to get in your mode with me."

My cheeks reddened from his blatant flirting. "Gavin, I told you. I don't know about all of that."

"It's just a dinner date."

"But I don't think I'm ready to start dating anyone just yet."

"Well, then drop the date, and let's just have dinner. That's not asking anything extreme. We all have to eat. It's for your nutrition and health," he coaxed, causing me to giggle.

Eyeing him skeptically, I pursed my lips. "I don't know what I'm going to do about you, Mr. Randall," I joked.

I'd only been there a little while, but already I knew more than most about Mr. Gavin Randall. He was my instructor in the ER where I did my clinical rotation as I worked on my degree. He'd been attracted to me from the start, though at first, he tried to keep it professional. His theory was that life was too short not to go after what you wanted, and what he wanted was LaMeka Roberts, hands down. I guessed he had a thing for girls with thick thighs and booty. I'd managed to lose my baby bulge, so I was thin up top with a flat stomach and skinny waist, but my thighs were still a little thick, and this Georgia-peach ass wasn't going nowhere. I had a permanent donk from LaMichael, but I didn't mind that. That was a Southern girl's thang.

Gavin was a cool man, though. Everybody loved him, and he was the best of the best when it came to nurses. He could've been a doctor he was so smart, but he said he liked being a nurse because he liked interacting with the patients and being hands-on.

He was single, had never been married, and didn't have children. His last relationship lasted two years but ended a year ago. They broke up because he wanted marriage and kids, and while she was for the marriage part, she didn't want any children. He was God-fearing and went to church faithfully. He had come from a single-parent household, but his mom passed away a few years back. What she couldn't provide for him while she was alive, she more than made up for in her death. Rumor had it that she left him and his brother a grip of money from her insurance policies. I believed it, being that he was pushing a Corvette, and ain't no nurses I knew balling around in Corvettes. His gear was fresh, and he stayed in the newest pairs of Nikes and Jordans, although that could just be from being single with no kids at 30 years old.

I ain't gon' lie. He was fine as hell. Six feet tall, muscular build with the prettiest light brown eyes I'd seen in my life. And Lawd did he smell good hella good. The kinda good that when you entered a room, you could still smell his scent even if he wasn't in there. We did have a lot in common. We liked the same gospel music. He was a big fan of Tye Tribbett, Da Truth, and J Moss just like me, and he also had a passion for dirty South rap just like me.

It wasn't nothing to hear him pulling up bumping a little old school Goodie Mob or even some Scarface.

And honestly, a lot of females wanted him. A lot. Nurses and doctors alike. He was just so fucking swaggeristic like that. Yeah, I said swaggeristic. It's my word meaning that you've got so much swag it's a part of your characteristic: swaggeristic. That was definitely Gavin Randall. It was also definitely why I didn't trust him. It was as if he had no flaws. Let him tell it, he had plenty of flaws, but your guess is as good as mine as to what they were. He was perfect. He seemed perfect for me, but was I ready to date again? More importantly, could I handle dating Gavin Randall?

"Is it because I'm white?" he asked me, breaking my thoughts.

"No. You know I don't even care about that," I said.

Okay, so I lied a little bit. Big deal. It wasn't the reason, but it was a concern, even if he was David Beckham fine with Snoop Dogg charm. Yeah, he was just like that.

"So, Miss Lady, if you don't care about that and we gel so well together, then why won't you give me a chance?" he asked me.

"I'm your student for one—"

"I can get you a new instructor," he cut me off.

"You better not even try it," I laughed.

"What's for two?" he probed, licking his lips like he was LL Cool J.

Those scrumptious-ass lips. I coughed to clear my thoughts. "Umm, two was, uh, yeah: we are good friends, and I don't want to mess that up."

"What friends do you know who don't hang out and go out to eat sometimes? I ain't never heard of dinner breaking up friendships unless somebody skipped out on the bill," he joked. "If it makes you feel better, we can split the tab. You pay for the drinks, and I'll pay for the food."

"Gavin!" another nurse hollered down the hall. "We need your help! We have a gunshot victim!"

"We'll finish this later. Let's rock and roll," he said as we took off down the hallway and entered the room.

The nurse gave us the details as we walked in. "Patient is a black male, twenty-three years old, shot twice—once in the leg and once in the back. He was carried in by two men in the waiting area."

"Are the police out there?" Gavin asked.

"No, I think they've been notified, though," another nurse said.

"Okay, we're going to lift him on three," Gavin called out. "One, two, three, lift," he called out as all of us moved the patient. Then the doctors rushed in.

It was my first gunshot victim, and I was nervous as hell. The sight was gruesome. Blood was everywhere, and his flesh smelled like it was burning from where he'd been shot.

"Anybody know the story? Any known allergies?" one of the doctors called out.

"No. The guys in the hall refuse to talk, and the victim was unconscious," the first nurse said as she prepared the saline and I helped Gavin gather the instruments.

When I turned to walk to the other side, I saw the man's face. It was Tony! "Oh God! You all be careful. I know this man. He's possibly HIV positive."

Gavin walked me off to the side. "Are you sure?"

"Yes," I said nervously. Gavin looked at me suspiciously. "Just trust me. I know him."

He nodded. "All right. Do you know anything else about him that'd be helpful?"

"He was a drug addict—cocaine and alcohol. He had surgery for his knee and has pins in the right leg. He's allergic to codeine."

"Okay, thanks. Since you seem to know him, go and see if you can find out any information from the two outside. Besides, you may be too closely related to this to work on him," Gavin instructed me.

I couldn't believe Tony had been shot, but I knew it was only a matter of time before his deeds caught up with him. It was the first time I'd seen him since he tried to kill me. It was ironic to me that the next time I saw him, he was fighting for his life after he'd tried to take mine. Part of me wanted to be happy, but the Christian in me was genuinely concerned for him. I'd always loved Tony and honestly wanted him to get his life together, and now his time to do that may have been up. As I began to approach the men who were pacing back in forth in bloodstained T-shirts, I heard Tony flatline, and instantly tears slid down my face.

Charice

"Make sure you boys are bundled up tight. I can't afford you all getting sick on me right now. Do you hear me, Ryan and Ray?" I commanded my boys as they put on their parkas and snow boots.

"Yes, ma'am," they said in unison.

"Shut the back door so snow won't get in the house," I added as I walked back into the kitchen.

"Something smells good," Ryan said after he walked into the kitchen.

"Yes, I put my foot into this lasagna, baby. It's almost done," I said, tossing the salad.

"I was referring to my lovely wife," he corrected. He walked up behind me and kissed me on my neck as he wrapped his arms around me.

"Why, thank you, baby." We kissed and I felt the impression of the rings on his hands. "You're really going to wear both Super Bowl rings?"

"At least for a little while," he laughed. "Are the boys getting ready so we can go outside and catch the last of this good New York snow and play some flag football?"

"Yes, they're putting on their parkas," I said and turned to face him and wrapped my arms around his waist. "You know, I say we should've made them take a nap and found something else to do to keep warm in this snow."

"Is that right?" he asked, wrapping his arms around my shoulders and leaning in for another kiss.

"Mm-hmm," I said as my mouth found his. We kissed passionately.

"D-scuh-ting," Ryan Jr. said, entering the kitchen.

Ryan and I laughed, and Ryan turned to his Mini-Me and started play boxing. "Shut up, boy. Just wait until you get a girlfriend."

"Yuck, Ryan has a girlfriend?" Ray came in and asked.

"No, your dad was just saying wait until he does," I corrected.

Ryan Jr. shook his head. "No way. Girls are crazy!"

"Yep, they are. Keep it that way," I agreed. "Now, all of you get out and do your thing before dinner is ready."

"All right. Who's ready for some football?" Ryan asked. The boys yelped in excitement, so Ryan grabbed his parka, and they all bounded out the back door.

I rushed to the oven to pull out the lasagna so it could cool down, and I was just about to put my breadsticks in the oven when I heard crying on the baby monitor. "It figures I wouldn't get a break for too long."

I washed my hands and rushed to the nursery. "Hey, Mama's baby," I cooed as I picked up my month-old little girl, Lexi McKenzie Westmore. Her middle name was dedicated to the memory of her older sister, Charity.

"Oh, you've made a stinky in your diaper," I said in my baby-talk voice. I cleaned her up, brought her in the kitchen, and sat her in the bouncer. Then I put one of her bottles in the warmer and put the breadsticks in the oven. I peered out the window and laughed as the boys ran and jumped on their daddy.

The pride I felt for my family made my heart swell. Ryan made a huge effort to keep us together after Charity's death, and with a lot of prayer, our marriage, and the love for our children, we'd done it. Not a day went by that I didn't think of Charity, but I made my peace with it more and more every day.

A month after the funeral, Ryan and I got married in a small private ceremony with only our parents and closest friends in attendance, and two weeks later, we were living in our new multimillion-dollar home on Murray Hill in Scarsdale, New York. I thought the move helped us out with the grieving process. It gave us a sense of normalcy when we didn't have to be met with all the tragedy we left behind.

Now that the season was over, Ryan vowed to devote every waking moment to the kids and me, and once school was out, we were going to take our honeymoon: a two-week vacation to the south of France, and I couldn't wait. Ryan and I had come full circle. It may have taken us years to find each other, but we had, and oh, how sweet it had been. The way that man loved me down was beyond any of my wildest dreams. I could've never imagined that after all I'd endured at his hands, he'd end up being the caretaker of my heart. And take care of my heart, he did. My heart, my mind, my soul—and my hot box was damn sure not hurting either. Indeed, everything I'd ever wanted and needed from Ryan he provided for me on a daily basis. Yes, I loved Ryan with my whole heart, and my life was blissful.

Just as I'd finished burping Lexi, I heard the doorbell. I laid her in her bassinette and ran to pull out my bread before I bounded to the front door.

"Note to self: extend the maid service through the weekends," I joked with myself on the way to the door.

"Who is it?" I asked when I didn't see anyone through the peephole.

"Lincoln."

My palms began sweating, and my heart plunged to my toes. I hadn't seen or heard from Lincoln since Charity's funeral. What the hell was he doing here in New York? How did he find out where we lived? And why would he be here even if he had a good reason to be in New York? My life was good. My marriage of five months was good. Why was he invading our lives again with his bullshit?

"Charice, I know that's you," Lincoln said, breaking my thoughts. "Please open the door."

Reluctantly, I pulled the door open. "What do you want?" I asked with my arms crossed.

"Hello to you too. It's nice to see you," Lincoln greeted.

"Lincoln, I do not have time for this. I have to finish dinner for my husband and my boys. Now how did you find us, and what do you want?"

"Nice," he said sarcastically. "How is your husband anyway?"

"He's great. You want me to get him so he can tell you for himself?" I asked with an attitude.

"There's no need." I heard Ryan say behind me. His footsteps quickened. "What the hell are you doing here?" he asked angrily. I stepped aside, and he stood face-to-face with Lincoln.

"You people sure don't believe in inviting people inside," he said, brushing off the snow that had collected on his trench coat. "Now is that any way to treat a former best friend and fiancé?"

"Cut the crap, Lincoln. What the fuck do you want?"

"Such hostility to an old friend." Lincoln smirked. "Oh well, since it seems I'm not going to get an invite inside, I'll be brief. I just thought I'd drop by to check on you all."

"Thanks. We're great. Now you can leave," Ryan huffed.

"You know, you should really be nicer to me if you expect me to block for you on the field, bruh," Lincoln said. He lifted a toothpick and put it in his mouth. His black leather gloves and black leather hat glistened with drops from the melting snow.

Ryan furrowed his brow. "What the fuck are you talking about?"

"Free agency is a wonderful thing, baby, and it looks like the Giants are willing to make a killer trade for me. Didn't you check my stats? My blocks and tackles were the highest in the league this year. Our QB was the least sacked the entire season. Had it not been for the injuries, I'm certain we would've made it that last game to beat you fellas to the Super Bowl. That's neither here nor there now. Why try to beat the best when you can just join them?" Lincoln gloated with a sneaky smirk on his face.

"Bullshit. They won't trade Parker—" Ryan was saying.

"It's a done deal. My salary just went up, my contracts are signed, and I'm house hunting. There's a for-sale sign about three houses down, and I'm meeting my real estate agent there in a few. We could be neighbors," Lincoln gloated.

"Get the fuck away from my house," Ryan yelled angrily. "If I catch you near here again, I swear to God—"

"Is that any way to talk to your teammate and neighbor, neighbor?" Lincoln laughed, cutting him off.

"What do you want?" Ryan asked through clenched jaws. I could see the anger welling up in him.

Lincoln's sarcasm faded, and his expression turned serious. "To let you know that I'll be in touch." He looked at me then. "Charice, it was really good to see you again. I look forward to catching up in the near future."

"I'm gonna whip your ass." Ryan moved toward Lincoln, but I grabbed his arm.

"I would not do that if I were you. If you hit me in my jaw, it might just come unhinged right now," Lincoln said with a wink.

I looked at Ryan. "What is going on with you two?"

"Nothing," Ryan said quickly.

"Have a nice Sunday, and enjoy your dinner. Oh, and you looking real good, ma," he said. He had a lustful look in his eyes as he shook his head and winked at me. Then he turned, got in his SUV, and drove away.

When Ryan closed the door and turned around, my hands were on my hips. "Do you want to tell me what that was all about?" I asked him angrily.

"No, because I don't know. He's just being stupid," Ryan said plainly and walked off.

"Ryan, something is going on, and I deserve to know what it is," I pouted as I followed him into the family room.

He ignored me and picked up his cell phone. "I can't deal with this now. I have to make a call."

Stomping in a fit, I demanded, "I want answers."

"Charice, please go and check on the baby," he said with aggravation. "You want answers, but we all have things we need to talk about when it comes to Lincoln, right?" he challenged.

Shame and hurt filled me as I bowed my head, too ashamed to speak.

"Shit, baby. Listen, I'm sorry—"

"Go to hell," I said angrily and turned to go get the baby, who had begun crying. I picked her up and rocked her. "It's okay," I soothed her.

I didn't know what the hell was going on between Lincoln and Ryan, but having Lincoln close by was not a good thing. He needed to be as far away from us as possible.

I placed Lexi back in her bassinette. "I swear you look just like your daddy. Let's just hope he doesn't ever come back to this house to find that out. It's bad enough he just got traded to the Giants," I said to myself, and I shook my head.

Lucinda

> *You Are Cordially Invited to Attend*
> *The Union of*
> *Ms. Lucinda Bree Rojas to*
> *Mr. Aldris Raymond Sharper*
> *on Saturday, June eighth at 5:00 pm*
> *Bethel AME Church*
> *Atlanta, GA*

The corners of my mouth turned upward, and I couldn't hide the blush that was radiating off me as I looked over my wedding invitations, which I'd just received in the mail. I simply could not believe that I was marrying Aldris. For the most part, everything in my life was perfect. I had my associate's degree and was going back for my bachelor's. Nadia loved Aldris, and more importantly, Aldris loved Nadia as his own daughter. To her, he was her daddy, and to him, she was his little *niña*. I was still doing well at my job, and Aldris had received a promotion. Between our two salaries, we were definitely straight in the finance department. I was best friends with my future sisters-in-law, and Ms. Lily and I were as close as ever, especially after I showed her a couple of little cute dance moves to put on her new beau, Mr. Franklin.

Aldris and his brothers weren't too thrilled about their mother having a boyfriend, but like I told Aldris, his mom needed a companion, especially now that all of her sons had their own lives. She was in her fifties, for Christ's sake, not her nineties, and she had plenty of life left to live and share with someone. My wish was that I could get somebody for my own mama. She was lonely, and she wanted to be back on the dating scene again. She needed someone in her life to offset the drama from my daddy. In fact, Raul and my daddy were still taking us through turmoil about child support payments, so even though I was happy, I still had drama.

Besides that, life as I knew it was great. I was on a euphoric high as I sat down on the sofa, holding my box of invitations with a big smile on my face, and I swore I was never coming down.

"Hey, gorgeous, what are you cheesing about?" Aldris said as he walked into our new house for his lunch break.

Once he made his way over to the sofa, I looked up and kissed him. "Hey, handsome. Our invitations came today. See?" I answered, giving him the box.

"Oh, these are nice. I like that," he said, admiring the invites as I opened up the rest of the mail. "What else do we have?"

"Can you pay my bills?" I paraphrased the hook from the Destiny's Child song. "My telephone bill, my light bill, and then maybe we can chill," I finished as I handed them to Aldris.

"Shit, I pay all of your bills and my bills anyway. I can handle it," he joked.

"I know you can, *papi,* and you always do," I said seductively.

"Oh, is that right?" he said, bending down and kissing me on my neck. "I'm thinking food ain't what I want for my lunch break." He brushed his lips against mine and sucked me into a breathtaking kiss.

Our intimate kiss was abruptly ended when my eyes caught some of the wording from the letter in my hand. Three words to be exact: "child support reduction."

"What?" I said angrily.

"Huh?" Aldris pulled back, trying to figure out what the issue was.

"Not you, baby." I patted him to get up so I could read. "Wait. This letter." I stood and paced the floor as I examined the paper in my hand.

What I read next nearly knocked me off my feet. Raul applied for child support reduction because of two more kids. The first child listed as a dependent of his was Rosemary Rojas, and the second child was Emilio Rojas, Jr. My damn stepsister and my new infant half brother. This bastard claimed he was the father of two of my dad's wife's kids. Now the irony in this was that as far as my dad was concerned, I felt he deserved it, if it was true, but I was pissed as hell for Nadia.

"This MF has some king-sized balls to make those kinds of allegations. He's lying to get a reduction. That's it!" I yelled, handing Aldris the notice.

Aldris peered up in shock after reading the letter. "Actually, he may not be. Remember when you were living in the apartment and he made that threat about a reduction? Then he made that comment about your dad. Do you think this is what he meant?"

Suddenly, I remembered when he claimed to have two more kids but not by Shanaya or Boop. This fool had been slippin' and slidin' with Maria. *Now how is that for*

my dad not wanting to get tangled up with Raul? Ha!
They say karma is a bitch, and she is bitch slapping the
hell out of Emilio Rojas right now.

"I wonder if my dad knows about this," I thought aloud.
"More than likely," Aldris said. "That's some shit, man.
Nadia's step-aunt and half uncle could really be her half
sister and half brother. Daaaaamn."

Suddenly, a big ball of laughter welled up inside of me,
and I cracked up until I cried. My dad—and I use that
term loosely—didn't want to provide for us and didn't
want to protect me against Raul because Maria claimed
to be looking out for his benefit when she was throwing
Raul her pussy to the left and right. I never liked her. All
of this glamorous life that he provided for Maria, and she
wasn't nothing but a $2 ho just like I tried to tell his ass.
That's exactly what he gets. I hoped Raul was the daddy.

After we finished chuckling about that situation, Aldris
got up to make a plate of the spaghetti I'd cooked, while I
finished opening the remaining mail. With the next letter,
the grin fell straight from my face. Just because I was
high on life, here it came trying to kick me down again.
Slowly, I got up and made my way into the kitchen.

"What's that?" Aldris asked, grabbing a soda from the
fridge.

"It's another letter from the State."

"Oh yeah? What about?" he asked, sitting at the breakfast table with his food.

"It's for you. You're being sued for a paternity test and
pending child support from Jennifer Brooks for a six-
year-old named Jessica Lily Brooks," I told him as I set
the paper down in front of him.

If Aldris had been of light complexion, all of the color
would've drained from his face. His mouth dropped open,

and the soda that he was holding slipped from his hand, spilling its contents all over the kitchen floor. Yep, that woman named karma was a bitch, and she was bitch slapping everyone in her path.

Pooch

Ain't this a bitch? Here I was in federal lockup, looking at 101 years of prison time with no possibility of parole. My nice-ass six-bedroom, six-bath crib with my plush-ass king-sized bed and plasma TV had been traded in for a one-cell, bottom-bunk cot, with a nerd-ass cellmate, one shitting toilet, sink, and a gray-ass brick wall for entertainment. My fly-ass gear was traded for this orange-ass DOC jumpsuit, and my five-star meals were traded for two hot plates of certified slop. And where was my bottom bitch in all of this? Missing in muthafuckin' action. Now you'd think I'd be worried about getting out this muthafucka, but I was so fuckin' mad that I didn't have time to concentrate on my appeals. My one mission in life was to find that bitch.

Word was when them muthafuckin' Feds raided my shit and froze my accounts, her ass was already ghost. Ain't nobody seen this bitch in Atlanta since, and she done disconnected her fuckin' cell phone. Even her moms and them done got missing, and her girls claim they ain't heard from her. Shit, they probably hadn't. I'll tell you who else ain't been seen from what my girl Chocolate Flava told me. Terrence. Now, what are the fuckin' odds that as soon as I went down for some federal bullshit, my girl, our kids, her siblings, her mama, and her baby daddy all disappear? Them muthafuckas ain't air or water, so they didn't evaporate. If I were a betting man, I'd have said that my girl lied to me when she said wasn't shit going on between her and that fuck nigga. Yeah, while she was acting like we were working on us and shit, she was really being his . . . li'l mama.

I couldn't believe my nose was so fuckin' wide open for this broad that I couldn't see what was right in front of me from the jump. She'd been creepin' with that nigga the whole time and biding her time until she could leave me. I swore to God as soon as I could find this bitch, she was as good as got. Got my fuckin' babies and gone with this nigga. I was murkin' for both of them niggas for real yo.

"Five minutes," my bullshit CO said to me as I sat down in the chair behind the glass. I wanted to roll my eyes at this broad sitting in front of me, but right now, she was my only connection to the outside world. So I had to put on my pimp hat and make it do what it do.

"What's up, baby?" I said sexily into the phone.

"Hey, baby. How you holding up?" Chocolate Flava asked.

"I'm fuckin' locked up," I shot back at her. "Whatchu think?"

"Attorney Stein and I are working on your appeal. I'm doing the best I can," she said sweetly.

Noticing the hurt flash in her eyes, I exhaled and tried to calm my aggression down. "I'm sorry. I'm just frustrated in here, man. I don't mean to take it out on you." Switching gears to make my apology genuine, I decided to bring a little smile to her face. "I got your letter last week. That shit was real sweet, and I got off real good on that fuckin' picture."

She grinned devilishly, and all was well. "I thought you would. Was you gon' write me back?"

"Yeah," I lied. "I missed mail call yesterday, but you know I appreciate everything you been doing for me."

"Well, you said I was your lady, right?"

"Yeah, my number one," I lied. "Speaking of, have you heard anything on Trinity?"

She rolled her eyes and sucked her teeth. "No, Pooch. I keep telling you. Ain't nobody seen or heard from that bitch. Why you keep worrying about her if I'm your lady?"

"I got my fuckin' reasons," I said, seething, but quickly eased up. "Look, you are my girl, but I really need you to put some effort into tryin' to find out where this bitch went or something. I need to get at her on some real personal shit. Can you please do that for me?"

She huffed. "Yeah."

"What's going on with my cousins' cases?"

"Both of them waiting on appeals approval."

"Damn," I mumbled. "Tell Stein that I'll consider his offer."

"You gon' snitch on Tot?"

"Shut your fuckin' mouth, Flava. Let the world know. Damn," I said angrily as I looked around to make sure nobody heard. "Look, it's every nigga for himself at this point, and I gotta get out of here. I ain't spending no hundred one years in lockup, and I got some unfinished business I need handled."

She shrugged. "A'ight. I'll tell him."

"Tell him don't come at me with no bullshit either. It better be right," I ordered. "Look, I need you to do me a favor, so can you come up here this weekend for a face-to-face visit?"

"I'm supposed to be doing this gig with Black Pearl in Tallahassee."

"Man, fuck that gig. I'm talkin' up on some real shit."

Crossing her arms, she leaned back with her attitude on go. "Pooch, I gotta live too. I'm paying your attorney fees and putting money on your books and shit. I need the extra money."

Bitch had a point there. "A'ight. Come next weekend then, and I mean that shit."

I caved 'cause I needed the money. She was already frustrating me, and I was locked up. I was gonna have to dump this bitch as soon as I got out of this hell hole because I couldn't tolerate no hardheaded-ass woman. *At least Trinity listened. Man, look at this shit. This bitch done left me to rot, and I'm still tryin' to remember the good shit about her. That fuckin' bitch always has been my Achilles heel. She gon' be the fuckin' death of me.*

"Time," my CO called out to me.

This punk muthafucka. "Listen, I gotta go."

"All right. Call me on Thursday to see if I came up with anything," Flava replied.

"A'ight. Bet," I said and gave her one of my million-dollar smiles.

"I love you, Pooch."

I rubbed my face to keep my laughter inside. "I love you too. Remember that shit," I lied. We hung up, and my CO got me.

I ain't gonna lie. Flava had been down for me. Throughout my whole case, she had my back. She was the only one of them fucking strippers who didn't snitch, and she testified on my behalf. She stood by a nigga like a true down-ass bitch was supposed to. A part of me wished I did love her instead of that fuckin' Trinity, because she proved she was the type of woman I needed by my side. But my heart was in shambles over Trinity. I would never love another woman again. Even if I did find myself caring for Flava, it would never be like how it was for Trinity. I was ashamed to admit it, but I truly loved that bitch, and in a lot of ways, I still did. The more I thought about her bending that ass over and letting Terrence tap that shit, the madder I got. I had to release some pressure.

I coughed. "Hey, CO Billings. I'm feelin' a little sick in my chest. Can you take me to the infirmary?"

"It's always something with your ass, Smalls. Damn, come on," he said as he escorted me to the infirmary. "Wait here," he said as he went to get the nurse. Soon, he escorted me into the room.

"I got him, Billings," Nurse Lisa said to him.

"You need me to wait in here?" he asked her.

"No, you can wait in the waiting area. He'll be fine. I'm used to Mr. Smalls coming here by now," she joked with him as he walked out.

"I don't like you flirting with him," I said once my CO was gone.

"I'm not flirting, Pooch. I just don't want him to get suspicious. I hid your money and food in your usual spot," Lisa said.

I winked at her. "Good. That's my girl."

"What's your issue today?" she asked, straddling my lap.

"I got built-up pressure I need to release."

"Stand up," she ordered as she helped me to my feet and removed my jumpsuit. She was about to slide down her panties when I stopped her. "Nah, babe. I just need a quick release."

"Oh, okay." She dropped to her knees and pulled out my dick.

"That's right, babe. Stroke him up real good," I moaned quietly as she stuck it in her mouth.

I swear this bitch's mouth was like resting my shit in a volcano. It stayed hot, and she made me cum so fuckin' fast. Within a few minutes, my shit was oozing all down her throat like hot lava as I gripped the back of her head and pumped in and out, making her take it all to the last drop.

"Feel better?" she asked as she cleaned her mouth.

"Hell yeah," I said as I sat down after she'd helped me pull my jumpsuit up. "You ain't nothing but the truth, I swear."

"Good," she said, giving me some cough drops. "I think you'll live," she said and got the CO.

"Time to go, inmate," CO Billings said in an authoritative tone to impress Lisa.

Really, my nigga? Fuckin' clown. I had to stifle a laugh. That nigga had been trying to push up on that bitch probably since before I got here, and within two weeks of my being here, I had her dropping her drawers, opening her mouth, and providing me shit, and I didn't have a fuckin' thing to offer her. Now you tell me whose game was tighter? At least this dumb muthafucka could give her money and some benefits, but she didn't want that shit. A chance to be with a certified bad boy and some good pipe was all she wanted. And they say men are shallow. It just proves ghetto birds and educated dimes all liked bad boys, baby. There was just something about us that turned them the fuck on, and hell yeah, I was gon' reap every benefit I could from it.

Right now, a bitch on the inside and a bitch on the outside was all I had, and I needed both them broads. It was time to get my pill game up on the inside so I could get some money in my pockets and make sure I could start giving back to Lisa and Flava. That was sure to keep them on my team and make them bend to what I needed done. And I needed them to keep handlin' my urges. I refused to be one of these shit-packin' muthafuckas, and if a nigga thought he was gon' pack my shit, he had another think coming. He'd better kill me if he tried it, because I damn sure would kill him. I was already serving 101 years. What the fuck else I had to lose?

"What took you so long to get back?" Wolf, my cellmate, asked once I was back inside the cell.

"I had to make a pit stop to the infirmary," I said, putting a cough drop in my mouth.

He laughed. "Boy, you ain't been here but four months, and you already pimpin' 'em."

"Got to, Wolf. How the hell you been in here seven years without hittin' somethin' I do not know."

"From time to time, I've had some female COs who've helped me out. But shit, I'm used to my right hand," Wolf said.

"Man, fuck all that. I'm gettin' me," I said. "You sure you ain't switched teams?"

He laughed. "Hell no, young buck, never that. But I got tried once in my first facility in Florida. That shit was bananas."

"Yo, so what happened?" I asked, not really believing his "tried" theory. This nerd muthafucka looked like he'd be anybody's bitch.

"I shanked that muthafucka in the neck and made him suck on it. Then I nutted and pissed in his face, bitch," he said seriously.

"Man, get the fuck outta here! You didn't do that."

Out of nowhere, this bitch pulled a blade from his mouth. "Yes, I did. I stay strapped, young buck. Always."

Nerd-ass Wolf was the truth. I was shocked. "Damn, man. A'ight. I hear you."

He released a slight chuckle. "It's best you learn real quick in here never to underestimate anybody. Once you learn that, you good to go."

We fist bumped. "Cool, thanks, Wolf," I said, taking in what he had to say.

"No problem," he said as I lay back on my bunk.

He bent down real quick, and the next thing I knew, the blade was at my neck. "As a matter of fact, I need a little suck now."

"You sure you want to do that? I think you might need to look again." My eyes darted to the side, where I had my shank pointed at his side.

"Fast learner," he said and stood up.

"Yeah, I am, and please believe I stay strapped too," I laughed as we fist bumped again.

"You gon' be all right in here," Wolf said, jumping on his top bunk.

"Nah, Wolf man. I'm springin' this bitch real soon."

"You caught up with your baby's mother?"

"Nope, but it's only a matter of time. If I don't catch her before I spring this camp, I'll definitely catch her when I'm out. You can bet that," I said, thinking back over all the things I did for her and how she just left me for Terrence. "Yeah, man, you can bet that."

I was gon' think of all the ways to get back at this bitch when I did, too. What else I had to do? I had nothing but time.

Stay tuned for

Never Again, No More 3:

Karma's Brew